BERLIN NOIR

EDITED BY
THOMAS WÖRTCHE

Translated by Lucy Jones

BROOKLYN, NEW YORK, USA
BALLYDEHOB, CO. CORK, IRELAND

This collection comprises works of fiction. All names, characters, places, and incidents are the product of the authors' imaginations or used in a fictitious manner.

Published by Akashic Books
©2019 Akashic Books

Series concept by Tim McLoughlin and Johnny Temple
Berlin map by Sohrab Habibion

The translation of this work was supported by a grant from the Goethe-Institut in the framework of the "Books First" program.

Paperback ISBN: 978-1-61775-632-0
Library of Congress Control Number: 2018960608

Akashic Books
Brooklyn, New York, USA
Ballydehob, Co. Cork, Ireland
Twitter: @AkashicBooks
Facebook: AkashicBooks
E-mail: info@akashicbooks.com
Website: www.akashicbooks.com

ALSO IN THE AKASHIC NOIR SERIES

AMSTERDAM NOIR (NETHERLANDS),
edited by RENÉ APPEL & JOSH PACHTER

ATLANTA NOIR, edited by TAYARI JONES

BAGHDAD NOIR (IRAQ), edited by SAMUEL SHIMON

BALTIMORE NOIR, edited by LAURA LIPPMAN

BARCELONA NOIR (SPAIN), edited by
ADRIANA V. LÓPEZ & CARMEN OSPINA

BEIRUT NOIR (LEBANON), edited by IMAN HUMAYDAN

BELFAST NOIR (NORTHERN IRELAND), edited by
ADRIAN McKINTY & STUART NEVILLE

BOSTON NOIR, edited by DENNIS LEHANE

BOSTON NOIR 2: THE CLASSICS, edited by
DENNIS LEHANE, MARY COTTON & JAIME CLARKE

BRONX NOIR, edited by S.J. ROZAN

BROOKLYN NOIR, edited by TIM McLOUGHLIN

BROOKLYN NOIR 2: THE CLASSICS,
edited by TIM McLOUGHLIN

BROOKLYN NOIR 3: NOTHING BUT THE TRUTH,
edited by TIM McLOUGHLIN & THOMAS ADCOCK

BRUSSELS NOIR (BELGIUM),
edited by MICHEL DUFRANNE

BUENOS AIRES NOIR (ARGENTINA),
edited by ERNESTO MALLO

BUFFALO NOIR, edited by ED PARK & BRIGID HUGHES

CAPE COD NOIR, edited by DAVID L. ULIN

CHICAGO NOIR, edited by NEAL POLLACK

CHICAGO NOIR: THE CLASSICS,
edited by JOE MENO

COPENHAGEN NOIR (DENMARK),
edited by BO TAO MICHAËLIS

DALLAS NOIR, edited by DAVID HALE SMITH

D.C. NOIR, edited by GEORGE PELECANOS

D.C. NOIR 2: THE CLASSICS,
edited by GEORGE PELECANOS

DELHI NOIR (INDIA), edited by HIRSH SAWHNEY

DETROIT NOIR, edited by E.J. OLSEN
& JOHN C. HOCKING

DUBLIN NOIR (IRELAND), edited by KEN BRUEN

HAITI NOIR, edited by EDWIDGE DANTICAT

HAITI NOIR 2: THE CLASSICS,
edited by EDWIDGE DANTICAT

HAVANA NOIR (CUBA), edited by ACHY OBEJAS

HELSINKI NOIR (FINLAND),
edited by JAMES THOMPSON

HONG KONG, edited by JASON Y. NG
& SUSAN BLUMBERG-KASON

INDIAN COUNTRY NOIR, edited by SARAH CORTEZ
& LIZ MARTÍNEZ

ISTANBUL NOIR (TURKEY),
edited by MUSTAFA ZIYALAN & AMY SPANGLER

KANSAS CITY NOIR, edited by STEVE PAUL

KINGSTON NOIR (JAMAICA),
edited by COLIN CHANNER

LAGOS NOIR (NIGERIA), edited by CHRIS ABANI

LAS VEGAS NOIR, edited by JARRET KEENE
& TODD JAMES PIERCE

LONDON NOIR (ENGLAND),
edited by CATHI UNSWORTH

LONE STAR NOIR, edited by BOBBY BYRD
& JOHNNY BYRD

LONG ISLAND NOIR, edited by KAYLIE JONES

LOS ANGELES NOIR, edited by DENISE HAMILTON

LOS ANGELES NOIR 2: THE CLASSICS,
edited by DENISE HAMILTON

MANHATTAN NOIR, edited by LAWRENCE BLOCK

MANHATTAN NOIR 2: THE CLASSICS,
edited by LAWRENCE BLOCK

MANILA NOIR (PHILIPPINES),
edited by JESSICA HAGEDORN

MARRAKECH NOIR (MOROCCO),
edited by YASSIN ADNAN

MARSEILLE NOIR (FRANCE), edited by CÉDRIC FABRE

MEMPHIS NOIR, edited by LAUREEN P. CANTWELL
& LEONARD GILL

MEXICO CITY NOIR (MEXICO),
edited by PACO I. TAIBO II

MIAMI NOIR, edited by LES STANDIFORD

MISSISSIPPI NOIR, edited by TOM FRANKLIN

MONTANA NOIR, edited by JAMES GRADY
& KEIR GRAFF

MONTREAL NOIR (CANADA), edited by JOHN
McFETRIDGE & JACQUES FILIPPI

MOSCOW NOIR (RUSSIA),
edited by NATALIA SMIRNOVA & JULIA GOUMEN

MUMBAI NOIR (INDIA), edited by ALTAF TYREWALA

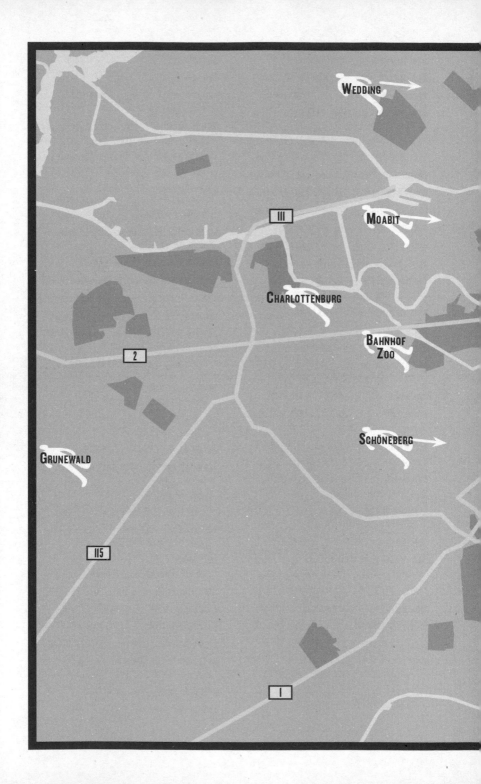

TABLE OF CONTENTS

11   *Introduction*

PART I: STRESS IN THE CITY

19   **ZOË BECK**   Bahnhof Zoo
Dora

33   **ULRICH WOELK**   Moabit
I Spy with My Little Eye

55   **SUSANNE SAYGIN**   Schöneberg
The Beauty of Kenilworth Ivy

74   **MAX ANNAS**   Neukölln
Local Train

PART II: COPS & GANGSTERS

91   **KAI HENSEL**   Altglienicke
Cum Cops

112   **MATTHIAS WITTEKINDT**   Friedrichshain
The Invisible Man

141   **MIRON ZOWNIR**   Kreuzberg
Overtime

163   **UTE COHEN**   Grunewald
Valverde

PART III: BERLIN SCENES

185   **JOHANNES GROSCHUPF**   SO 36
Heinrichplatz Blues

204   **MICHAEL WULIGER**   Charlottenburg
Kaddish for Lazar

221   **KATJA BOHNET**   Mitte
Fashion Week

239   **ROBERT RESCUE**   Wedding
One of These Days

259   **ROB ALEF**   Tempelhof
Dog Tag Afternoon

286   **About the Contributors**

INTRODUCTION
BERLIN, YEAR ZERO

Berlin does not make it easy to write noir fiction—or perhaps Berlin makes it *too* easy. Noir tradition casts a long, influential, and even daunting shadow.

Alfred Döblin's and Christopher Isherwood's works, some of Bertolt Brecht's plays, the *Morgue* poems by Gottfried Benn, M by Fritz Lang, and many other narratives from the first third of the twentieth century, all of which are tinged with noir, set high intellectual standards, and literary and aesthetic benchmarks that are hard to surpass. Perhaps this is why Berlin barely existed as a setting in noteworthy crime novels after the Second World War, with a few exceptions such as Ulf Miehe's *Ich hab noch einen Toten in Berlin* (1973) and some other disparate texts. For Anglo-Saxon authors, Cold War Berlin was more interesting: John le Carré, Len Deighton, Ted Allbeury, and Ross Thomas all knew better than most German crime writers how to turn the divided city into a story, and even today's "historical" Berlin crime wave, set against papier-mâché backdrops from the 1920s and 1930s, was ushered in decades ago by the British writer Philip Kerr. It took until well into the 1980s and 1990s before Berlin was inscribed onto the crime fiction landscape of unified Germany—by authors like Pieke Biermann, Buddy Giovinazzo, and D.B. Blettenberg, even though their works defied strict crime fiction classifications.

In the proud tradition outlined above, this legacy is continued in *Berlin Noir*: neither Döblin nor Benn, Brecht nor Lang, for example, catered to any crime fiction formats. They merely steeped their literary projects in a great deal of noir. And so it is with most of the stories in our anthology: they do not necessarily follow the usual patterns of crime fiction, but regard noir as a license to write as they wish, a certain way of approaching the city, and a prism through which its nature is viewed.

As Franz Hessel, the flaneur and spiritual brother of Walter Benjamin, once noted: Berlin is a city that "is not," a city that "is always on the move, always in the process of changing." Stagnation, you could say, leads to death, as illustrated by Robert Rescue's story included in this volume, "One of These Days." Written in a style that might best be described as stoic madness, it is set in the heart of Wedding (paying homage, as it happens, to a real-life bar called the Mastul), a traditionally working-class district that has increasingly become the target of gentrification. In "Heinrichplatz Blues," Johannes Groschupf's elusive hero suddenly vanishes after years of having drifted (to the delight of many women) through the bars of Kreuzberg's Heinrichplatz, a setting that is now a veritable tourist hot spot. Nothing ever remains the same—but what does remain in this case is a mystery and the echo of a bygone libertarian lifestyle.

This famed lifestyle is, in turn, an echo of the roaring twenties, the first age of sexual emancipation, which was experienced in the "laboratory of modernity" and has now been abbreviated into the raunchy-sounding product "Babylon Berlin." Sodom and Gomorrah, in Ute Cohen's toxic, modern-day story "Valverde," has degenerated into a dull game played by the rich—and not necessarily beautiful—in chic, exclusive Grunewald. There is no hint of emancipation here, but inevitably greed, profit, and exploitation, which only an insane work of art can adequately express.

There is play with smoke and mirrors in the hip district of Mitte, which is itself increasingly transforming into an artificial hot spot of luxury and fashion, much to the ire of the long-established population. Even if the hipsters are progressive, politically correct, and ecologically minded, well-known capitalist practices emerge as soon as the surface is scratched. And in Katja Bohnet's "Fashion Week," they also reek.

Naturally, Berlin is also a place where people lose their minds: what really goes on in the head of Dora, the eponymous character in Zoë Beck's story—one who is practically invisible too, as it happens—remains unclear. What can be said for certain is that some aspects of modern life are not easily endured, even if a person's background is, at first glance, solidly bourgeois. Dora, in any case, appears to favor the sexual violence she endures as a homeless woman around Zoo Station than the straitjacket of a "normal" existence. And if the urge to impose "normality" arises, obsessive tidying can quickly veer from the neurotic to the psychopathic, as Susanne Saygin's story "The Beauty of Kenilworth Ivy" shows. Here, a marauding killer in Schöneberg tries to clean up the city by eliminating representatives of the "bourgeois"; this, in her view, is the only way to protect social diversity in the botanical biotope of Berlin—by weeding out these undesirables once and for all. What an evil paradox. The frustrated film critic in Ulrich Woelk's "I Spy with My Little Eye" has long since lost touch with reality and logic; he just doesn't know it yet. His perceptions of what is real and what is illusion have been radically tampered with by the cinema, alienating him from the foundations of his own existence. As he tries to write a "human interest" story set in a run-down area of Moabit, it is clear that he is living his life through the movies, even when he . . . But why not just read it for yourself!

And when it comes to the much-vaunted subject of identity, the labyrinthine possibilities that Berlin offers are not easy to navigate. Upright man by day, killer by night, to paraphrase Karl Marx. A cruel strategy of survival in Friedrichshain, perhaps, a district particularly tyrannized by party tourism, especially around Boxhagener Platz. To get to the bottom of it all, it may be a good idea to have an outsider look at the goings-on in Berlin, as the Italian investigator in Matthias Wittekindt's "The Invisible Man" dares to do.

Berlin is a relatively peaceful city, at least compared to other capitals around the world. This is partly because organized crime—which is just as endemic here as elsewhere—observes strict rules that aim to inflict as little collateral damage on bystanders as possible. Which does not mean that cops and gangsters do not appear in *Berlin Noir*. Kai Hensel's satirical story "Cum Cops," about the unusual rehabilitation of a police officer from conservative Altglienicke, is based on actual events: In summer 2017, a Berlin police unit became the laughing stock of Germany when it was sent back to the capital from Hamburg following a scandal involving public sex and heavy drinking. The Berlin unit had been deployed there to assist with the expected G20 summit riots. And the consequence in Hensel's story is a fatal reverse thrust.

Blood is also spilled in Miron Zownir's story "Overtime," about a clash between corrupt cops and genuine gangsters. The fact that this story moves back and forth between Kreuzberg and Neukölln is not supposed to suggest that these two districts have a particularly high crime rate: Berlin's fifteen districts are mere political entities, whereas specific neighborhoods are the socially relevant entities—and in these neighborhoods, huge differences in lifestyles and crime exist. That's why Max Annas's Neukölln introduces us to a completely different kind of world than Zownir's. And Annas's characters, although certainly not squeaky-clean Germans, are part of the fairly standard diverse population of a big city. The guy in the (metaphorical) sack in "Local Train" is not happy about this. That's why he belongs in the sack.

What's left is history. It is omnipresent in Berlin at every turn; the city is saturated in a history full of blood, violence, and death. The echoes of the Nazi era can still be felt in Michael Wuliger's "Kaddish for Lazar," even though the relationship between Jews and Germans is highly contemporary and ironic in this story, and felt especially keenly in the "new West," particularly Charlottenburg. Rob Alef's "Dog Tag Afternoon," on the other hand, deals with the consequences of the Second World War—more precisely with the 1948/1949 Berlin airlift, which had more to do with Germany's Western connections than many other actions by the Western Allies. History forces its way up into the present from a past that can't be buried, surfacing at the exact spot in Tempelhof where American and British aircraft punctured the Soviet blockade.

Berlin, as we want to show, is a "SynchroniCity" (Pieke Biermann), a city of the most disparate and diverse simultaneities, firmly attached to the rigging of its political and literary history and always moving forward in the present. And noir, in its very essence, does that too. In this respect *Berlin Noir* is a snapshot; and as I write this today, I fully expect that everything will look completely different in just another year's time.

Thomas Wörtche
Berlin, Germany
February 2019

PART I

Stress in the City

DORA

BY Zoë Beck

Bahnhof Zoo

Take a look at her. Even if it's hard.

You won't want to look at her because she stinks and is filthy from head to toe. You think you know what you'll see but take a look anyway.

Don't wait for the woman from the rescue mission to help her to her feet and prop her up so she doesn't fall over again, then bring her to the homeless shelter where she'll have to cut the clothes off her body, wash her, and give her something new to wear. The clothes aren't new, of course, just castoffs from strangers, but they're new to her. She'll wear them for a day or two and then they'll have to be cut away again, because she won't be able to take them off: they'll be so stiff with filth and grime and blood and sperm and vomit that the only way to remove them will be to cut them from her body and throw them away.

They know her here; they know how it is. They're happy when she shows up. Sometimes a person from the rescue mission finds her and brings her in. Sometimes she screams and lashes out for hours and they have her taken to the clinic, at least for a few days until she discharges herself or simply disappears. Here they hope she'll stay longer in the hospital until she's fully recovered and healthy, if there is such a thing. Ever since someone from the mission saw her by chance after she'd been in the hospital for five days in a row, and told everyone that he didn't recognize her at first because she looked so young and beautiful, that's what they all want here.

So, take a good look at her. Somewhere under the dirt and the stench, it's still her.

In her early twenties, she took her meds. Not always, but there were stable phases. Sometimes entire months went by without incident. A year and a half ago, I remember that we thought everything was going to be fine and that our lives and hers would return to normal. We thought: *She'll take her meds for a while longer, and then this whole topic will be a thing of the past.* We longed for normality. As if anything had ever been normal. A year and a half ago, when we'd been lulled into a sense of security, the call came from one of her friends.

"Come here immediately," he said. "Just come, now." Then he hung up.

I heard voices in the background, loud and confused. Students, I figured, the cafeteria. I was in the library not far away, and I jumped on my bike. When I reached the Math Institute, one of the nightmare scenarios that I'd been trying to block from my mind was taking place in front of the building.

Dora was standing on the steps leading up to the entrance. In each hand she was holding a glass bottle, which she aimed like weapons at other students who were gathered at the bottom of the stairs. At the same time, she was yelling: "I'll kill you! You fuckin' Nazis!"

I felt sick—not because I was afraid she'd really do her classmates harm, but because I saw that she had wet herself and didn't seem to have noticed. I saw a guy standing at the edge of the group who was taking pictures with his cell phone.

As a big brother, you have responsibilities and you have to make decisions. My decision was to take the guy's cell phone first, then grab my sister. The guy didn't want to hand over his phone just like that, so we scuffled a bit, but the others barely noticed. Then I put his cell in my pocket, latched onto my sister's arm, and dragged her into the building. There I grabbed her bottles, put them by the door, led her to the toilet, and told her to clean herself up. If you spoke English to her, it worked just fine. Another student rested his hand on my arm and handed me her backpack. I thanked him and looked for her meds inside the bag, but only found a month-old pre-scription. Luckily, I also found her gym bag, which I handed to her in the bathroom so that she could change. She was still cussing Nazis, but sounded a little calmer and at least didn't want to kill anyone anymore.

We went to the nearest pharmacy in the village of Dahlem. In the Luise beer garden, I gave her one of her pills, saying they would protect her against the Nazis. As always, she was suspicious at first, but eventually swallowed it. It would take a few more hours until the voices in her head went quiet, and a couple more days until she was stable.

When you look at her, remember how young she is. You'll think she's at least twenty years older than she actually is. That's because of all the dirt on her haggard face. Her hollow cheeks. Her empty eyes. She hardly eats, and drinks instead to block out the voices, and when she gets hold of some money, she sometimes buys drugs—any old kind. She doesn't care as long as they're stronger than the voices.

Dora heard the voices for the first time in South America. At least that's what we think. We weren't with her, and she never said much about it, but the friend she was traveling with during the semester break thought so too. This is what we figured: somewhere, somehow, she took the wrong drug.

She'd had almost no experience back then, and it must have triggered something in her brain. The doctors we spoke to said that she must have been going through the early stages of her illness for a long time and it would have eventually happened anyway.

After returning from South America, she seemed really stressed. She was always turning around, startled, spoke in a low voice, and refused to use the telephone. She took the radio and television out of her room and locked away her computer and cell phone. Blacked out her window. Talked to herself.

We brought her to see the best doctors and made appointments with the most renowned therapists. She regularly took her prescriptions until a therapist told her that she didn't have to if she didn't want to. Three weeks later, she started hunting for Nazis in the backyard. We brought her to a different therapist and sued the man who talked her out of taking the meds. There were bad phases, but also good ones. She was able to carry on studying and heard the voices less and less often. She even used a laptop and warmed to the Internet again.

In the past, it had been one of her obsessions. In the past: before South America, the period that the doctors kept digging up for some kind of explanation. In the past, Dora had taken pictures and posted her every move online. She didn't do anything without telling the whole world where she was and why, what she'd eaten and drank, why she was laughing and with whom. Her Instagram account had several thousand followers. She was a minor celebrity. She used to be outspoken, cocky even, and our brother Bela called her an attention junkie. If she'd had a musical streak like him, she would have made a perfect diva. He, on the other hand, always hid behind his double bass.

In the bars on Ku'damm she was a real hell-raiser, but her favorite hangout was the Lang Bar in the Waldorf Astoria. She'd gather there with the admirers who could afford to join her. Or with those who'd do anything to post a selfie with her. She herself wasn't afraid of approaching real celebrities at the Lang to take photos with them, with the Memorial Church or Zoo Palast cinema in the background. On summer nights, she would sit on the rooftop terrace and snap shots of herself and her followers with the floodlit construction sites around Zoo Station as a backdrop. She loved it there.

That's why she often sleeps there, under the railway bridge next to the bakery. If you look around, you'll see very few women. They try to stay off the streets at night. Or they look for nooks and crannies where they can't easily be found. Most try to find a place to stay—in homeless shelters or women-only facilities. Some go home with any old guy and stay for as long as they can stand it; they let the guys do whatever they want with them, just to have a roof over their heads. Shame is often greater for women than men—shame, but also fear of sleeping on the streets. Because they are attacked more often. Because they are raped. I've done my research.

Dora feels no more shame. She has nothing left to protect or hide. She sometimes spends the night in shelters and the like, but whenever we look for her she's mostly here; and when the rescue mission contacts us, we're often told that they found her just around the corner. They know her and they know us. Once she disappeared for several weeks, and no one around here could tell us where she was or when she'd last been seen. We asked around in all the shops and dive bars, even showing her photo to passersby. We called hospitals and every single emergency shelter. We made inquiries with the police. Finally, we stood, exhausted, in front of the Zoo Palast and Bela burst into tears. I could tell he thought she was dead. No one would contact us, he said. No one would recognize her. Perhaps she had been buried in some anonymous grave. The glass pane reflected the brightly lit Waldorf Astoria. I left Bela and crossed the street, let angry motorists honk at me, made it to the other side unscathed, and stormed into the lobby of the luxury hotel. I asked about my sister. Showed photos. Looked into their helpless faces. She was a regular here, I said, up in the Lang Bar. They'd long since forgotten her.

Then the concierge, a woman, remembered that a homeless person had been thrown out a few weeks ago. A young woman, she said, but it had been hard to tell at first, because she had looked so old. I nodded encouragingly and asked her to tell me the whole story. She had been pacing about on the sidewalk in front of the hotel, then finally huddled on the floor near the main entrance. Of course, she was immediately shooed away, but that same night, a colleague had found her in the underground parking lot, where she'd settled in a corner to sleep.

No one knew what had happened to her after that; no one could even remember the exact date. I went back to my brother, who was still standing in front of the Zoo Palast, crying silently. I hugged him and starting crying too. I knew she would have never gone home with some guy just to have a roof over her head. I couldn't think of anything else to do. Now we both thought she was dead.

I happened to be at the Lang Bar when she gathered her followers together for the last time. I'd not planned to go out that evening. This was right before my law degree exams, and I had other things to do; but then the attorney from the firm where I'd done my internship invited me there, and with an eye toward my future career, I wasn't going to turn him down. I was hoping not to meet my sister; but, of course, she was sitting there happily in the midst of her admirers with a non-alcoholic cocktail in front of her—she barely drank at that time because she didn't like the taste—and waved to me excitedly. I said a quick hello, mentioned my business meeting, and sat down with the attorney. A good hour later, she got up to leave, but the lawyer asked her to join us at the table; I found it embarrassing, though it couldn't be avoided, especially as Dora was so gregarious. We were drinking tea and talking about a case that I'd worked on as a legal clerk. He offered Dora a cup, which she accepted with a shrug. I remember this because she never used to drink tea or coffee. But I understood that she wanted to appear more grown-up, to somehow reduce the eight-year age gap between us. She was pretending that she didn't think it was stuffy and conservative to drink tea. Smiling, she threw back her hair and answered the attorney's questions about her majors and exam subjects, and what she was going to do later on.

Then, all of a sudden, I noticed that she had grown tight-lipped and distracted. She stared into her tea, looked around nervously, then stared back into her tea. If she'd been shy, I wouldn't have thought anything of it, but this wasn't typical of my sister. I asked her if she was okay, but she only muttered that something was wrong, then stood up and left the bar, even forgetting her purse.

"Young girls at that age," was all that the lawyer said, and we resumed our conversation.

When I returned to our father's roomy apartment in Uhlandstrasse, where I still lived for financial reasons, I found her sitting on the bed in her room, staring into space. There was something in the tea, she said. I asked her to elaborate, and she said that something had appeared on the surface and had risen with the steam. It had been impossible for her to drink. I asked why she hadn't ordered something else, and she said, "Because I had to leave. It didn't want me there."

I thought I'd misheard, and to this day I'm not sure if that's what she really said, or if I'm just imagining it in hindsight. But from then on, something changed. She became quiet and introspective, sometimes sitting for long stretches with a far-away expression on her face, as if deep in thought, and only reacting when we shook her or said her name very loudly. Her grades suffered and she complained of trouble concentrating and insomnia. Dad took her to a doctor, who prescribed her sedatives, saying it was due to the pressure of high school exams; apparently, he had many such cases.

On some days she was better; on others, worse. But none of us thought that she was seriously ill. Dad thought she might simply be growing up, and that perhaps she'd even take after him in the end. "Like you, Adrian," he said to me. "Like you and your brother."

I think that's what he wanted to see, because she reminded him too much of our mother—our mother when she was young.

As far as I know, she never went to the Lang Bar again. From her Instagram pictures, I gathered that she frequented a café at the Bikinihaus; she obviously liked sitting in front of the large window, from which she could see straight into the monkey enclosure. She posted fewer selfies, and I read the concerned comments from her followers: *Is everything all right? What's happened to you? What about the Lang Bar?* She replied that she was stressed by her exams, and I admit that it put my mind to rest.

A few weeks later, Bela called me from the hospital. He had burned his wrist, he said. When I picked him up and asked him how it had happened, he said: "It was Dora. I was making myself tea in the kitchen when she passed by, stopped, looked at my cup, then knocked it out of my hand."

He'd been advised not to play the bass for a few days. He wasn't badly hurt, and had he been studying a subject other than music, chances are that he wouldn't even have bothered going to the emergency room. But Bela's hands were his pride and joy, and he returned home in a foul temper, slamming his bedroom door.

I knocked at Dora's door, wanting to know what had happened. She wasn't crying. "I didn't mean to hurt him," she said. "But he mustn't drink tea." She looked at me and I saw the fear in her eyes. "Adrian, what's wrong with me?" she asked.

"You're stressed out," I said. "That makes people do strange stuff."

I didn't know at the time that she thought she'd seen something in the rising steam, like at the Lang Bar. Something she was afraid of and saw as a threat. I didn't know because she didn't tell me or anyone else. Maybe I should have been more insistent. Maybe I was even afraid of what she would tell me.

The next day, she apologized to Bela. Then she left the house. She wanted to go to the zoo. "To listen to the animals," she said. "It calms me down."

Yes, she even sleeps out here in winter. Until they pick her up and bring her somewhere warm. But she never wants to stay. She's afraid of the others—that they'll give her a hot drink. Most of the mission staff know about it. But the volunteers frequently change. She's already scalded some hands. And one woman's face. The winters in Berlin are long and gray, and they can get very cold.

Dora managed to get accepted to the math program, and after the first semester Dad rewarded her with a trip to South America—the trip which caused her complete transformation. She thought that someone was giving her orders; she could hear them in her head. The commands came from American intelligence agencies. In her mind it was 1945, and she was a soldier whose mission it was to liberate the city. We don't know how she managed to get through the return flight, because just as we arrived at the airport to pick her up, we saw her jump onto the back of an older woman and swear at her violently.

We thought the incident was the aftermath of some wild drug trip, because the friend she was traveling with said something like that. It wasn't for a few weeks that we realized it was more.

Things got quieter when she started on the meds. We became hopeful. Everything seemed to be going well. A few blips whenever she did not take her pills—sometimes on purpose, sometimes out of forgetfulness. Then we'd have to pick her up from some place to stop her from chasing imaginary Nazis and make her take her medication again. Yet things didn't go too wrong. The thing at the Math Institute was a bad relapse, but after that it was quiet again for a few weeks.

Until a therapist tried to convince her that she felt guilty about our mother's death. Dora came home distraught and wanted to know everything. Dad had always spoken vaguely of a fatal accident; Bela and I knew better. Now Dad thought it right to tell her the truth, something he himself didn't like to talk about. He told her about Mother's suicide shortly after

Dora's birth. How or even whether the therapist knew wasn't clear: she refused to talk to us about it. We made sure that Dora was transferred to a different doctor. But the truth about Mom's death preoccupied her for a long time afterward, of course.

One evening she knocked on my door, sat down on the sofa, and said: "What other things don't I know?" I told her as factually and calmly as possible about our brother Carl, who had died only a few days after his birth. He had had severe birth defects, but Mom hadn't wanted to terminate the pregnancy under any circumstances, and immediately after his birth, she fell into a deep depression. It had been her wish alone to get pregnant again. Why she had killed herself shortly after the birth of a healthy girl was something none of us could understand. She'd always wanted a girl, as I knew from Dad.

"Why wasn't I named Carla?" Dora asked, and I couldn't answer that. I hadn't even thought of it myself. I told her to talk to Dad.

She disappeared that very day and never returned to our apartment.

She often walks by but only sometimes recognizes us. She doesn't say hello or address us by name; she just registers us and responds to our voices. She occasionally even agrees to come with us if we offer to take her to the hospital or try to get her into one of the shelters, just so she's off the streets for a few hours at least. And when we come back to pick her up, she complies. But she never comes home.

Lately, the voices seem to have died down again. In any case, the thing about believing she's an American soldier on a mission to kill Nazis hasn't happened for at least two months. But we've heard that she often takes walks around the zoo.

She walks along Hardenbergstrasse and Budapester Strasse, stopping and listening. She listens to what the animals tell her, as a woman who works at the zoo ticket office told us. "Sometimes I let her in," she said. "I'm not really allowed to, but if she doesn't look too bedraggled and is having a good day, I turn a blind eye. She wouldn't hurt a flea."

Bela gave the woman a hundred euros and thanked her.

Once we brought her to our front door. When we got to Zoo Station, she went berserk in Dad's car because she wanted to get out. As soon as we stopped in Uhlandstrasse and opened her door with the child-safety lock, she jumped out of the car and ran back to Ku'damm. We knew where she was running and let her go.

If you saw her, you wouldn't believe that men sexually assault her. You'd think: *She's dirty and stinks, who'd want her?* You don't understand what these men want. They want to punish her. For being what she is. For some, she's just a piece of meat that happens to fall into their hands. She probably has every STD going. Syphilis is back in Europe, I've heard. When you see her, you won't believe how often it happens. Sometimes they only beat her up, and when I see her afterward, when they cut away her clothes at the rescue mission, I wonder why she didn't lose her will to live long ago. I've forgotten how many times they've broken her ribs. And her fingers. Her shins twice, I know that. Once she had a serious head injury. Not one of the usual gashes—this was worse. But she managed to survive that too. Her nose has already been broken three times, and once her left ear had to be sewn on again. She's not an isolated case. It's not her fault. The rescue mission says that anyone else out there would experience the same thing. That's why most women try to find a place to stay at night. But not Dora.

* * *

When she killed Bela the day before yesterday, she'd been to the zoo that afternoon. Since Bela gave the ticket office woman a hundred euros, she started calling him every time Dora showed up. I don't think it was because she cared, but Bela always felt reassured, and I knew he kept tabs on Dora's zoo visits to give the woman money again as soon as he could. Money for her tickets, he said, all added together and rounded up. "That woman's lining her own pockets," I said. Bela didn't care. Somehow it eased his conscience.

There was no reason to go looking for Dora that evening. I don't think Bela intentionally walked past her. He'd been out with his orchestra colleagues, and they parted at Zoo, where most of them caught trains and buses home. But Bela walked. The day before yesterday the weather was mild, and Bela liked to go for a stroll after concerts.

So he passed Dora, and maybe that evening she recognized him. Everything might have gone fine, but Bela was carrying a plastic cup of tea, which he'd just bought at the station and had taken off the lid to drink, the steam rising to his face. They say that Dora ran over to him and yelled: "You're going to die!" Then she sprang toward him and knocked the tea out of his hand, and he fell backward hard, hitting his head on the sidewalk. Dora kneeled over him, hitting him and shouting, "You're going to die!"—over and over again. And that's exactly what happened. The head injury from his fall might not have been fatal, but Dora's shaking and beating certainly were. By the time they pulled her off, it was too late. The paramedic could only confirm his death. Our sister had long since vanished.

So, if you see her, and if you take a close look, you'll know she didn't mean to kill him. She was trying to save him. I still don't know what she sees in the steam, or what's reflected in the surface of hot liquid. I don't think I have to either. When you see her—before the woman from the rescue mission picks her up, brings her in, washes and dresses her, then calls the police—remember: you mustn't be brutal. So many men have already been brutal with her. Be gentle, do it quickly. Bela would have wanted her to have a decent grave with her name on it.

I SPY WITH MY LITTLE EYE

BY ULRICH WOELK

Moabit

This much is certain: things would have turned out differently if Hauser hadn't gotten sick with an acute gallbladder problem. That's why the morning editorial meeting was held without him, a delicate omission, as soon became obvious, because crimes don't care about journalists' gallbladders—they happen anyway. And that morning an incident took place that a newspaper like ours (admittedly not the classiest) had to report.

I wasn't very focused during the meeting, because I'd had yet another fight with Irene the night before over custody for our daughter Chloe. It had been nerve-wracking and messy as usual, but gradually I had to face facts. There was no longer any doubt about it: Irene wanted to take Chloe away from me. She had decided to move to her new boyfriend's place in Frankfurt—and take Chloe with her, of course. And then all that I would have of my daughter would be short, irregular weekends and a few meager vacations.

As always, Irene had become hysterical and had hurled all the usual insults at me: I'd never had time for our daughter and, anyway, wasn't capable of empathy when it came to the mental and emotional needs of children and teenagers. To top it all, she presumed to claim that Chloe would be only too glad to get away from me and was looking forward to starting a new life in Frankfurt with her and her new partner—a boring but apparently very hip homeopath, or hands-on therapist, or miracle healer for Frankfurt bankers (or rather their wives).

Maybe that's why my ears pricked up when Menning, in his morning analysis of the news we had to cover that day, started talking about Janina, a pupil from Moabit who had been missing since the previous day. She had been on a bus on her way home, this much was known. But she had never arrived. She may have been sighted again near the bus stop, and perhaps she had even got into an unknown car, but these were just the usual unconfirmed rumors and conjectures that always happen in such cases.

Anyway, it was clear that the story had to be published in the local section of our paper, or even on the front page, which meant that someone had to take care of it—talk to the relatives and get in touch with the police press office. And since Hauser, whose specialty was crime reporting, was now in the hospital with gallbladder problems, someone else would have to take care of it, which wasn't easy to organize, given that we journalists are notoriously overworked. But before Menning could push the story onto any reasonably qualified department, such as the local section, I said I was interested in the case.

Menning did not answer right away. Admittedly, my involvement was unusual since I normally write for the feature pages of our newspaper (calling it the culture section would be an exaggeration), mostly about movies and movie stars. I guess Menning assumed that by volunteering, I was seizing the opportunity to write about a real atrocity rather than a screen crime for once—and, well, why not? Maybe after all the CinemaScope adventures and Dolby catastrophes I'd seen and reviewed in the past two decades, part of me was yearning for real life, real drama. As a tabloid news editor, Menning was up to every trick; maybe he was wondering if my leap into crime reporting might add an interesting movie-like touch that would make it stand out from the usual stories about runaway teens. He looked inquiringly around the table and no one objected.

On the way to Moabit, my quarrel with Irene ran through my mind again. Like every Tuesday I had gone to my former apartment, which I moved out of less than a year ago, to pick up Chloe for our movie night. But then Irene had nailed me down in the hallway, announcing her plans to move to Frankfurt, which was probably a subconscious (or conscious) attempt to sabotage my Tuesday ritual with Chloe, and which she ultimately succeeded in doing. In the end, Chloe and I only managed to have dinner together, because all the films that we were interested in had already started, but that wasn't such a bad thing. I've always enjoyed sitting with Chloe at an Italian or a Greek restaurant, noticing how the nature of our conversations has gradually changed over the years. Whereas they used to revolve around Chloe's imagination as a child, they have become increasingly serious talks about all kinds of things, the more Chloe's horizons expand beyond things that directly affect her. The idea that she might suddenly disappear or be torn from my life is the ultimate nightmare, and probably what drove me to sign up for the Janina story. It was prompted by the same psychological drive that makes us read cruel fairy tales or watch horror movies: the desire to somehow escape our worst fears and fantasies by experiencing them in a virtual way.

Janina lives in one of those four- or five-story 1950s Berlin tenements with unadorned gray facades that were built to fill the many gaps made during the war. I slipped into the building behind a pamphlet deliverer, who did the usual trick of pushing all the doorbells and waiting for someone to open. The stairwell was dark and had a musty smell of old plaster. Janina lives on the second floor with her mother and grandmother, who came to Berlin from some distant Russian province in the early 1990s as ethnic Germans. The door of their apartment was open: perhaps they had assumed that it was me who had rung the bell, as the editorial office would have announced my arrival. But perhaps it was to air the place, which smelled of some kind of fried breakfast.

To draw attention to myself, I gently knocked on the living room doorframe, but the grandmother, who was sitting on a tattered plush sofa, staring at the TV, did not respond. She was hard of hearing, as I later learned, and barely spoke any German. What's more, both Janina's mother and grandmother were in an apathetic, even paralyzed state, as I soon discovered. They could go about everyday things like preparing an elaborate breakfast or opening the door, but rather robotically, without much interest or energy. To use the old-style film jargon that I had already mentally noted for my article, the scene was . . . spine-chilling.

I sat down in one of the cheap brown armchairs and looked at the grandmother, who stared blankly through me at the TV. There was a video game playing on the screen—*Super Mario*, as I knew from the movie in the nineties, whose banality was not easy to bear, even for a well-meaning critic like me. And squatting in front of the TV was an eight- or nine-year-old girl, who was steering the Mario figure up and down through a world of ruins and swaying tropical plants, in which flashing treasure chests sometimes appeared, or bulging-eyed monsters with small claws and large jaws full of pointed teeth, which opened and closed voraciously. For a while, the girl managed to dodge the monsters deftly and grab one treasure chest after another; but then a monster emerged from behind a fern bush and seized her in its jaws. The screen froze and words flashed to a simple jingle: *You lose a life. Game over.*

The mother came in with two plates of bacon swimming in grease next to some slices of dark bread. I apologized for my intrusion—the door had been open, I said. But when I saw the latest issue of our newspaper on the table, I somehow felt welcome.

"Perhaps," I said, "your daughter is only at a friend's house. Most cases of missing persons are solved harmlessly within forty-eight hours."

Janina's mother turned to the grandmother and spoke in some language at great volume: I assumed that she had translated my comment. The grandmother nodded silently, but I did not have the impression that my thoughts were particularly comforting. For a while, I took in the artificial sounds and simple loops of the video-game music and said nothing. I was not here as a psychologist, but as a journalist, an observer of the monotony and anxiety of waiting. In my article, I would definitely mention the way the girl fled her oppressive reality into the artificiality of Super Mario's world. That's what the readers of our newspaper would want to know—the story of the people behind the headlines. A human-interest story, as we say in the trade.

"May I have a look at Janina's room?" I asked. The mother translated, and the grandmother nodded.

The room was small and narrow, with barely enough space for the bed and low cupboard. Pictures of horses and cats were stuck to the walls, along with childlike drawings, which the girl hadn't wanted to part with yet. The blanket was still lying there, probably just as she had flung it to one side yesterday morning; everything generally looked as if Janina might come in at any moment and resume her life like nothing had happened. And maybe she would too, because what I had said was true: most missing persons' cases turned out okay in the end.

At the desk, I opened one of the school exercise books and, with a certain frisson, felt like an investigator or detective from one of the many crime films I'd seen over the years. Having said that, I had no idea what I was looking for. It only happened in movies. I thought briefly of *The Girl with the Dragon Tattoo*, in which the journalist discovers more than the police. I looked around, but it was clear to me that, aside from the fact that I don't look like Daniel Craig, I'm never going to be Mikael Blomkvist in search of an entrepreneur's lost grandniece.

Soft footsteps at the door made me look up. Janina's sister came into the room, although I didn't actually know whether she really was Janina's sister, or a half- or stepsister, or just a girl who, for whatever reason, had been sitting in front of the TV in the living room, eating and playing Super Mario. She stopped and looked at me sadly.

I put the exercise book back on the desk and said, "It's going to be okay."

She nodded weakly, came closer, and said, "I'm so scared."

"I understand," I said, trying to comfort her. "But you know, we often imagine the worst, and then it turns out quite differently."

"Do you have to go now?" she asked me.

"Yes, I just wanted to see how you all are. You, your mother, and your grandma." (She didn't correct me and so this confirmed that she really was Janina's sister.) "Many people are interested in you and I'm going to tell them. That's my job. People are scared just like you, and if they all keep you in their thoughts, you won't feel so alone."

The girl nodded again. "But I'm scared all the same."

By now she was now standing in front of me, looking up. I suddenly realized that she wasn't just trying to describe her feelings but was trying to convey a subtle message, trying to make me understand something. After all, what was she so afraid of? I realized that it wasn't just a vague premonition tormenting her—she was afraid of something concrete. In other words, she knew something. Yes, maybe she even knew what had happened to her sister and was afraid that the same might be done to her.

I squatted down and hugged her gently.

"What are you afraid of? Can you tell me?"

She was shaking with cold and looked clammy. She was breathing softly, and I had the impression that she was struggling to decide whether she should say something or not.

But she stayed quiet, and in the end I said, "It's going to be okay."

What else should I have said? I'm not a cop or an investigative journalist. I didn't want to use the child to get information. Besides, the police had already questioned the girl. How seriously would they take my hunch that she knew something? Not seriously at all was my guess.

When I pulled away, a tear ran down the girl's cheek, which I wiped aside gently. A crying child—now I had my story.

Half an hour later I walked into the park by the Moabit Poststadion, unaware that something of the kind even existed. The spacious sports grounds had fallen into disuse long ago, and over the years had transformed into an inner-city waste-land. Meanwhile, the site had become a hangout for teenagers and local drug users. According to one lead, Janina had been seen here shortly before her disappearance, so the area had been sealed off. Policemen with dogs had moved in and were scrutinizing and sniffing every square inch. Occasional barks echoed across the grounds, where a dense wilderness of shrubs and trees extended in all directions.

The policeman posted at the entrance to the grounds paid no attention to me after I held up my press card with the logo of our newspaper: its initials were instantly recognizable all over our city, and its magical open-sesame effect had often procured me favors. I nodded briefly to the officer to give the impression that this was all part of my daily routine, and as I walked into the grounds, the same movie-like feeling over-came me as it had in Janina's room, of being a journalist in the role of an investigator, which felt a bit exaggerated and inappropriate. I only knew these things—the forensic search, interviewing witnesses—from the comfortable perspective of spectator and critic. But to be honest, as distressing as Jani-na's disappearance was, I was enjoying the invigorating thrill it gave me.

Maybe that's why I started taking photos of the grounds, despite knowing they would be of no use to our newspaper. A crying child—yes, that would have been a possible pic-ture for the front page (I hadn't photographed Janina's sister yet)—but trees and shrubs on a wasteland that used to be a post-office sports stadium? Perhaps the close-up of a police-man with a sniffing dog might have made it onto page seven or eight, but without knowing why, I pointed my phone at a clump of bushes about twenty or thirty yards away that may or may not have already been searched, I didn't know. For some reason, I thought I saw something significant there, but I couldn't put it into words—a detail I had missed, although it was visible.

After taking my photos I went over to examine the group of bushes more closely, but was interrupted by shouts and the rumble of several approaching vehicles. I wheeled around and saw that the city's police commissioner had arrived with an entourage of journalists and photographers: he wanted to show his face at the round-the-clock sniffer dog search party, which he had personally organized, and to answer questions about the case and security in our city more generally. As he did so, his assumed an expression that was both concerned and assertive; and now my career as a film critic did help after all. I immediately saw that his concern was just a sham. He was playing a role—pretty well, admittedly. Had I been a real crime reporter, I would have known about the impromptu press conference, and now wondered if I should join my colleagues to pretend I knew how to play the game—but something held me back. Somehow—and maybe this feeling was just my naivety as an out-of-touch film buff—I felt I was closer to the truth.

I went home to write my article, my human-interest story. After breaking up with Irene I had moved to an overpriced, modern, three-room apartment on one of the constantly congested main streets, complete with honking cars and roaring engines at night from street racers. I didn't need three rooms all for myself, but I wanted Chloe to be able to stay overnight, which she rarely did. After all, the public transportation runs all night, so it's not a big deal to hop from one place to the next at any time of day or night. Of course, I always pretended that it wasn't a big deal when Chloe got ready to leave at around midnight, but it stabbed me in the heart every time. So yesterday, at the Italian place, I had used Berlin's unbeatable nightlife to illustrate the difference between Frankfurt and here. "You know," I'd told her, "Frankfurt is a real backwater compared to Berlin."

"Mom says it's really nice," she said.

"She has to say that, but all Frankfurt really has are banks and big corporations. People run around all day in their suits, ruining the world. You should know that."

"Mom said it was a lot cleaner than here."

"Well, that's not quite true. Frankfurt has more prostitutes than anywhere else in Germany. It's really hard-core. I think Frankfurt has the highest crime rate compared to all other cities. If you're interested, I can ask my colleagues in the police department—they'll know for sure. They're constantly comparing how safe big cities are, and Frankfurt normally comes out at the bottom of the pile. All in all, I think can you consider yourself lucky to be a Berliner."

"Mom thinks people should see something different once in a while."

"Of course—you have to be open to new things. But not to everything. It's not like you're going to take a quick look at the bankers and hookers and then check out again. Mom wants to move there for good, and then you won't be able to cruise around whenever you feel like it, the way you do here. I'm not even sure if it has a subway—a real one, I mean, not just a few shabby train cars. And if you're sick, you'll have to go to Mom's new boyfriend, the miracle healer, with his useless tinctures and potions, and just hope that your body beats the virus on its own somehow. Don't get me wrong, I don't want to make it all seem lousy from the outset, but someone has to tell you what you're getting into."

I was aware, of course, that the picture I was drawing of life in Frankfurt was not exactly objective. But it wasn't completely fake either. No doubt Irene would paint a picture of Frankfurt as paradise on Earth, and who else could counter it with a little reality if not me?

When I entered my apartment, I remembered the photos I had taken at the sports grounds. I plugged my phone into my laptop and opened the files. As someone who grew up with bulky SLRs, I remain stunned by the quality of photos casually shot on devices that were invented to make phone calls and now fit into your pocket. The bushes and shrubs that had seemed so odd to me on the sports grounds appeared clear and sharp under the hazy blue of the sky. I scanned the screen, searching for something—a detail or a clue—but I didn't know what I was looking for. The whole thing was a crazy notion, that was already clear to me. After all, the grounds had been combed by a canine unit, yet I was obsessed with the notion that I might discover something in the photos that would give me clues about Janina's disappearance.

I knew from our photographers that some details are more visible in black-and-white than in color. So I opened the pictures in an image editor, erased the color information, increased the contrast, and improved the sharpness. I enlarged a section of the photo where I had glimpsed some object in front of the bushes to 400 then 800 percent, but at this size, only the individual pixels were visible, and there was no meaningful whole. I played around for two hours with the enhancement and optimization possibilities, but nothing helped. At some point I grew convinced that I could actually make out the sole of a light-colored sneaker lying on its side, then I thought it might be a bare foot, the ragged edge of the object resembling a row of pretty toes. But I rejected this idea and imagined that the shape was a small bag, the kind that some women use for makeup.

Eventually, my eyes got tired from staring at the small screen; it occurred to me that I could continue my investigation on my sixty-inch curved 4K TV, which I had bought a few months ago after my marriage had finally collapsed. Why hadn't I come up with this idea right away? I blew up the area of the photo on the screen and was thrilled, as expected. Brilliant brightness and stunning contrasts! The quality was fantastic—in principle, anyway. It turned out, however, that the exceptional zoom feature of my TV wasn't able to tease out any more detail from the pictures than the maddening pixels from my laptop screen.

I panned across the screen, screwed up my eyes, stepped back from the TV as far as possible, then almost crawled into the fantastic high-tech display—but none of this helped. The memory of an old children's game that I had played with my mother during long, boring car rides came to mind: "I spy with my little eye." That's how it felt right then, with me in the role of the one blindly guessing. "I spy with my little eye . . . something that is dead . . ." But that too was nonsense. A foot, a sneaker, a makeup bag, a discarded tissue, or just a tattered old newspaper—it was impossible to make out one thing or exclude another.

At some point I gave up. I realized that I had gone way off track. The whole thing was ridiculous, an obsession, the root of which wasn't even clear to me. I was not a police officer or a detective, nor had I ever wanted to be one. I turned off the TV, tried to calm down and be reasonable. I was a journalist and I had a story to tell. That was my job, not analyzing photos of potential crime scenes. And I *had* a story, after all:

an apathetic mother, a silent grandmother who wasn't able to speak German, and the younger sister taking refuge from her fear in the colorful fantasy world of a video game. What more did I want? That's what my readers expected of me; that's what I had to deliver.

I sat down at my desk. I had wasted a hell of a lot of time with my photos—my deadline was in an hour. But, hey, I'm no rookie. If I know what to write, I can do it quickly. And the articles in our widely circulated if rather simple newspaper are neither too long nor too deep. Without mulling over the sentences too much, my fingers flew over the keyboard. I had every word in my head and knew that there would be little editing required. I finished the text twenty minutes before we went to press, so I wasn't doing too badly for time. I'd had tighter squeezes in the past.

That night, I slept badly. I had a confusing, downright scary dream. I was in a huge luxury hotel, but the lobby was deserted, and when I set off in search of staff or other hotel guests, I couldn't find anyone. I walked down seemingly endless corridors lined with soft carpeting, went into sophisticated parquet lounges, a lobby with an open fireplace, sprawling ballroom, and even an upscale, orange-paneled bathroom—but I did not come across one single guest or hotel employee along the way. At some point I realized that I was completely alone in the hotel, but just then, I heard old-fashioned dance music coming from the ballroom. A 1920s salon orchestra was playing, and there were guests present, but no one noticed me; it was as though I didn't exist. I sat down at the bar to calm myself with a drink, but that didn't work because the bartender looked at me meaningfully as I pulled out my wallet and said that I, of all people, did not have to pay today . . . and the way he said it held an eerie message that I could not decipher.

Finally, I stood up to go to my room. In the corridors I was completely alone again, and on the way back to the elevator I didn't meet a soul. Feeling I still had to do something that couldn't be put off until tomorrow, I turned into a corridor with an elevator at the end—but as I approached, a torrent of a bloodred liquid came gushing from inside it, spraying like sea surf before turning into a wide current, sweeping up the sofas that rushed inexorably toward me . . .

I woke up drenched in sweat with my heart pounding. Outside dawn was breaking and, because I assumed I wouldn't be able to fall asleep again, I got dressed and drank a cup of coffee. Gradually I calmed down. I traced the nightmare back to yesterday's events. I had no experience in dealing with real crimes, and so my film critic's imagination had run wild in the night.

After coffee I drove to the newsroom. It was way too early, but I decided to focus on Janina's disappearance one more time, intensively and calmly. Perhaps there was new evidence from the police; I couldn't shake the feeling of having overlooked something important. As usual, I grabbed a fresh copy of our newspaper at the door and thumbed through it. To my amazement, I didn't find my Janina human-interest story on page three where I expected it to be, nor in the local section. Confused, I scanned each page a second time, and then there could be no doubt: the article I had quickly typed a few hours ago had not been published.

I was, to put it in our newspaper's jargon, completely stumped. What had gone wrong? All our articles are automatically uploaded to our editorial pool when we save them; perhaps the system hadn't worked. But then why hadn't an impatient, irritated colleague from the editing room phoned me and requested my article? It was very strange. I searched the text pool for my Janina story, not finding it, as I had feared, but I did locate it right away on my laptop. Obviously, I had been thrown out of the system, for whatever reason. But why? And who was behind it?

My pulse quickened. Could it be that Janina's case had stirred up interest among the powers that be? A girl had disappeared and reports were being selectively removed. I didn't need to suffer from paranoia to suspect some dark, mysterious forces behind this operation. How often had it been proven that evidence of sexual offenses reaches up to the highest echelons? And how many films had I seen in which exactly this or something similar had been the case?

I opened the article on my laptop to print it out just in case. But when the text appeared, I got a second shock. I'd given my article the headline "The Beauty and the Beast," which I thought was justified by its content, as well as being a clever allusion. Or at least I was convinced that this is what I'd done. But now the title read, "I Spy with My Little Eye." Not a bad choice, thought the journalist in me, but not the one I was convinced I had made eight or so hours ago. And that was not all. My entire text, my atmospheric human-interest story on Janina, now consisted of one sentence, endlessly strung together: *I spy with my little eye. I spy with my little eye. I spy with my little eye . . .*

I stared at the screen, and what happened next is not the kind of hyperbole that often finds its way into our newspaper, but the plain truth: I broke out in a sweat. Someone had accessed and tampered with the document on my laptop and replaced it with a line repeated a hundred times: *I spy with my little eye.* Which amounted to the blatant threat: *I know who you are. I know what you're doing. I see you!* Or a little less formally: *Don't stick your nose into things that are none of your business.*

And I realized something else—my third shock—at that very moment: whoever had swapped out the article knew about my meeting with Janina's sister. Because the short conversation with the girl had been the highlight and culmination of my piece:

> *Janina's sister comes into the room. She has interrupted her video game, and now she stands hesitantly at the door. It seems as if she wants to say something, but then she is silent. At some point a tear runs down her cheek. Does she know something? For a moment it seems so. Perhaps the mystery of Janina's disappearance lies hidden deep inside her.*

Of course I was aware of the lurid and highly speculative nature of the last sentence, but that's the style of our newspaper. You have to go easy on allegations, but speculation is the spice of journalism. In this particular case, however, I couldn't rule out that I had endangered the girl with my suggestion that she might know something about her sister's disappearance. Because whoever had harmed Janina was now alarmed. Because of my article, Janina's sister was now a potential witness, a risk to the perpetrators, and someone who needed to be eliminated. Somehow I had to warn the girl, and somehow—without having the vaguest notion how—I had to protect her. With that in mind, I left the newsroom as quickly and discreetly as possible.

Maybe that was my destiny: protecting girls from the uncertainties of life. And I could only hope that I would have more success with Janina's sister than with my own daughter. I had tried everything the night before the editorial meeting to make it clear to Chloe that it would be a mistake to go to Frankfurt with Irene; but for some reason I couldn't get through to her. I had talked and talked, but apparently Irene had worked on her for so long in advance and had stirred up the mood against me that Chloe didn't believe a word I said— on the contrary. At some point she actually claimed I was only against the move to Frankfurt to spite her mother.

"Why is it so important all of a sudden for me to live with you? You've never really taken an interest in my life," she said (and her words sounded as if they were coming straight from Irene's mouth). "What do you know about me? Do you even know what I like? Let's be honest: whenever things got difficult, you left all the upbringing stuff to Mom. Sometimes I feel like I'm just a character in a movie to you. Okay, it's the movie of your life, and I play your daughter in it, and I guess that means something. But I've never had much of a role. You're kidding yourself if you think you can give me what I need. No, Dad, really. The two of us here in Berlin wouldn't work."

Her accusations hit me hard. I had always thought we had a reasonably smooth relationship, but now I realized that Chloe saw it very differently: in her eyes, we had no relationship at all. I felt wronged. In contrast to the never-ending, hysterical quarrels she had gone through with Irene, I had always considered myself the sensible, quiet influence in her life. Whether it was her clothes (she had only worn black for some time), what she did during the weekends (I assumed an interesting mix of drugs were in play), or her academic pursuits (they could hardly be called achievements), I did not interfere. But here she was, accusing me of just that, as if my comparative coolness on these issues (we all had our clothing fads, drinking bouts, and slack phases at school) were merely apathy. I couldn't believe it. She actually preferred a life with the eternally cantankerous Irene to a few quiet years with me.

"You're not serious," I said, hurt. "I've always been there for you."

"Forget it, Dad," she said. "You don't even know who I am."

With these words she had turned and crossed the street to enter the subway on the other side. Her black clothes blended into the Berlin night, shimmering against the traffic lights and neon signs. I wanted to call after her, but I didn't know what to say. Then the light changed and the approaching traffic became an insurmountable barrier between us. I watched powerlessly as Chloe entered the station and eventually disappeared.

I stood paralyzed on my side of the road and stared dejectedly at the blue subway sign. Cars lurched past in the traffic. And then, after I don't know how long, I couldn't stand it any longer. I ran blindly across the street in the hope that the train hadn't yet arrived and that I'd be able to catch Chloe. But I didn't get that far because all of a sudden, I felt a violent blow to the side of my body. Tires slid across the asphalt with a shrill squeal, the lights of the night whirled around me kaleidoscopically, I flew, I hovered . . . and then, after time seemed to stand still for a moment, I ended up across the street underneath the blue station sign.

I hardly knew what had happened, but the impulse to stop Chloe was still strong. I ignored everything that was going on around me, ignored the passersby who were staring in horror because of the accident—*my* accident, that much was clear to me—ignored the onset of horns because the traffic had come to a standstill, and somehow scrambled to my feet. Yes, I could still walk; yes, I was conscious. Miraculously, I was unhurt. I rushed down the stairs and reached the platform out of breath—but I was too late. All I could see were the taillights of the train pulling away and then I was alone.

Only now did I become aware of the raging pain in my skull. I sat on the cold wire-mesh benches in front of the tracks and my head was empty. Gradually the platform filled up with people who paid as little attention to me as I did to them. It was a disaster—not the accident, but my life. My daughter had left me; she had gone, disappeared, was no longer there. I hadn't been able to stop her. I was seized by the panic that I would never see her again. She had put it into plain words: it didn't work with the two of us. At some point, the next train arrived. I got on, sat down, and let myself be rocked through the stone guts of our city, on the way to somewhere, a night ghost, already dead, a dead man walking . . .

I can barely remember entering my apartment, but at some point I was lying in bed, awake and desperate—perhaps that's why the next morning at the editorial meeting I had been so quick to take up Janina's case. I wanted to undo a human disappearance—Chloe's disappearance. My dedication was an obsession. It was a fight against the most painful defeat I had ever suffered.

Something—a sixth sense or a vague desire to save Janina's sister—dragged me back to the Moabit apartment once more, and when I got there, everything was the same as the day before: the apartment door was open, breakfast eggs were being fried, and I could smell bacon. Life had to go on, even without Janina. I hadn't announced my arrival, but Janina's mother and grandmother stoically accepted my presence, just like on the previous day, as if a journalist's visit was as much a part of their everyday life as a fried breakfast.

I went into the living room with the gray, diffused daylight and the hectic color changes of the video game. Janina's sister was sitting in front of the TV steering the multicolored Mario through the same enchanted world of treasure chests and deadly monsters as yesterday. However, it struck me that not only the setting of the game was the same, but all the moves were the same too. Once again, a monster emerged from behind a fern bush, the screen froze, and the text appeared: *You lose a life. Game over.* The girl, I realized, was not controlling the character, but sitting in front of a demo version.

Though this struck me as weird, I was mostly relieved to even see her there. After all the worries and the blame I'd given myself for the article, I was able to say that she was fine. And when I stepped a little closer, she was the only one who took any notice of me. She turned around and I saw that she was glad to see me, and that made me especially happy. In the peculiar state I had been in for the past two days, she was a ray of hope: the only person who truly saw me and valued my presence. How good that felt.

She got up, took my hand, and brought me into her sister's room. I assumed that she wanted to show me something and already had the feeble journalistic hope that I might learn something new about Janina's disappearance.

"What's your name anyway?" I asked her.

She stopped and looked up at me. "Janina."

"Janina? Like your sister?"

She looked at me in surprise. "My sister?"

"Yes . . . who . . . the day before yesterday . . ." I did not quite know how to put it without hurting her too much. "The one who everyone is looking for right now . . ."

She shook her little head. "I don't have a sister. But I know that people are looking for *me*. You are too."

"But . . ." I did not understand. Had she repressed what had happened? Was her belief that she was her sister a way of dealing with the incident? Did she want to help Janina by sacrificing herself in her imagination? Only a child psychologist could tell.

"I'm so glad you found me," she said. "I was so terribly alone after . . ."

"After what?"

She was silent for a long time, but then she said softly: "After the man hurt me."

"Hurt you? Who?"

"He did something to me . . . and he held my mouth shut and I couldn't breathe . . . He was much stronger than me, and I couldn't stop him . . . There was nothing I could do . . . I couldn't breathe for ages and then I was suddenly able to move again. The man was still standing in front of me, but I was able to get up and walk away. And do you know what I saw then?"

"No," I whispered.

"I turned around and saw myself, the man . . . doing that . . . to me . . . And I ran away very fast . . . all the doors were suddenly open . . . I ran here, but my mother and grandmother can't see or hear me . . . No one can see and hear me, only you . . . I'm so happy!"

She wanted to hug me, and I crouched down. Endless questions swirled through my head, and I couldn't answer a single one. When the girl threw her arms around me, I felt the coolness of her body, which I'd already noticed yesterday. And I became aware of something else: my body was cool too. But whatever that meant, I didn't want to think about it right then. Because I was bursting with happiness that I meant so much to this girl. She wanted to be with me and I felt the same way: I wanted to be with her, protect and shelter her, share my life with her. And yes—even if it sounds completely exaggerated and pathetic for the short time that we had known each other—I wanted to be like a father to her. I wanted to start all over again.

THE BEAUTY OF KENILWORTH IVY

BY SUSANNE SAYGIN

Schöneberg

"Do I look like a hustler?" A question, not in the least aggressive, as if he were asking me the time or the weather forecast. The man was too close to me, his crotch at eye level.

I raised my eyes. "Do I look like I can tell?"

He studied me for a moment, then his gaze flickered, as if he had only just realized who was sitting in front of him. "Sorry," he said. He turned away and walked down the road in the direction of Tempelhofer Feld: late twenties, about five feet nine, still well-toned but with the first signs of running too fat. His jeans were cut off just below his butt. The setting sun made the blond fuzz on his thighs glint.

I stayed sitting on the bench and leaned back. The moment when the target singles itself out is like a gift, every time. The building touching my back was still hot from the sun.

Someone had sprayed *Fuck gentrification!* on the wall opposite. Until recently, even down-at-heel bohemians could afford spacious apartments with exposed floorboards and stucco ceilings in Berlin for next to nothing. But now well-off people were suddenly taking over, people who could afford higher rents, or who simply bought their own apartments—go-getting young lawyers with their blond, supple wives, whose children wore zany, multicolored organic prints; or software developers at some start-up or the other, who spent all their money on minimally furnished apartments, costly Nikes, and racing bikes with bamboo frames.

I'm relaxed about the topic of gentrification. Of course all things wild and wonderful are slowly vanishing from the city center, slipping to the fringes before they disappear completely. But why should things in the city be any different from nature? Out there too, every stretch of wasteland is first populated by enterprising plants that drift in on the wind: the South African ragwort, the common mallow, the red poppy. All these species make up for their weak substance and lack of assertiveness with flashy colors and infinite fertility. "Poor but sexy," to quote a former Berlin mayor. However, by the following spring at the latest, the first tree saplings shoot—maples, poplars, robinias—and soon their canopies are so dense that nothing can grow beneath them anymore. In the end there will be a forest. At least until the first storm or bark beetle rips a hole in it and everything starts all over again. In ecology, it's called succession—a natural process, no big deal.

Not for me anyway. Rather, it makes things easier. Take accommodation, for one. Hotels aren't suitable for my missions, of course. But thanks to gentrification, over the past few years I've been able to check into an Airbnb in any neighborhood of my choice, register via a strategically maintained Facebook profile, transfer the fee with a prepaid credit card, collect keys from a storage box, wear latex gloves in the apartment—no traces, no contact. It's vastly more convenient than before, when I had to resort to apartment shares for my missions, only to find myself, more often than not, in messy Kreuzberg kitchens alongside people who eyed me (if at all) with contempt because I did not fit into their ideas of wild unorthodoxy. Which, of course, suited me down to the ground but also made me laugh, because the unorthodoxy of these ex-country-bumpkins-turned-city-slickers was humdrum and superficial.

Have you ever heard of bombweed? In the first summers after the war, this plant—the rosebay willow herb—sprung up everywhere on Berlin's derelict ruins and gutted walls. Bombweed, which had only grown in fields up until then, took over the devastated city. As far as the eye could see, its vivid blossoms blazed in identical garish pink. In late summer, its white, velvety swathes of seeds drifted over ruins, settling into every crack and making new purple clusters. Then the gaps in the cityscape were closed as Berlin underwent reconstruction and bombweed was slowly driven back. Now you can count yourself lucky if you spot a lone flower along the subway tracks. Meanwhile, more discreet species have gained the upper hand in the city: common knotgrass, white man's foot, and—in particularly favorable conditions—Kenilworth ivy, which turns its shoots just so that its tiny seed-bearing nuts can germinate in the minute cracks in walls. Do I have to spell out how much I relate to this plant?

But I'm digressing. Once a year, my missions bring me to the capital for four weeks. My qualifications for this task are incontestable: studies in botany, followed by a PhD in phytochemistry and plant sociology—observing, typifying, systematizing with great tenacity over the years. Finally, I switched to the police force, first the uniforms, then criminal investigation. And then more of the same: observing, typifying, systematizing. But I also identified and eliminated potential threats. As far as the latter is concerned, I had some serious conflicts—not so much with my colleagues, who generally shared my views, but with my superiors. At that level, people like to resort to expressions such as "powers of intervention," "police law," and "disciplinary action"—all terms that are hardly reliable when it comes to depicting the reality in the field. The transfer to a desk job was a blow, no doubt about it. So now, it is all the more important to do my missions, because they maintain my equilibrium. They help me keep up active practice of my strengths: observational powers, solution-oriented thinking, consequences. And no, it's not what you think: the missions are explicitly *not* about tidying things up. On the contrary, nature shows that an ecosystem is more stable the richer in species (i.e., the messier) it is. You're probably familiar with this from the instructions for natural gardening that are endlessly reiterated in every women's magazine: musty corners, broken clay pots, and piles of brushwood make a home for those light-shunning creepy crawlies without which all the hard-working bees, fluffy blue tits, and cute little hoglets that townies associate with pristine nature can't be had. In a nutshell: no harmony without disorder.

But there are always factors that upset this natural disorder. Take the greater dodder, for example: a climbing species from a genus of the bindweed family in the order of Solanales; no roots, its leaves degenerated to scale-like tips, incapable of photosynthesis, hence an obligate parasite that prefers to prey on stinging nettles. The dodder barely sprouts before its seedling tendrils start searching for a host, taking their cue from the volatile odors secreted by nettles. Once the seedling has picked up the scent, it grows swiftly toward the host plant. Having found its target, it entwines itself around the nettle, driving thorn-shaped suction shoots deep into the host's tissue, tapping its flesh for water and nutrients, and, over the course of the summer, increasingly engulfing its weakened victim in an obscene flesh-colored web.

You will argue that the greater dodder is a rare plant species, affecting only nettles. And, of course, you're right. But don't you find that its modus operandi has an unbearably cruel touch? And is this cruelty relativized in your eyes by the fact that we're only referring to an evil weed? If so, what happens when we map its behavior onto a human scenario? Would the world be poorer without the greater dodder? Would you be sad to see this parasitical plant terminated *before* it managed to strangle the nettles?

I already settled these questions for myself long ago—which brings me back to my missions. This year, I opted for a site in north Neukölln, just within the subway ring, surrounded by old buildings and linden trees lining the street. The Airbnb hostess had advertised her place as being within easy walking distance of Tempelhofer Feld. This might be a bonus for others, but I don't come to Berlin to gaze at parched inner-city grassland. What was decisive for my choice of site was, firstly, the apartment's location and, secondly, the facilities: front-facing building, ground floor, large flower tubs and a bench on the sidewalk in front of the door. Ideal conditions for a discreet field survey.

In fact, I've spent the time since my arrival three weeks ago mostly on this bench. In this phase of the mission, I can't emphasize enough that it is a huge mistake to be guided by stereotypes like wealthy Wilmersdorf widows, rich Russians in Charlottenburg, bearded hipsters in Mitte, old-school punks or limousine liberals in Kreuzberg. Of course, such generalizations can be justified to a certain extent, in a similar way that you draw on characteristics of plant communities to systemize them; but, ultimately, they reveal little about local conditions. I'll spare you the usual clichés of Neukölln: extended Arab families, a parallel society, an underclass of excluded have-nots. Not that I don't see all this from my observation post—I do. But if I had to name a typical taxon, I'd say: native German, male, welfare recipient, over fifty years of age, in a death-metal T-shirt tightly stretched over a paunch, drinking problem. The morning noises of clinking bottles and dry heaving are just as typical as the screeching tires of a young Arab with a carefully trimmed jihadist beard taking off at top speed in his black Merc.

Besides these stereotypes, there are many normal working people in my survey area this year: they are German rather than immigrant, young rather than old, and more likely to be in the lower wage bracket than in management positions. In addition, you have a flock of German, Turkish, and Arab mothers who drop off their children at one of the three kindergartens, housewives who take their dogs for walks, students who get their rolls from the Turkish baker, a tenement block of Bulgarian Romani, a handful of American expats, a few moderately successful artists, a café, three 7-Elevens, a vacant dive bar on the corner, two brothels and four pubs under southeastern European management, two gambling dens that are always empty, a Lebanese greengrocer, an Arab hairdresser, an esoteric shop, and a thrift store. Comparable social groupings can be observed in every average German city.

That pretty much covers empirical values. Let us now turn to the determination of variance, i.e., abnormalities caused by the behavioral deviations of individuals. A very high number of lone figures feature prominently in this year's target area. For example, there is the woman in her midseventies who bares her withered breasts every few days in the Turkish bakery, her face void of expression; or there are the two ageless and sexless figures who stand out prominently due to their incessant combing of the streets for empties and cigarette butts, always hand in hand, but never seeming to say a word to each other; and there is the hulking man in his forties who gazes at himself every few feet in the reflection of ground-floor windows and slicks his hair back over his square skull with a plastic comb. The list could go on forever.

The number of potential targets in the intake area therefore appears to be very high. But this—and I'm always having to point this out—this is precisely where the real work begins. Not every "wacko," as my colleagues like to call such characters, makes a target. Rather, what has to be determined is the extent to which outsiders like these actually represent a significant deviation from the local average. In other words, if an intake area proves to be a biotope for crazies, this is by no means a license to indiscriminately weed them out. It merely means that the survey parameters have to be adjusted. What has to be examined in particular is the degree to which deviation from the norm is still tolerated in the specified area. For me, this step is perhaps the most fascinating of every mission: prejudices are revised, scenes shift, and new perspectives emerge.

Let me clarify using the above examples. From the conversations of coffee drinkers in the Turkish bakery, I deduced that the old exhibitionist had previously run the dive bar on the corner that is now closed. The hapless flaunting of her body was met with embarrassment, because many still remember the days when the bar lady's bosom was nothing other than a covered, tautly ripened promise. As for the bottle-collector couple, it should be reported that worried neighbors formed a search party after they hadn't been seen for more than a day. And the man with the hairstyling compulsion was a taciturn but well-liked regular at the welfare café around the corner.

Although the behavior of oddballs such as these may appear strange to onlookers, their social environment does not perceive them as nuisances; in fact, they are even part of a social structure in which they fulfill a function of sorts. Therefore, they no longer comply with the requirements for potential targets, because these stipulate—let us call to mind the example of the greater dodder—that a target should not only make no identifiable contribution to the local community, it also has to represent a threat.

Let me also illustrate this with an example. Last year I stayed in the Rheingau district in Wilmersdorf. Even in this refuge of well-groomed bourgeoisie, an astonishingly wide range of potential targets turned up within a very short time, although most of them were rejected in a similar way to their counterparts in Neukölln this year. Meanwhile, Ms. B rose higher on my list every day. Tall, in her late forties, with a severe hairstyle and unfashionable glasses, she had already come to my attention on the morning of my arrival, when she harshly rebuked a man bent double with age who accidentally brushed against her in the bakery with his walker. The following evening, just as the blue hour was starting, I spotted Ms. B on a balcony on the other side of Rüdesheimer Platz, directly opposite my Airbnb. There she stood and, in an increasingly shrill voice, shrieked at the patrons of the Rheingau wine festival to be quiet. This was an evening ritual, as I soon understood, which contrasted sharply with the peaceful mood of the visitors.

Nonetheless, I only determined Ms. B as my target a full three weeks later when I witnessed her shooing away a homeless person who was sitting peacefully in the morning sun on a bench at the Siegfried fountain.

The next day I saw Ms. B again at the bakery. On the way back to Rüdesheimer Platz, I caught up with her, as if by accident, and praised her unwavering campaign against the wine festival. For a moment, Ms. B eyed me suspiciously, but then she took the bait: the noise was so intolerable, she said, that she was only able to calm her nerves with homeopathic drops. I feigned an interest in alternative medicine: which preparation could Ms. B recommend? She relied on strychnine tincture, combined with a tablespoon of wormwood formula at bedtime. A methodological no-brainer. I would have liked a bigger challenge. But it's not for me to choose. I dragged out our conversation. When we said goodbye at her house shortly afterward, Ms. B invited me to tea the coming Saturday. That left me three and a half days. Tight but doable, especially as I had a supply of strychnine seeds from an earlier mission.

Producing an extract of *Strychnos nux-vomica* in the required concentration is somewhat exacting; yet with expertise, the right equipment, and a little bit of practice, it can be carried out in any regular German kitchen. So, when I rang the bell at Ms. B's. on Saturday afternoon, I was well prepared.

I should make myself comfortable on the balcony while she brewed the tea, she said. On the balcony: a teak table and chairs, porcelain, silver spoons, tea biscuits. The red of the geraniums clashed with the orange of the awnings. Down in the square, girls were French-skipping. I closed my eyes, listening to the monotonous rhythm of their counting rhymes, and for a moment I was thrown back to the early seventies.

Shortly afterward, Ms. B sat down across from me at the balcony table. Even while pouring tea with a stiff, straight back, she embarked on an endless litany about the wickedness of the world. Soon her mouth turned into a bright-red, ranting slit before my eyes.

I asked to use the bathroom. On the way, I took in Ms. B's kitchen: an aged but scrupulously clean kitchen unit, no dishwasher, a neon tube light on the ceiling. On the Formica table, a place was already set for supper: a place mat, a little wooden board, a butter knife with a plastic handle, and, next to the water glass, a bowl of soaking prunes. I digested this still life. For a fraction of a second, I doubted my mission. This involuntary hesitation in the face of the existential loneliness of my targets has always occurred at some point on every mission. But over the years, I've learned to see these glitches for what they really are: a sentimental reflex.

Of course my targets are lonely, but that applies to many people; I'd even go as far as to say that loneliness is the essence of the human condition. Which, in turn, explains why it touches us so much to see someone else's isolation. The question, however, is how we deal with our personal limitations. We can try to overcome them in our relationships with others. We can accept our loneliness and become stable. Or we can settle somewhere between these two poles. But no one—I repeat, NO ONE—is compelled to be malicious due to loneliness. The decision to be malicious is always a conscious one and it always has a serious impact on our social environment. I keep this fact in mind whenever I run the risk of getting held back by sentimentality.

In the case mentioned here, such self-discipline wasn't necessary. Ms. B's wooden chair scraped abruptly across the balcony tiles. The next moment, her already familiar shrill cries for silence rang out across the square. The counting stopped, the children's shoes clattered across the asphalt, then it all went quiet. My hostess straightened her chair and leaned back, sighing.

I pulled on my latex gloves, went into the bathroom, and opened the medicine cabinet: inside there was cream for mature skin, mascara, lipstick, a whole battery of homeopathic remedies, and the wormwood formula. I left Ms. B's strychnine tincture untouched—the bitterness of my extract would stand out immediately. The pervasive taste of wormwood formula, on the other hand, would mask the strange new undertone sufficiently. I flushed half of the formula down the toilet and filled up the rest with my extract. Then I pretended to wash my hands, peeled off my latex gloves in the hallway, and went past the kitchen to the balcony.

I sat back down and praised how quiet the building was. Ms. B shrugged. Unfortunately, she said, she would only be able to enjoy the silence until the end of next week, when her neighbors returned from holiday. Then everything would go back to the usual pandemonium. The ranting slit was off again.

Half an hour later I said goodbye. There was no one in the stairwell; no one saw me exit the building. I disposed of the latex gloves and the remainder of the extract in a trash can. I bought bread and some cheese and sat on my balcony with a bottle of Riesling. At around half past eight, Ms. B pulled up the awning. She moved into the kitchen, ate her supper, and washed up. At around nine o'clock she returned to the balcony and began her usual screeches for quiet. "Go get laid, you dried-up old hag—go have some fun!" came a loud riposte from below. There was restrained laughter down in the square and a few people clapped. Ms. B slammed her balcony door.

Shortly afterward, the light went on in the bathroom. For a while, shadowy outlines could be made out against the stippled glass window and then, abruptly, nothing, even though the light in the bathroom was still on. I sat in the dark on my balcony, drank my Riesling, and listened to the soft chatter drifting up from the wine festival. At around midnight I went to bed.

The next morning the light in Ms. B's bathroom was still

on, but the balcony door remained closed and the awning up. I packed and did my usual thorough cleaning of the guest apartment. For the first time since my arrival, not a peep was heard that evening from Ms. B. I enjoyed a glass of sparkling pinot by the Siegfried fountain in peace. Twelve hours later I left. I followed coverage of the case from afar.

You will argue that death by strychnine is one of the most horrible things that can happen to a person. That is correct. However, no herbal toxin causes a gentle death, except perhaps opium. And if you muster too much compassion for a target, and wish him or her a gentle passing in their sleep, then you should ask some fundamental questions about the intent of your mission, or at least the choice of target.

This brings me back to the young man in the tight shorts who featured in my opening remarks. In fact, I'd had him in my sights as a possible target since the morning of my arrival and nothing had altered my opinion so far. The list of his peculiarities starts with his sitting in the lotus position every morning between the bike racks and the dumpster in the yard, dressed only in a black kimono, staring at the courtyard wall while the other tenants walk past him to work.

As I quickly found out, he has no gainful employment. Instead, "#holzhammer" or "#h," as he calls himself, stylizes himself as a performance artist, filming his interventions with a cheap webcam, then posting them on social media. In one of these videos, #h uses dog shit to smear the words *money = feces* on the facade of a neighboring building in protest of the displacement of vulnerable tenants due to luxury renovations. The house was repainted not long ago, in fact, but the light-yellow paint coat is already cracking again and the apartment balconies are dominated by satellite dishes, laundry racks, and empty beer crates. In another video, filmed against the backdrop of the refugee camp on the Tempelhofer Feld, #h philosophizes about his tough fate as the grandson of German refugees from Sudetenland. His latest activity is to hammer handwritten notes into the trunks of the linden trees that line the street with thick nails. On these notes, #h attests to the refugees' moral depravity due to lack of parental love, provoking bleak, orthographically shaky counterspeeches, which are pasted to our front door overnight. Mostly, however, #h's interventions have produced a rather muted response. His number of Facebook friends is in the lower double digits; his videos get a hundred views at most, and the comments below do not mince words. #h attributes the failure of his work to the exclusion mechanisms of the international art market where, as an autodidact, he doesn't stand a chance.

In short, #h had already qualified for the prime position as a possible target before he came over to me in his shorts with his hustler question. Let me make one thing clear at this point: I have no problem with homosexuals. To tell the truth, I have never understood sexuality at all. Other people's desire, no matter what its persuasion, simply baffles me. Rather, what intrigued me most about #h's latest pose was his timing. At the end of July, Berlin was gearing up for its Christopher Street Day parade. So, it was clear which front #h was getting ready to fight on next.

I went inside and powered up my laptop. And there he was: not even two hours earlier, #h had uploaded a shaky video where he was standing in front of a relevant establishment in Schöneberg. On the soundtrack he rapped against the "sado/maso fascism" of the gay community and promised to commit a "radical act" at the CSD.

Well, there are certainly enough people who would find nothing wrong with that—roughing up a mass rally of, at best, scantily clad leather slaves, bears, and beefcakes; but I tend to agree with that old Prussian faggot, Frederick II, that everyone has to seek heaven in his own fashion, even if your particular heaven is the darkness of a smother box. That's why I felt #h's agitation was all the more offensive, and his choice as a target became even more certain. I watched #h's video again, then went to the bathroom and made some necessary changes to my appearance.

Two hours later I was at Nollendorfplatz. I left the subway station with its rainbow-colored dome and turned onto Motzstrasse. It was Saturday night; the day had been hot and the night did not promise any relief. It was rush hour on the streets. I drifted through the pubs without a specific goal, trying to pick up the target's trail, studying the window displays of piercing salons, casting stolen glances into massage parlors, and losing myself in side streets. At some point, I spotted #h. He was standing in one of the fetish stores, being shown a black shiny latex suit with a long devil's tail. Afterward he tried on a stocking mask covered in spiked studs without mouth- or eyeholes.

When he took the things to the cashier, I slipped away from my lookout post and moved on. In Fuggerstrasse I drank a Hefeweizen beer next to German pensioners and Balkan boys with emaciated faces and plucked eyebrows. Later, I stood on the mezzanine in a gay disco and watched the activity down on the dance floor. For a moment I thought I had identified #h among the dancers, but I wasn't sure.

At dawn I returned to Neukölln. I slept briefly and then took up my position on the bench. In the early evening #h left the house with a backpack. I followed him to an abandoned community garden between the subway tracks and the south perimeter of Tempelhofer Feld. #h squeezed through a hole in the fence of a deserted lot. He set up his webcam on the terrace of the arbor and unpacked a pile of old sheets. For the next hour and a half, he was busy with spray cans and a stencil. Afterward he retreated with his camera into the garden hut.

When #h stepped back onto the terrace at nightfall, he was wearing the latex suit. He packed the sheets into his backpack, pulled on the mask, and forced his way back through the hole in the fence. Soon after, he made a hole in the fence to the subway tracks with a bolt cutter and disappeared through it to the other side. Silently, I slipped through after him. #h fastened his sheets all along the subway fence in the direction of oncoming trains. The black lettering of *Stop homofascism!* stood out in sharp contrast to the white background of the sheets.

After about two hours, all the banners were up. #h crossed the subway tracks, produced his webcam, and sat down in a white garden chair that someone had left on the embankment. There he set up the camera, surveying his work. Occasionally he cracked his latex devil's tail in the air like a whip. When a train approached, the rivets on his mask shone, making it look like a weird horned helmet. Otherwise, nothing happened. At some point, I went back to my apartment and fell into a fitful sleep.

When I started up my computer the next morning, #h had already uploaded the video from last night: inflammatory tirades against "homofascists," a confused confession of his own (unclear) sexual orientation, and another announcement of a radical intervention at CSD.

An hour later I squeezed my way through the hole in the fence of the deserted garden and checked the hut. #h was not there. I put on gloves and sneaked over to the door. It was not locked. Inside there was a musty smell. A camp bed, a fifties bedside table, a kerosene lamp. Next to the lamp was a dog-eared photo of a child: a boy in a black suit with a bow tie—#h at an earlier stage. On the back: *Congratulations on your first Communion from your nana, who loves you very much.* I put the photo back and turned around. The latex suit and mask were hanging on a hook on the door. The mask was made of very thin black gauze, which it was possible to see and breathe through even without the holes. Next to the camp bed was a plastic bottle labeled, *Mojito Latex Dressing Aid.* The greenish gel smelled of peppermint and cheap booze. I made a note of the ingredients. Then I opened the bedside drawer: ecstasy, speed, a bag of crystal—the entire arsenal of synthetic drugs to ensure entry into today's artificial paradises. Suddenly, all I wanted was to get away from this hut and the community garden.

On the way back, something like a plan formed in my mind, though it remained vague and beyond my grasp. Then, on the embankment on the other side of the subway tracks, near the spot where #h had sat the night before, I spotted an almost ultraviolet glow. Suddenly, my mind sharpened. I looked for the hole #h had cut in the subway fence, crossed the tracks, and soon afterward found the source of the blue glow. Among the gray mugwort and the dark-green blackberries on the railway embankment, the blue flowers of a devil's helmet were swaying in the wind. I thought of #h sitting with his horned mask in the white garden chair and cracking his whiplike latex tail. I thought of what I'd seen in the garden hut. I thought of the way devil's helmet works. And everything fell into place.

Back in my apartment, I took my folding spade and thick

lab gloves. Half an hour later I had cut off a length of the devil's helmet root on the embankment. I spent the afternoon preparing the root extract. When I was done, I ordered an Afro wig in rainbow colors from eBay. Then I sat outside with a beer.

It wasn't long before #h headed off in the direction of the garden. I followed at a safe distance. When I reached the garden, he was already inside the hut. Hidden by a thicket of weeds, I slunk up and peered inside. The kerosene lamp was burning. #h was sitting in the latex suit and mask on the bed, looking at his childhood photo. His shoulders were shaking as if he were crying. The familiar doubt drifted through me. Suddenly #h jumped up, tore up the photo, and stamped on the tattered remains in a rage.

"Nazi cunt!" he shouted. "Fucking old Sudeten Nazi cunt!" I ducked away from the window and slipped back through the overgrown garden and the hole in the fence. That night, I slept deeply and dreamlessly.

Two days later it was CSD. I packed the wig into a bag and sat down on the bench. Unlike I'd expected, #h did not leave the house for the parade in the afternoon, but only when darkness fell. He went with his backpack to Nollendorfplatz and disappeared shortly afterward into a massage parlor on Motzstrasse. Half an hour later, #h reappeared without a backpack but with a banner under his arm, and then mingled with the party people on the street. In the general CSD costume madness, he barely stood out in his latex suit and mask.

I put on my wig and followed #h, who drifted aimlessly in and out of the bars and among the caipirinha vendors. *"Getcha getcha ya ya da da!!"* blasted from giant speakers. Two men wearing nothing but white angels' wings danced Viennese waltzes to a song by Hildegard Knef. There was a smell of poppers and limes in the air.

#h disappeared in the club where I thought I'd seen him a few days earlier. I followed him and fought my way up to the mezzanine. Strobe lighting flashed across sweaty bodies, which fused into a mass of people pounding in time to the techno beat. For several minutes, I thought I'd lost track of #h, but then I saw him whipping an aisle through the dancers with his devil's tail. Once he made it to the middle of the dance floor, he unfurled his banner and circled it over his head: *Love Hitler! Hate cocksuckers!*

For a moment he seemed to be completely isolated in the crowd, a dervish in a shiny black latex suit and faceless spiked head. Then everyone surged toward him, tore away his banner, and #h's head and body were pummeled by severe blows. By the time security intervened, the only thing holding him up were the people running riot around him. I watched as #h's limp body was carried out of the club, then I traveled back to Neukölln.

For two days #h disappeared from sight; I was afraid that the dancers in the club had beat me to it. On the third day, #h uploaded a documentation of the injuries that "homofascists" had inflicted on him. The next morning, he dragged himself with his backpack in the direction of the community garden. He filled an old zinc tub with water and washed the encrusted blood from the latex suit and mask. Then #h sat in an old sun lounger, drinking vodka, dressed only in boxer shorts. His body was covered in bruises and cuts. When the latex suit was dry, #h rubbed it with a cloth until it shone. He moved about it as if he were caressing a lover, not just an empty rubber suit with a flaccid appendage.

I had seen enough. As soon as his wounds healed, #h would get back into his suit and smooth it over his body like a second skin. I went back to my apartment. The extract of devil's helmet was on the windowsill. The root pulp had sunk to the bottom of the laboratory glass. The alcohol above it shimmered an oily yellow in the sun. I pulled on my lab gloves and poured the solution into a plastic bottle. After that, I treated myself to an early dinner in an excellent Thai restaurant on Bergmannstrasse, which I knew from previous missions.

The next morning at five I was back at the deserted hut. The bottle with the dressing gel was on the bedside table. I filled up the gel with about fifty milliliters of my root solution and shook it vigorously. Using the rest of the solution, I drizzled the inside of the mask. In an hour or two at the latest, the alcohol would evaporate, leaving only a fine pollen-like residue on the material.

For the last time I went back to Neukölln via the embankment. I packed up, did my usual thorough cleaning routine, deposited the key in the safe, and headed for the subway. Spilling from a crack in the wall, there was a blossom of Kenilworth ivy. I tore off a sprig and stuck it behind my ear. I caught my reflection in a store window and saw for a fraction of a second what others see: an unassuming woman whom people tend to overlook.

LOCAL TRAIN

BY MAX ANNAS

Neukölln

"Over there." Kareem pointed through the shrubbery in front of them. "The local train . . ." His body tensed. From the direction of Hermannstrasse Station, distant headlights appeared, followed by the buzz of the train a moment later.

"Hmm . . ." Issam stuck his hands into his pockets. Said nothing. Didn't budge.

"It's too late now anyway." Kareem relaxed again.

"We need to talk about how we're going to do this exactly," Issam said.

The headlights came almost level with them, and then passed under the bridge. Kareem and Issam stared after the commuter train. Its lights flickered through the leaves in front of their eyes and lit up the greenery on the embankment next to the track.

"What's there to talk about? We've covered everything."

"Well . . . whether we should make a move when we first see the lights. For example."

Kareem didn't say a word.

"Or if we run. I mean . . . we don't want to take too long in case anyone sees us. Or if we—"

"There." Kareem pointed toward Tempelhof, where the first train had disappeared. Flickering headlights, buzzing. There was a train coming from that direction too. "But we wanted to take the one on the other side."

"Hmm . . ." Issam pushed aside a few branches near his head. "Like, do we wait by the railings? How often do they run at this time? And how late?"

"How should I know? Pretty often. Waiting by the rails is too dangerous. What if the train doesn't come? We can't just hang around like this. Over there . . ." Kareem pointed north. "People."

"Are they coming this way? But they stop running at some point. People?"

"Looks like it. Yeah . . . the trains stop running at some point."

"What do we do?"

"Just be quiet." Kareem's voice was flat. "But it's Friday . . . don't they run through the night?"

"Nnnnnnnnnn . . ." There was a rustling sound in the bushes behind them. "Nnnnnnnn . . ." it went again. Kareem turned and kicked the bundle hard in the side. "Ng . . ." it went, then stopped moving.

Kareem bent down and checked the gag. His football shorts were as tight as a vise between the guy's teeth. He stood up and gave him another kick.

"Are the laces holding up?" Issam asked quietly.

"Tight as a vise." Kareem gave the thumbs-up but checked the guy's laced-up hands and feet all the same.

The people had gotten closer. By now they could clearly hear what they were saying. Kareem could make out three figures. Three men. Swaying slightly.

"Otherwise it's as neat as a pin," one of them said.

"The beaches?" That was the second one.

The third was a few feet behind and looked around. He was searching for a place in the bushes. Kareem tapped Issam. Put a finger on his lips.

"Everything in Antalya. The people, nice and polite. Clean beaches, not too crowded. And no one talks about politics."

"Come on," said the second, turning round. The third caught up with them.

From Hermannstrasse, which lay eastward, the next train was approaching. "Too late," said Kareem. "Look, you can hear when it's leaving Hermannstrasse. That's our cue."

"Hmm . . ." Issam turned and looked down at the bundle.

"We can't do a test run. No practicing. Train leaves, we pull this thing off."

"We can do a test run. When we hear the train leaving, we walk over to the railing. That way we'll see if we have enough time. It's like . . . what, a hundred feet?

Kareem said nothing.

"He can't get away. Right?

"You're not into it anymore.

"I am . . . but . . . I mean . . . Washington's getting out of the hospital soon."

Kareem shook his head. "He was in a coma for a whole week."

"Yes, but he'll be back soon."

"For the next few months he's gonna walk around with splints on his legs. No football or any of that shit."

"The doctors said—"

"Man, this guy almost killed Washington. You forgotten that?"

"Course not."

"It was touch and go whether he'd survive. They said it was curtains."

"Yeah . . ." Issam went quiet.

"Over there, next train's on its way. Come on." Kareem stooped and grabbed the bundle's feet.

When Issam didn't move, Kareem straightened up again. The train approached and then passed them.

"Look," said Issam.

"What?"

"Over there . . ."

"The dog? It'll be gone in a minute."

"That's not a dog."

Kareem looked more closely. Four legs, quite short, thick fur, brown or red, pointed little ears, and a bushy tail. He hadn't seen it coming. It glanced down the street, then over the bridge.

"A fox," said Issam. "Saw one on YouTube."

"What kind of shit do you watch on YouTube?"

"Shit like that . . . all kinds of shit."

A car engine started up nearby. Way too much pressure on the gas pedal.

"When they're sick, they even attack people," said Issam. "That's what it said. Really interesting."

The fox turned its head and then disappeared in the direction of Tempelhofer Feld, taking its time.

Kareem watched the intersection from the bushes. The engine was still revving but the car wasn't moving. Its headlights weren't on yet. Behind them was the expanse of Tempelhofer Feld, all greenery and community gardens. On the other side, residential buildings with way too many balconies for his liking. The small bridge over the train tracks was part of the T-junction. It was roughly 150 feet to the bridge railing. Maybe only a hundred—Issam might be right. Now the car headlights were switched on. The sound of the engine got louder as it approached. The car cruised around the corner. For a moment, the light dazzled him. He was glad they were both wearing dark clothes.

When the car had disappeared around the bend onto Emser Strasse, a figure, whom Kareem thought he recognized, appeared at exactly the same spot. The guy briefly got his bearings and then fixed his sights on the green verge where they were hiding. Then he looked at his phone and headed straight for them.

Emeka had showered and smartened himself up since football. It really was him. When he reached the bushes where they were hidden, he checked his phone again. "Hey," he called.

Kareem grabbed him and pulled him into their hiding place. "What's up?"

"GPS," said Emeka. "Totally easy." He thumped Issam on the shoulder.

"Yeah—easy, man," said Issam. "I sent him a photo."

"A photo?"

"Here." Emeka handed Kareem his phone. The bundle was visible. Tied up with the gag in its mouth. *Amazing how good photos are these days*, Kareem thought. You could make out the yellow Dortmund shorts, even in the dark. They were spilling out of the asshole's mouth.

"Sick," said Emeka in appreciation, looking at the real bundle: its shaved head and thin sideburns were barely visible in the reflection of the streetlamps. "Where did you pick him up?"

"On the way home," said Kareem. "We were on our way to Hermannstrasse. Then we saw him."

"He spotted us and crossed over," Issam said.

"No, he didn't see us. We just followed him."

"And all of a sudden we were chasing him."

"All the way here."

"And then I pulled him into the bushes."

"*I* did, actually."

"Whatever . . . we both did."

"But who is it?" Emeka hadn't taken his eyes off the bundle yet.

"The guy who almost killed Washington," Kareem said.

"No shit." Now Emeka looked up. "That's him?"

"Hmm . . ." Issam said. "Seems that way."

"Yo!" Emeka raised his foot and kicked the bundle in the side.

A rasping sound came from behind the yellow shorts. Emeka kicked again, twice. The rasping got weaker.

"And now what?" asked Emeka.

A train rattled past. Kareem looked around and watched its lights disappear.

At first Emeka didn't say a word. Then he slowly blew the air out through his lips. "Okay," he said.

"And now that there are three of us, it'll be much easier. Watch out—people."

A group of young women were approaching. The last of them, who was trailing behind the others at a distance, stopped right in front of where they were hiding and took a long swig from a bottle of fizzy wine. The other three had already gone on quite some way, but now stopped as well. One of them doubled back and took the bottle. She said something quickly in Spanish, then glugged back some of the wine. Then something else. Kareem didn't understand it all. Something about a job. She took a last gulp, gave the bottle back, and rejoined the others. The girl at the rear followed her slowly. Silently, the women moved away. Two trains passed each other under the bridge while the women were still visible. The phone Kareem had taken from the bundle buzzed in his pants.

"One of you grab his feet." Kareem stood so that he could

hold the bundle's tied hands. "I think I can hear the train. Come on!"

"Someone's coming." Emeka was half standing on the sidewalk and peering off to the side. A man had stopped on the bridge. He was wearing a gray jacket, which was much too big for him. Kareem pulled Emeka back into the bushes. The man took a few steps, stopped, looked up and then to the side. He moved closer still.

"What's he doing?" Issam asked.

"Shhh!" Kareem put a finger on his lips.

"Nnnnnnnnnnnn . . ." went the bundle on the ground.

Kareem kicked it in the side.

"Krrr . . ." came from below.

Meanwhile, the man had crossed the bridge and was looking into the first parked car opposite the verge. A station wagon. Then he checked out the next car, a Golf. Then he looked into the next. Bent down. Kept going. When he reached a small sports car, he squatted. Under the halo of the streetlamp, Kareem saw that his pants had a rip in the crotch. His shoes were almost falling apart. The man stood up and glanced around again. Then he raised his arm and whacked his elbow against the window of the driver's door.

Nothing happened.

He raised his arm a bit higher and tried again. Now the pane broke.

"Jesus!" said Emeka.

Kareem waited for the alarm. But it didn't go off.

The man reached into the car. Quickly slipped whatever he pulled out into his jacket and walked away. He didn't even look back.

"Wow," said Issam. "That's not his first time either."

"Can you make a living from that?" asked Emeka.

A train coming from Tempelhof passed under the bridge. Another immediately followed coming from Hermannstrasse.

"What now?" asked Kareem as he bent down.

Issam and Emeka were standing beside the bundle.

"Okay then, I'll take his feet," said Issam.

"I don't believe it." Kareem stood up again.

"What?" Issam was next to him in a flash. "Who's that?" he asked as his eyes adjusted.

A woman was heading straight for the bushes. She was leaning on a walking stick. One step long, one step short.

"Auntie Mo," said Kareem. "Did you send her the photo as well?"

"I don't know even know her." Issam.

"I showed it to her." Emeka.

"Shit. Just what we need." Kareem turned away and stared at the bundle.

The stick clacked loudly as Auntie Mo approached. She was already standing in front of the bushes. "Where is he?" she asked, without bothering to lower her voice.

"Shhh . . ." Kareem glanced at a nearby house as the woman trampled through the bushes.

"Is that him?" she asked at the same volume. Then she spat on him. She lifted her stick above the bundle, but thought better of it before bringing it down.

Kareem exhaled. "Let's be quiet please, Auntie."

"She's Washington's aunt," said Emeka to Issam.

"I am not," said Auntie Mo, still at full throttle. "I happen to know him from Lagos."

"Okay." Kareem put his free hand on Auntie Mo's shoulder. "Not his aunt. But we still have to be quiet."

A car was slowly approaching. In too low a gear, it cut out, started up, then cut out again. The windows of the old Toyota were wound down. Kareem made a soft "Pssss!" Immediately everyone went quiet.

Four young guys were sitting in the car. Staring out. One was a skinhead; the others looked like everybody else. The car was light green, but with rust-brown doors. The roof was dented. For a moment, the engine spluttered as the car passed the bush. The driver looked into the footwell and stomped on the gas pedal with all his might. The engine choked, then caught again. The car turned the corner.

A train was approaching from Hermannstrasse. Then another from the opposite direction. Kareem looked around at the others. They made no sign of helping him: Issam was gazing out at the street, Emeka was in his own world, and Auntie Mo was looking down. She shook her head. The arm holding the stick twitched.

"We can do it real quick now," Kareem said. "With four of us, it'll be simple."

Emeka bent down and Issam turned to the bundle.

"I can't," said Auntie Mo. "My leg."

Steps were heard coming toward them.

"Nnnnnnnnnn . . ." From the ground again.

The four turned toward the street.

"Nnnnnnnnnn . . ."

The footsteps could be made out clearly now. Fast and light. Not sneakers.

A train drowned them out for a moment. When the noise had died away, a figure appeared coming from the direction of Emser Strasse.

"Fuck me," Kareem said. "Where did she turn up from?"

"Tanja." Emeka seemed less surprised.

"The photo?" asked Kareem.

"Yeah . . . her too."

"Where are you?" called Tanja.

"In here." Emeka held out his hand through the bushes. Tanja jumped through the gap he made with his arm.

"They're after me." Tanja was out of breath.

"Who?"

"Skinheads . . . Nazis . . ." Tanja exhaled. "A whole car of them."

"Crap," said Issam.

"They stopped. And . . . talked shit to me. It was totally gross."

Kareem wanted to know what they'd said but didn't dare ask.

"That him?" Tanja had gotten her breath back and was pointing down.

"Hmm," said Kareem. "The scar."

She bent down and smacked the bundle around the head several times.

"Nnnnnnnnnnn . . ." went the bundle.

Tanja kept on whacking until she was out of breath again.

"Hnnn . . . hnnn . . . hnnn . . ."

"Come on," said Emeka, and wrapped his arms around Tanja. "Enough."

"And the Nazis?"

"Didn't follow me."

The spluttering engine could be heard again in the distance. Coming closer. Rock music had been added to the mix, getting louder along with the engine.

"Assholes." Kareem waited for the car to appear. "We could just go and beat them all up."

"Are you crazy?" Tanja said. "They're probably armed."

The car came down Emser Strasse and stopped in front of the bushes where they were hidden. The driver turned off the music and opened the door. He got out, stood next to the car, and glanced up and down the road. "She has to be here somewhere," he said.

"Or she lives around here," someone called from inside the vehicle.

"Come on." Another voice. "We've got other stuff to do. Like finding Björn, remember?"

The driver stepped into the car and turned the music back on. The din was deafening. Beside him, Kareem heard someone giggle.

In the room behind a balcony on the other side of the street, lights came on. Second floor. A tall man stepped out and looked down into the street. He stood at the balustrade and lit a cigarette. The four men drove away. The guy on the balcony leaned over the railing so he could catch a glimpse of the car.

"Very quiet now," Issam said.

"Hnnnnnnnn!" went the bundle. Kareem aimed a kick backward.

Another light came on, same floor. Another man came out. He too lit a cigarette. The two men did not look at each other. Not a word passed between them. When the first one had finished his smoke, he flicked the butt down and went back in. The other did the same shortly afterward and also disappeared.

Emeka was still holding Tanja in his arms when Kareem turned around. He saw her struggle free and place her heel at the center of the bundle.

"Iiiiiirrr . . ." came from behind the Dortmund shorts. "Iiiiiirrr . . ."

Kareem knew that the tied-up guy was a Nazi, but it hurt him to watch all the same. He instinctively clenched his balls.

Tanja kicked him again, then once more. The bundle scrunched itself up as best it could. Kareem pulled her away. She was panting with fury. "First they said that Washington would never be able to get it up again. That's how hard they kicked him. He was already lying on the ground. And then . . ."

"How many were there?" Issam asked.

"Three. One guy held me down. The others beat up Washington. When he was down, they kicked him in the head. And then . . . it was horrible. *He* did it."

"And then?" Issam asked.

"One of them slapped me. Really hard. But I didn't even realize. I was just watching Washington. Then they took off."

A train coming from Tempelhof passed under the bridge.

"Now?" asked Kareem, letting of Tanja.

Issam grabbed the feet. Tanya gripped under the knees. Kareem bent down and waited for Emeka. Auntie Mo stood there and said nothing. The bundle squirmed. In pain or in an attempt to fight back.

"Another one's sure to come soon," said Tanja.

"Hurry up," said Issam.

"It's coming now," said Emeka.

When they all had a firm hold, the bundle's resistance waned. Kareem checked whether the road was clear. "Now," he said.

They rushed out of the bushes and hurried to the bridge. The guy was thin and light.

At Hermannstrasse, a train was waiting on the platform. They could see its headlights. The announcement was just about audible. The bundle began to convulse and writhe. The doors of the train would be closing now. They still had a good grip on him as the train pulled away.

"We have to lie him on the railing," said Emeka.

"Use a bit of force then." The train was already way too close for Kareem's liking. Now they had to hurry. "On three," he said. "One . . ."

"Two . . ." said Issam.

"Stop!" shouted Tanja. "That's not him."

Everyone let go at the same time. The bundle slammed against the railing and then landed at their feet. The train rattled past below.

"What do you mean that's not him?" Emeka was standing right in front of Tanja.

Auntie Mo shook her head.

"There," said Kareem. He pointed to the guy's face. "That's the scar."

"It's on the wrong side."

"What do you mean?"

"Wrong side, that's all."

Everyone leaned over the bundle.

"There . . ." said Tanja. She traced the scar under his right eye. It was short and thick, making his eye look like it slanted at an angle. "It should be here." She pointed to his left cheek. "From here . . ." she traced from his eye to the corner of his mouth, "to here. Totally different."

"You sure?" asked Auntie Mo.

"Yeah. Real sure. He kept grinning at me while he was kicking Washington between the legs. You don't forget stuff like that."

Everyone straightened up again.

"So what do we do now?" asked Issam.

Silence. A train was coming from Tempelhof.

"He's definitely a Nazi," said Emeka. "No doubt about it."

"Did you see the other two?" Kareem asked.

"One of them, not at all—the one who was holding me. And the other, not very well."

"And those guys in the car?" asked Auntie Mo.

"No idea. I couldn't see them."

"You know what?" Issam held up his index finger. "Let's just leave him here. The police'll come and find him. He's sure to have a record . . ."

"What if the police don't even care?" Kareem said. "Well, okay, but . . ." He was thinking. "How about we all go to the Schiller quarter? One last beer?"

The group set off. At the intersection near the bushes where they had been hiding, Kareem remembered something. He went back to the bundle.

As Kareem bent over him, the boy's eyes widened. He was still scared. Kareem yanked the Dortmund shorts out of his mouth.

The boy's eyes narrowed. Kareem saw the muscles around his mouth tense. *"Kanacke,"* he spat out hoarsely.

Kareem took the Nazi's phone from his pocket. He threw it onto the tracks just as a train was setting off from Hermann-strasse. Then he turned around and followed the others. He was looking forward to that beer.

PART II

Cops & Gangsters

CUM COPS

BY KAI HENSEL

Altglienicke

Berlin/Hamburg—One of the biggest police scandals in recent years. Three mobile squads from Berlin have been expelled by the Hamburg police forces. The reason: lewd behavior!

The 14th, 15th, and 32nd riot police departments, a total of more 220 law enforcement officers, arrived last Sunday in Hamburg. Their mission was to support their colleagues at the upcoming G20 summit.

The Berlin police force was housed in units within a fenced enclosure. Security guards allegedly observed two police officers having sex in public. Other police officers are said to have urinated in a row by the fence after a rowdy party.

In a chat group between the police later on, other incidents were also mentioned, such as "dancing on containers, fucking, stripping with weapons, and pissing in line." A spokesman for the Berlin police has said: "Our colleagues' behavior is shameful!"

—Bild, June 22, 2017

1.

"How could you do a thing like that?"

Vera was standing at the kitchen window with her back to him, staring out at the lilac bushes, the birdhouse, and Timo's bike, which was lying in the grass next to the path.

"We all—"

"You all?!" she screamed. "Since when has that been a reason? Doing the same as everyone else? Going along with something and not taking responsibility for your actions? Shame on you!"

Shame. Jens had never heard her that word coming from her mouth. The newspaper was lying on the dinner table.

"It's not just the photo," she said. "What about the eye-witness reports? The jokes they're making on the radio about you all. About what you did."

"Not everyone," he said. "Not everyone did—"

"In a line! You did it in a line! What difference does it make whether one was naked and the others weren't? Whether some just watched and the others . . ."

Her fingers clenched her coffee cup. She bent her head low so that her neck went crooked, like a crow's, which was something she didn't normally do. Jens thought it did make a difference that he hadn't been naked. He hadn't danced on the container. And he had definitely not—she had to believe him—

"You have to believe me," he said.

"What?"

"That I didn't . . . like Steffen."

"Do I have to?"

She turned around. Her mouth was twisted into a smile that was meant to be mocking. But Vera was not the mocking type. She always said everything plain and outright, in the way that you knew she meant it. That's why the smile didn't suit her, the woman he'd have like to have kissed while asking for forgiveness with tears in his eyes. But he didn't feel tears in his eyes. He felt, if he was honest, nothing at all.

"Then that ridiculous excuse . . ."

Yes, that had been a mistake. Saying that their early return from Hamburg had been due to there being more officers than necessary, that they were needed more urgently in Berlin. Jens had never lied to his wife. It had hurt, that lie. He had tossed and turned all night. In a few days he would have definitely told her the truth. But that morning, the photo was all over the newspapers and the lie had burst like an egg splattering all over the wall.

"And Timo . . . if I even *think* about how they teased him at school today . . . *Dick Daddy*, that's what they said. *Your Dick Daddy!*"

"Children forget things like this."

"The Internet doesn't forget! This is going to hound him all through high school, all the way to university . . ."

It wasn't yet clear whether Timo would study or not. Their son was eight, his personality not yet fully developed. But Vera had pictured him at university since he could walk, as a physics or chemistry student. She always planned everything way in advance.

She rinsed her cup and put it on the drip tray. "We need time."

"Time? For what?"

"For everything. To think. About where things should go from here."

"Well. Okay. Where should things go from here? I mean, I'm just asking."

"Just give me some time." She rested her hands on the counter and took a deep breath.

He stood up. He wanted to put his hand on her shoulders. But she bent her neck again, almost into a hunchback, and he dropped the idea.

"I'm off for a workout," he said. "With Steffen."

2.

"It'll blow over in a couple of days," Steffen said, increasing the speed of the treadmill. "I love my wife. She knows I love her. But she also knows . . . I'm a man, goddammit! Things were a little out of the ordinary. Alcohol, the tension in the air before we went in!" He took a sip from his water bottle. "It's all about politics anyhow. Just politics. Hamburg has always been second best. They just wanted to take us down. And the G20 summit? They can shove it up their asses! Up their asses, I tell you! Did you know that Donald Trump has German ancestors? It was a put-up job, I tell you."

Jens was running beside him, slower but on a 5 percent incline. He wasn't sure what Donald Trump's ancestors had to do with the G20 summit, or the G20 summit with the rave between the housing units. What was certain, however, was that Steffen was well and truly screwed. Melanie might have forgiven him if he had just stripped down. But getting his rocks off with Biggi afterward? And that someone would take photos, even make a video, not for just a few seconds, but a full four minutes—well, that was obvious. He hadn't been that drunk and should have seen it coming. And that the video would be circulated among their colleagues and their wives, finally ending up on Melanie's phone . . .

"What does your old lady say? You're off the hook. Doing a prissy little piss in a line . . . Every mother-in-law's dream . . ." Steffen guffawed, shaking his head, so that a few drops of sweat sprayed in Jens's direction. "But tell me something: how come you were standing nearer the fence than all the others?"

"Why?"

"It's obvious in the photo . . . You're, like, a foot closer . . .

like you were afraid you wouldn't hit the fence . . . like you couldn't spray far enough . . ."

"Nonsense."

"Take a look at the photo! Not very in focus, and if I didn't know it was you . . . But the others noticed too."

"Who?"

"Matthes, Gerd . . . *How come that guy is standing so close to the fence?*" The treadmill slowed for the cooldown phase. Steffen started walking, drinking from his bottle, wiping a towel over his face and neck. "I'm not saying that I'm proud of that video. Sure, you can see that Biggi's having a good time. And you can see that I . . . Still, if I catch the motherfucker who filmed it . . . and sent it to my babe's cell phone . . ."

"Probably not the same guy."

"You don't *do* stuff like that!" The treadmill slowed and stopped. "Have to make it up to Melanie. Weekend in Usedom, that kind of thing. On the other hand, the bottom line is that you were all hot for Biggi, and Melanie's tears will dry fast . . . The fuck was worth it."

3.

Tears were streaming down Melanie's cheeks. "I never want to see him again!"

"Don't do anything rash," said Vera.

"I'm seeing a lawyer tomorrow," said Melanie, swigging back her third glass of Vera's mother's homemade ginger liqueur. "He's going to pay, I swear. He won't see a cent of the house. And I'm not going to work before Jasmina starts school . . . I'm going to bleed him dry!"

She pushed her glass toward the bottle, an invitation for a refill. And why not, thought Vera, on a day like today? She had watched the video. Not the whole thing, but the first three or three and a half minutes. She had searched for Jens among the jeering, beer-drinking, cheering spectators—but he wasn't there.

"Am I that ugly?" Melanie sobbed.

"Nonsense."

"Three kids . . . a cesarean section with Fabian . . . Of course I don't have the figure I used to . . ."

"That has nothing to do with it."

"Then what *does* it have to do with? What?" She glared at Vera over the edge of her glass, looking hostile for a moment. "You can hardly make out Jens in the photo. Looking so shy, just standing there in line, peeing away."

"Melanie."

"Sorry, I take it back." She sipped her drink. "I don't understand the peeing thing anyway. I mean, how do thirty adult men hit on the idea of pissing against a fence in public . . . ?"

"It wasn't in public, you know that. It was in an enclosure of housing units almost in the woods. And if the security guards hadn't taken that stupid photo . . ."

"Are you defending your husband on top of everything else?"

"I'm just saying there's a lot about this that's hard to understand."

"Damn true!" Melanie slammed her glass on the table. "Anyway, we don't know the half of it. We only know the tip of the iceberg. The tip of the tip. You really believe that your husband only had a piss? Do I really believe that my husband only fucked that one whore? How do we know? Do you think our husbands are telling the truth?"

Vera closed her eyes, feeling sick for a moment. Jens had lied to her after they returned, that couldn't be denied. Had he perhaps not told her the whole truth yet? Maybe he wasn't in Steffen's video simply because he was off somewhere with some other woman . . .

"I've watched my figure for eight whole years . . ." Melanie moaned. "Zumba five times a week, Callanetics—does he think it's fun? That horny bastard! Taking care of the house, the pediatrician three times a week because of Anton's asthma . . ." She jumped up, her body taut, and tossed back her long, bleach-blond hair. Then she stretched her upper body and picked up her fringed leather jacket that was hanging over the chair.

"Where are you going?" Vera asked.

"I'm not going to sit around here waiting for my husband like a cow for the milkman. Where am I going?" Melanie shrieked. "To live it up a little!"

4.

Jens switched off the engine. He looked up at his house, the garden, the blue tit in the birdhouse pecking at the bird feed. There was no need for bird feed now, not in summer. Timo had bought it with his allowance and put it in the birdhouse. At school, he was learning about taking responsibility for living creatures. How nice it was here. How quiet. The houses weren't too big or too small. The front gardens were neat but not conservative. No garden gnomes, no German flags. Children's toys lay scattered on lawns here and there. They had been lucky with this house in Altglienicke on the outskirts of Berlin; they had bought it when interest rates were still low and real estate was affordable. "We moved in for the kill," Vera had said at their housewarming party, which had made Jens wince inwardly. Moving in for the kill wasn't a phrase that suited either of them.

There was a bouquet of roses on the passenger seat, although Vera's favorite flowers were marguerite daisies. But there was much too yellow in them, and yellow was not an option, not on this occasion. Hence the red roses. Vera would understand, even though she didn't like roses. She would surely recognize it as a gesture of his goodwill. And that he was really sorry about all of this.

Just as he was getting out of the car, the front door opened and Melanie came out. She was walking fast, determinedly, her face flushed. At the gate she noticed him and stopped, her hand on the latch.

"Good evening, Melanie."

"Huh."

"Everything okay?"

"What do you think?"

"I'm just asking because—"

"You think about it."

She pushed open the gate and walked past him. Her breath smelled of ginger liqueur. She crossed the street, stopped at her Fiat Punto, and rummaged in her pants pocket.

"Are you leaving?"

She pulled out her keychain, pressed the car key angrily— three, four times—then the knob popped up.

"Do you think you should drive? In your state?"

"State? Did you say *state*?"

Then she noticed the bouquet of flowers in his hand and snorted. "Little Manneken Pis! Seriously? Roses?"

"You've been drinking. You shouldn't drive."

"Screw you, officer."

She got into her car, slammed the door shut, and started up the engine. Backward, forward, tires squealing . . . Her taillights were already disappearing into the distance, the rumbling of the engine fading.

The fragrance of roses wafted from the cellophane paper. He couldn't call one of his colleagues. The headline "Wife of Party Cop Caught Drunk at the Wheel!" wouldn't go down well right now. But "Wife of Party Cop Drunk at the Wheel—Fatal Accident!" would be even worse. He hid the roses under the gorse bush behind the gate and quickly walked back to his car. He'd better take care of Melanie. He owed her that—owed Steffen that. Despite everything.

5.

He saw the taillights of the Punto on the expressway heading toward the city center. She was driving fast but keeping to the limit; signaling, changing lanes, overtaking. She wasn't that drunk. Perhaps he needn't keep an eye on her after all. It'd be better if he turned back. But something in her face—rage, determination—had alarmed him.

In the distance, the TV Tower gleamed in the evening sun like the stinger of a wasp. But maybe that was just his overwrought imagination. Or because he never really liked the drive into Berlin, especially not in the evening, when he had a night shift or had to step in for sick colleagues. People thought it was exciting being a police officer on call, always going to demonstrations, football matches, and rock concerts. But in truth, he usually assisted in the local offices—Kreuzberg, Neukölln, Hellersdorf, wherever they were undermanned. And they were nearly always undermanned, everywhere, all the time; they had been hopelessly short of staff for years. Berlin, the capital of crime. Burglaries were reported less frequently or not at all. But murder, sexual offenses, and assaults were all on the rise. And the crime rate was worse than in any other German city. What disturbed him the most, though, and sometimes even made him afraid of his job and afraid for the city's future, was something intangible, a feeling. Fear was on the rise. In the subway, on the streets, even in people's own homes. The police were called because someone thought "something was moving out there." Teens stabbed each other because "someone was looking at me funny." A police officer was an enforcer of the law, an idea he had always loved. But what kind of law was he enforcing? What kind of law would he have enforced at the G20 summit in Hamburg? The newspaper with the photo was lying on the passenger seat. Jens couldn't be recognized because all the faces were blurred or had been pixeled out. But he was closer to the fence than the others, that was true. Perhaps not two feet away. But at least a foot. What had gotten into him? What had he been trying to prove to his colleagues? Or himself?

Melanie's Punto was signaling in front of him. She continued on her way into the city center.

6.

"Is my wife with you?"

"She left half an hour ago."

"Did she say where she was going?"

"Home, I guess."

"But she's not here." There was an edge of worry, almost anxiety, to Steffen's voice. "The kids' food is in the fridge. Anton needs his medication. I have no idea how—"

"You can manage alone for one evening, Steffen."

"A whole *evening*?" He gave a forced laugh, as if trying to make a joke. "You're right. An evening on their own with their dad. The kids'll love it."

Vera could hear a child crying in the background. "I think she wanted to go to Callanetics."

"Now?"

"The late class."

"Did you talk?"

"Yeah, a bit. Women's stuff."

"Women's stuff, hmm. Nothing to do with us men, eh? Well, if you speak to her . . ."

"She's bound to be home soon."

Vera hung up. There was no reason for her to get mixed up in other people's marital crises. She didn't believe in divorce, if only because of the children. On the other hand, what if Melanie had been thinking about separating for a while? Perhaps this was just a convenient occasion to get rid of Steffen for good. She looked at the clock: it would soon be ten. Jens should have been home long ago. But was she going to call him? Pretend she was worried? Like hell she was.

She heard the sound of bare feet on the stairs. Timo was standing by the door in his pajamas. In his hand, he held the tablet which his grandmother had given him for Christmas, against Vera's wishes.

"Mom," he said, "what are Cum Cops?"

7.

The district of Wedding. Arabic music, women in veils, the smell of hookah pipes and barbecued meat. Jens was sitting in the car by the side of the road, his window wound down halfway. He was watching Melanie standing at a Turkish takeaway across the street, eating a doner kebab. No, she was wolfing it down. Her teeth tore off thick pieces of Turkish bread, while grease and sauce dripped down her chin. Well, good for her. Melanie was a highly disciplined woman. She worked out five times a week and went from one diet to the next. Not that she wasn't successful. You couldn't tell she'd had three children. In fact, she looked totally hot in her tight bleached jeans and leather boots. She was just letting her hair down tonight. Out to party, and Jens didn't intend to stop her. But why in Wedding?

He didn't like coming here to settle fights between youth gangs and Chechen clans; or to enforce laws no one wanted and no one understood.

"You can't beat up your wife/daughter/cousin."

"What's it to you, you unbeliever/Nazi/faggot?"

A colleague had had a bottle of absinthe thrown at his head. For the past two weeks he'd been in the hospital with a concussion, and was lucky it hadn't been a skull fracture.

Jens's stomach felt empty. Before his workout he had eaten a banana, and nothing since then. He could just get out of his car and go and stand next to Melanie in the kebab shop. Just pretend it was a coincidence. No, bad idea, she would see right through it. She wasn't stupid. She opened a can of Coke and clinked it with a black guy in mechanic overalls. She guzzled her drink down. Coke: everything was back on the straight-and-narrow. It was only just after ten o'clock, so Jens did not have to look after her. He was about to start the car when his telephone rang.

"It's me." Steffen's voice sounded forcibly cheery. "Have you made up yet?"

"What do you mean?"

"You and Vera. The photo. Has she forgiven you?"

"She's getting there."

"Mine too, I think. Women remember a lot, but they also forget fast. In one ear, out the other. You already home?"

"On my way."

"Do you think our wives might be in cahoots? Are they plotting against us?"

"What makes you think that?"

"Melanie's disappeared." Steffen's voice trembled. "Your

wife says she's at Callanetics. But she's not, because her sports bag is here. It's a fucking lie!"

"Have you called her?"

"She's not picking up."

For a moment, Jens considered telling him the truth: that his wife was chomping down her second kebab. That she was tipping a bottle of vodka into her Coke can and clinking glasses with the mechanic again. "Maybe her battery's dead."

"Not if her phone rings."

"Maybe she just went to the sauna and borrowed a towel from the gym. She'll be home before midnight."

"You think so?"

"I'm sure so."

Jens hung up. Before midnight. Now he had made Steffen a promise. Melanie gargled her Coke, choked, and the mechanic patted her on the back. Jens had to take care of her. He couldn't leave now.

8.

"There are good guys and bad guys," Vera was saying. "The good guys get rewarded and evil guys get punished. "

"By Daddy?" Timo asked.

"Exactly."

"And who rewards the good guys?"

"Daddy is one of the good guys. His reward is money. For doing his job."

"A lot of money?"

"Not a lot. Not heaps of money."

"But more than the bad guys?"

"Yes. No. Sometimes the bad guys make a lot more money."

Timo frowned, which looked cute, then leaned back into the large folds of the pillow. "If the good guys get rewarded and the bad guys get punished . . . but then the bad guys get more money . . ."

"The world isn't fair."

"Why isn't Daddy a bad guy instead?"

"He's not the type."

"So Daddy isn't a Cum Cop?"

"Go to sleep now, will you? It's late."

"I can't."

"We're all tired."

She kissed Timo on the forehead, turned off the light, and closed the door. She leaned against the wall. They didn't earn anywhere near enough. If the interest rate on the house went up, if Jens's promotion didn't work out because of that damned photo . . . Now Timo wanted to join the karate club . . . could they even afford it? *Berlin—poor, but sexy.* How she hated that phrase. The others were sexy. A police officer was a sewer rat. On the outside, it looked great, but on the inside, it was an uphill battle through shit. And she had to put up with all the stupid things people said to her when she was out shopping or at parent evenings. *Someone stole my son's/daughter's bike again; my dog/cat has been missing for days; teenagers are smoking pot/swapping porn in front of the school gates—and what is Jens doing about it? You live off our taxes, after all!* Vera stared at the wall and had a vision: The G20 summit in Hamburg. Violent offenders running riot through every part of the city. Storming hotels, taking politicians hostage. Because no one was there to protect them. Because her husband, whom she loved more than anyone else in the world, was sitting twiddling his thumbs in Berlin. Because of a harmless photo of him peeing!

She looked at the clock. Half past ten. It was really muggy in and outside the house. Why hadn't Jens come home yet?

She didn't get him; she didn't get the world. She wanted a thunderstorm to break out. She wanted something to happen that night.

9.

He was watching her standing by the slot machine. Lights were flashing, she was pressing buttons, then more lights flashed, a whole row. She hesitated, held her hand in the air, leaned forward as if she wanted to swat a gnat—then the lights went out. She slammed her fist against the machine, threw in more money, and took a sip from her beer bottle.

Jens was sitting to the side at the bar in semidarkness. On the jukebox—one that played real records, which he didn't know still existed—"White Rose of Athens" was playing. He rarely went to bars like these when he was on duty, ones with names like Zum Biermichel or Babsi and Bernd's, behind whose brown- or green-tinted windows overweight old men and women hung about for hours on barstools. There were occasional fights between drunken pensioners, or perhaps a coked-up streetworker might chuck a glass against the paneled wall—but rarely, even in those cases, did someone call the police.

"Another Futschi, please."

Coke with brandy, two euros a glass. It tasted both disgusting and not so bad at the same time. It was his second today. And his last. After all, he had to get Melanie home; she was no longer fit to drive. He still wasn't sure how to approach her. Chance encounter? In this bar? She would never buy that.

His cell phone vibrated in his pocket. Steffen. Bad timing. He sent him to voice mail. Because what was he supposed to say? That his wife was being hit on by a young man in a silver-gray suit with slick black hair? The young guy, who was good-looking in a sleazy kind of way, playfully pressed a few buttons on the slot machine: lights flashed and flickered, a tune played. The man smiled and pressed the button next to the coin slot: the coins fell in a never-ending *ching-ching-ching*. Melanie clapped her hands to her cheeks like one of those candidates who wins on *Who Wants to Be a Millionaire?* even though they have only guessed half of the answers.

The waitress set his glass in front of him and drew a line on his beer coaster. It wasn't true that all police officers were alcoholics. They weren't all corrupt or violent either. Most of them had slipped into the profession out of naivety, idealism, or stupidity (Jens did not exempt himself), and then tried to survive with a sense of decency. A wife, a house, children: small dreams in a big city. They hadn't planned for Timo to be an only child. But what in life was ever planned? If interest rates rose, if he was suspended—not likely but not out of the question either—what would be left of his plan? Or of his marriage?

The guy in the silver suit looked over as if he sensed competition. Not that there was any. But he would see what happened if he dared leave the bar with Melanie. Jens would intervene, that was for sure. Because his job was to protect things that did not belong to him.

"Gypsy boy, gypsy boy, he played guitar by the fire" was blaring from the jukebox.

Take the gay Mormon who was robbed by Romani boys in the Fugger neighborhood. If there was a benevolent God, Jens had asked, why did he let the Fugger hood exist? That had convinced the Mormon. He had said goodbye to Jens and his colleagues and gratefully left them his brochures. At moments like those, Jens was happy being a cop, as it gave him the feeling he was doing something for the city and its people.

But those moments were scarce. And becoming scarcer. He took a long sip from his drink. People believed that the life of a police officer was exciting; but in fact, they always had to sacrifice their lives for others. They were the whores of the republic, that's what they were! And whores wanted to party too sometimes, right? To have a bit of fun now and then!

"Another Futschi!"

A third made no difference. Because a realization was dawning on him, a dim feeling he could hardly put into words. When they had been standing there at the fence like schoolboys, peeing and laughing, was it simply life they had felt coursing through their veins for a few precious moments? Their own lives? And the sense of freedom, of being law enforcers doing something forbidden, something outside of the law, standing on the other side of the fence, as it were—wasn't that just their human side, goddammit? Part of their dignity?

He looked around. Where was Melanie? She had disappeared. Likewise the stud in the silver suit. Jens stood up, holding onto the bar for a moment. His heart was pounding. She couldn't have left the bar: he was sitting next to the exit and would have noticed. But she wasn't at the slot machine. And not at the bar either. She wasn't on the small dance floor next to the jukebox. There was another exit, a doorway with a beaded curtain. Not that it was any of his business. But on the other hand, it *was* his business! It was Melanie's life. And Steffen was his friend!

"*Just a gigolo, everywhere I go . . .*"

He crossed the dance floor and pushed back the curtain. He entered a dark corridor with two doors. On one, there was a brass plaque depicting a squatting girl with pigtails. On the other plaque was a boy standing and holding his wiener. Jens quietly opened the door with the squatting girl. There

was a sink, a paper towel rack, and two cubicles. He listened—
nothing. He kneeled on the floor and looked under the
doors—empty. He went back and opened the other door.
Snuck past the sink to the urinal. Pretended he needed to
pee. Actually, he really did need to pee. But then he heard
a smacking sound and a moan from one of the two cubicles.
The one on the right. No, on the left. He quietly opened the
right-hand door—the cubicle was empty. He locked it without
making a noise.

"Oh . . . yes . . . *yes* . . ."

He recognized the voice. It was Melanie's life and he had
no right to interfere. But as a paying guest, he also had a right
to use the bathroom. There was a small hole in the partition,
and he leaned down to peer through it. It was blocked with
something on the other side, probably chewing gum.

"Great job . . ." he heard the stud say.

Jens flipped down the toilet lid and sat down. If he was
right about the sounds, they weren't properly at it yet, but just
on the verge. He could use his car key to push the gum out of
the hole. But how would that help?

His phone vibrated in his pocket: a WhatsApp message
from Steffen.

Why aren't you picking up?

I'm already in bed.

She isn't back yet!

A moaning, smacking, and gagging sound came from the
other side of the partition. She had the stud's cock in her
mouth. No doubt about it, she had him in her mouth. A cell
phone rang, there was embarrassed laughter, and then the
ringing stopped abruptly.

She's blocking my calls.

Maybe she has no coverage.

It rang! Then it went dead!

I'll see you tomorrow.

Can't stand this!

From the other side of the partition he heard the stud's voice. Quiet but demanding. Telling her to kneel on the toilet lid. That it was time to get down to it. Because he wanted to. And because he wanted to, Melanie wanted to as well.

What if she's fucking someone else?

She's not.

How do you know?

Jens urgently needed to pee. He heard thrusts and moans. Then he got an erection.

What a fucking life!

She'll be back soon.

You said she'd be here by midnight!

Jens put his phone away. He was hot, he was shaking. He didn't have to put up with this. Not from his best friend, not from anyone! Let them go ahead and ruin their marriage, what was it to him?

He stood up, quietly opened the door, and tiptoed over to the urinal. He opened his fly and tried to pee. His cock was as hard as a rock. It twitched in the cold light of the energy-saving bulb on the ceiling. He couldn't jack off here. What if someone came in? *Party Cop Caught Masturbating in Toilet!*

"Yes!" yelled Melanie. "Yes!"

That was his life right now. Not able to pee and not able to jack off. And tomorrow, suspension. Then foreclosure on the house, and Vera moving out to her mother's with Timo. That was the law that he enforced. A law that mocked him. A law where he was nothing but dirt in the cracks.

Melanie panted, "Do whatever you want to me!"

Jens stowed his cock in his pants and pulled up his zipper.

He took a running leap and kicked open the cubicle door: "Hands up! Police!"

Melanie shrieked, the young man spun around, reached into his jacket, and a gun flashed in his hand—

10.

Cold light. Whitewashed walls. Smell of flowers and disinfectants. Pain in his chest, dizziness in his head. A cannula stuck in his hand. A monitor that he couldn't see beeping next to him.

"He's opening his eyes," he heard a child's voice say.

He turned his head. Vera and Timo were sitting on two chairs next to his bed. Vera was holding the hand without the cannula and had tears in her eyes.

"How are you?"

"I dunno . . . fine . . ."

"I'm so proud of you," she said, smiling through her tears.

"Look, Dad! That's you!" Timo showed him the front page of several newspapers on his tablet: "Party Cop Shoots Germany's Most-Wanted Gangster!" "Mafia Boss's Life Ends in a Toilet!"

Jens turned his head and closed his eyes. He couldn't remember anything. Wait, he'd been at the bar. The slot machine. "White Rose of Athens." Melanie and the stud with the slicked hair . . .

"You hero." Steffen's voice, coming from the doorway. Next to him, Melanie, smiling, tired, her eyes fixed on Jens with a touch of panic.

"You're all over the Internet. You have your own fan page."

"I don't remember . . ." says Jens.

"The painkillers. The bullet just missed your lung. You were really lucky, buddy. Damn lucky!"

"And the other guy?"

"The investigation is just a formality. Not surprising after you blew his brains all over the tiles."

Through the fog of the painkillers, he could smell the blood again, hear the splintering of cranial bones.

"They didn't catch the tramp who was with him. But who cares! Drugan Mirković! You took out Drugan Mirković!"

Drugan Mirković . . . The Black Angel . . . Drug boss and sex trafficker. Villas in Switzerland and the Black Sea, private jet, dozens of fake passports. The guy Europol had been after for years.

"At some point he'll tell us everything, the whole story. Won't you, darling?"

"Definitely," Melanie said, and again Jens saw panic in her eyes.

Everything felt numb in his head. Drugan Mirković. Who covered his tracks like no other. Who was allegedly dead, lived in South America, or in a Tibetan monastery. Why in Wedding? Why in a bar for the jobless, taxi drivers, and aging whores? A man who could afford champagne and the most expensive women? In a bathroom in Wedding with a mother of three . . . Had Drugan felt life coursing through his veins too? Real life? Perhaps he hadn't found it in his villas or fancy brothels. Perhaps life was never where you happened to be. They were all looking for it: Melanie, Drugan, Jens. And his expression, as Jens had kicked down the door, knocked the gun out of his hand, and grabbed his head . . .

"Is Dad a Cum Cop now?" Timo asked.

The faraway laughter, as if from another world, made his head ache. Vera buried her face in the pillow next to him and whispered into his ear, "I love you . . . I love you . . ."

Sometimes, he thought, we do things that don't suit us. And perhaps then, and only then, are we really the good guys.

THE INVISIBLE MAN
BY MATTHIAS WITTEKINDT
Friedrichshain

F ew people on the streets. No one in the cafés or restaurants. Garbage men picking up bags of trash. Lights on in some apartments. A young Pakistani in plaid chef's pants sits on a stone stoop. First he gazes in the direction of Grünberger Strasse, then toward Boxhagener Platz. There a woman sits on a bench. She's wearing a white dress, light-gray ballet flats, and a white hat.

The day is just beginning and it's going to be hot. Later in the afternoon, children splash around in the concrete kiddie pool. Droves of people cross the square. Some stop before they move on, others sit on the benches. Those who know each other look at one another. When the evening sky is tinged with red, first one, then two women scream. Their shrieks reach the highest pitch that human vocal chords can achieve. Days later, many point to the now empty bench and talk about the woman in the white hat.

And he?

Should he have considered in due time that sooner or later it would come down to whether or not anyone had seen him? There was so much he hadn't considered, because everything had happened so suddenly.

The people he had met on Boxhagener Platz and Grünberger Strasse didn't remember him. Someone might still recollect that they'd had seen him on Kopernikusstrasse, a route he often took. Like he had done on the night in question. The news had already spread. Pictures of her hung in store windows. Her white hat was mentioned in many conversations.

Had he at least worked out routes, times, and places, or woven them into a story that he would be able to tell later on? Had he covered his back, gotten himself what they called an alibi? No. He had not had much in mind; he was no different from the others, after all. And yet it had happened, between him and her. Something like a shock wave had come over him.

It has been Fabian's fate for about a year now that no one ever remembers him; being constantly ignored has landed him in quite a few amusing situations. Just the other day, something happened. When he'd gone up to pay at the bar with friends, the waitress had forgotten to settle his tab. He was standing there, just like the others, but eventually the waitress had looked up and said, crossly, "I'm sorry, boys, but there are still three unpaid beers." Fabian was standing almost in front of her at the counter, holding a clearly visible bill in his hand.

Why hadn't she seen him? Is Fabian unattractive? Or perhaps even disfigured by a childhood accident? Do women look away at the sight of him, or close their eyes because they can't help it? No, no woman has ever looked away or closed her eyes. They just look straight through him. Or slightly to his left or right, sometimes just by a few centimeters. Just enough not to make eye contact. He noticed this after he had begun to analyze what had gone wrong.

Why do they do that? He has often asked himself this question and has inspected himself more than once from all angles in the mirror. But there is nothing wrong with him. He's no different from the men who women do look at, or even chat to now and again. He's noticed often enough how easily they indulge other men this way.

Fabian's fashionably cut hair is dark brown, almost black, and no one can say that it's an ugly or nondescript shade. Aren't some actors conspicuous, even memorable, for having just his hair color? His face is shapely too, and he has a healthy, unspoiled appearance—if perhaps a little naive.

So why is it that women always look straight past him?

I'm normal, damn it! He sometimes says things like this to himself while standing in front of the mirror, styling his hair and trying on different clothes, undergoing a complete transformation before checking himself from all angles. He really makes an effort with his looks; recently, in fact, he feels as if he's almost offering himself up to women. Sometimes he has an urge to go up to the nearest female and say, "Look at me, damn it!"

In the summer—and it is summer—Fabian mostly wears black, gray, or olive-colored T-shirts with dark, well-fitting jeans. There is usually a cool saying or the name of a band he's seen live printed on the front. That's because he likes going to concerts and listens to the same music that many here listen to, and claps in the same way as those around him, and knows in other ways too what's going on. Were a spontaneous conversation to arise, he would be able to join in and make a good impression. An encouraging look, a little smile as if to say, *Oh, and who are you?* is all it would take. Fabian is anything but tongue-tied. His friends in Giessen even thought he was quick off the mark.

Perhaps it is beside the point to mention what are mere details, but Fabian has exquisite, even carefully manicured fingernails and clear skin. As he frequently goes rowing, his skin is darkly tanned, so he has a healthy appearance. He has an upright gait, his stride is masculine and not shy by any means, and when he sits down, he always sits up straight. And his chin: that is definitely a manly chin. His body says it all. He gives off these kinds of vibes the whole time.

But no one has noticed him for a year now. Ever since he moved to Friedrichshain, that's how it has been. It makes him sad and sometimes angry.

Now it's possible, of course, that it has nothing to do with him at all, but with the women in this city or at least in this district. Once, he even thought about touching a particular woman's face—she happened to be wearing a striking, colorful scarf like a cape—putting his fingers on her eyes.

Do you see me now? he almost said out loud just as she passed him by.

We will probably never know exactly how much or how little is required for a person to change so that even those who know him fail to recognize him. And then people tend to say that surely the change didn't just come about, something must have led up to it, and this just happened to be the moment when it broke out. Like a fever breaks out after an infection. So it's not surprising when the word "sick" crops up in contexts like these.

Oh, if only someone could be his witness and let him off the hook. After the first call from the police—apparently, he had been noticed by more people than he'd realized—after the first, still-tentative call from the police, he had very much hoped that someone would remember him, speak up for him, and provide him with an alibi. Because, as he said: "I didn't hurt her. I'd never do a thing like that to a woman or a girl. Whoever did that is sick, and . . . what happened to her eyes?"

That's what he said at the first round of questioning. He disassociated himself from the sick, perverse side of it all in clear terms, although he took the word "sick" from the newspaper reports, as that was how they had described the perpetrator. *Sick.* Nothing else came to mind. Besides, he told the truth when Inspector Rotter interrogated him and when they brought him in for questioning a second time after someone had shamefully betrayed him.

"Yes, I hang out on Boxhagener Platz now and again, like many people do, I guess."

"Which days?"

"Only Sundays."

It's the truth. Fabian only goes to Boxhagener Platz on Sundays because, until recently, he has been studying and working to finance his studies and afford the rowing-club fees. He looks forward to these Sundays, because on the square with its tall trees and flower-lined borders, he feels a little like he does at home with his parents, among friends and his three sisters. The large shady trees, and sandy but firm ground . . . an ideal place to play boules. None of Fabian's friends or drinking buddies want to play with him because they all think it's a pastime for old men. So he asks strangers if he can play. And mostly they let him.

He always brings his own balls. There are good, heavy balls, worthy of a seasoned player like him. And it's true, the men he plays with on Boxhagener Platz are much older than him. But there's a group of younger players too, including a few women. So why doesn't he ask if he can join them if getting their attention is so important?

After an hour, Inspector Rotter let him go. It seemed that the police lacked any firm evidence. In any event, the officers hadn't taken a swab of his saliva. He assumed that the whole thing was over—but he was wrong.

When Inspector Rotter calls him two days later and says

that there is someone else who wants to talk to him, guilt and shame hit him with such force that he is unable to speak for a moment. His mouth goes dry, his heart hammers so hard that he can hear it, and he even starts quivering—well, his chest does. Just above his diaphragm. In other words, right where his anger sits.

By this time, he has long since found out that it is about the young woman who had stood out from the others.

How had it happened? What was the trigger?

She had only been making herself comfortable. She hadn't wanted anything. She hadn't been expecting anyone to look at or talk to her. Having said that, the place she had chosen to take a rest was unfortunate because it was a tram stop. And what was worse, it was one o'clock in the morning, when young people were sitting at tables with friends or standing around near the small park, drinking beer. She did not seem to belong to any of the countless groups you saw everywhere.

There, under one of those urban shelters made of plexiglas, she had chosen the sculpted plastic seat to the far right. There was nothing striking about the sight of her—people often choose to rest under those tram shelters. Some of them are drunk, some are lost, and some have no place to stay. He had noticed right away that she wasn't homeless. She was young, even if dressed in a slightly old-fashioned way.

How did they identify Fabian? Photos showing the face of the girl found on a park bench on Boxhagener Platz had been photocopied and hung up. They said that she was probably Italian. First, the clues had matched him as well as quite a few others. And then, after he'd been questioned twice, an anonymous caller had identified him by name. How had this reprehensible person known which street he lives on?

An Italian police lieutenant was allowed to question him

because, ten days earlier, another Italian woman had been attacked. She too had been sitting on a park bench, this time on Mariannenplatz in Kreuzberg.

In this case, the attack had also taken place around midnight, and she'd similarly been injured from a blow to the head with a heavy object. When she had regained consciousness eight days later, she thought she remembered a young man who had been skateboarding around the square and had come very close to her a couple of times.

"He was practicing jumps. The same ones over and over again, like he'd wanted me to watch him and clap."

Some newspapers had printed this statement word for word. Perhaps to point out that, by doing the same thing over and over again, the alleged offender had manic tendencies. Unfortunately, she had only been able to describe the man on the longboard in very vague terms.

"Medium height, dark hair, black clothes, not brand new. And he was wearing a baseball cap, but with the brim facing forward. I only got a brief look at him and thought he could be Italian."

The story had received a lot of coverage in the newspapers because she had been attending an international congress for her party. So this was an attempted murder of an Italian politician, whose political leanings were somewhere between the center and moderate left. She was still very young for her position and classically beautiful.

Lieutenant Gobin had already been on his way to Berlin when they found the next deceased woman on Boxhagener Platz. So far, despite the hesitant testimony of the first victim, they had been looking for an Italian or an Italian-looking man in his early twenties.

* * *

"Mr. Arnold?" Lieutenant Gobin recognizes Fabian immediately.

"Yes. You're the inspector who wants to speak to me?"

"I'm Lieutenant Gobin. Don't get up." The man takes a seat and puts his hat on the table in a way that makes Fabian nervous.

"They told me on the phone that someone had been sent from Italy, but you're expecting too much. And why are we meeting here, in a bar?"

"I'd like to clarify some details that have to do with routes and locations. I have to start somewhere, don't I?" Lieutenant Gobin turns his head slightly to the right, taking his eyes off Fabian for a moment. "Is there a pool table back there?"

"Four tables."

"Do you play pool?"

"I'd never do a thing like that. I have three sisters, one of them her age."

"You know how old the deceased was?"

"I've already been asked when and how often I was there. And there are signs up everywhere."

They are interrupted when a waitress comes to the table. First she looks at the lieutenant, her eyes practically glued to him. He orders a carafe of white wine and Fabian orders a beer, announcing: "I don't normally drink beer at this time of day."

"Nervous? There's no reason to be."

"I've already said everything."

"And I'll ask you many of the same things over again. Where do you work, Mr. Arnold?"

"In the copy shop over on Warschauer Strasse."

"But you're not from Berlin." Lieutenant Gobin takes a pair of gloves out of his jacket pocket and puts them next to his hat.

"I'm from Giessen. I studied engineering and material technology here at the TU and just finished my master's. You can call me Fabian, by the way. No one has called me Mr. Arnold in a long time."

"How old are you, Mr. Arnold?"

"Twenty-one."

"And you've already finished your studies?"

"I skipped a grade in elementary school, and was quick at studying because of my dad . . . I already knew most of it. He taught me everything."

"Any plans on what you want to be?"

"A mining engineer. We have a small company. I mean, my dad does, of course."

"There are mines in Giessen?"

"My father works in Johannesburg."

"How long has he been there?"

Fabian has to think. "I don't know exactly. Twenty-five years?"

"So your father was away a lot."

"Someone had to earn money. And it didn't make him less of a father, just . . ."

"Of course. Besides, you still have your mother and sisters. You have three sisters, right? Will you now go back to Giessen?"

"For the time being."

"And then to South Africa? You used to live there?"

"Until eleventh grade. In Johannesburg."

"And now just your father is there?"

"My parents are divorced. Apparently, he was having affairs. But no one really knows for sure. He sometimes disappeared for a few days and wouldn't say where."

"And now that you have your master's, you're going to go and live with him?"

"Yes, we . . . have always gotten along well, and my dad wants me to take over the business from him, the way he did from his father. But before I do that, I wanted—"

"A bit of adventure, a bit of experience in Berlin, and then off into the big wide world."

"But nothing like this."

"Nothing like what?"

"Murdered women."

"Is there more than one?"

"I meant in general—and because they found one on Mariannenplatz too. But she's still alive. Has she completely recovered? She hurt her head, right?"

"You heard about that? Do these kinds of things interest you, violence against women?"

"It was in all the papers. Besides, there were posters up everywhere. The police were looking for witnesses."

"You say, *There were signs up everywhere.* So you often go to Mariannenplatz?"

"There's an open-air cinema there."

"Do you work out? Do you like playing sports?"

"I'm in a rowing club. Why do you ask? Because you think I'm strong enough to have done it?"

Lieutenant Gobin smiles. And, as always when he smiles, he shows his teeth. It makes him looks open and friendly. But even when he isn't smiling, his face is mysteriously attractive. Even though he is no longer young and his skin has had a lot of sun and scars over the years, at least twice needing stitches. Fabian is overcome by a powerful wave of affection. Then his emotions suddenly flip to the opposite extreme, and the lieutenant's way of looking at him with his feminine eyes puts him on edge. It's as if every inch of his body were being examined, as if he's being touched.

"Was she murdered in a way that would take strength?" Fabian asks. "Was she strangled? Is that why you wanted to know if I work out?"

"Oh, no, it was just a very random question. You're wearing a T-shirt and I see what I see."

"I would have been strong enough, but it wasn't me. I just passed her by." Why did he say that? He had made up his mind not to do just that.

"Do you live alone?"

"Alone, yes. But I didn't take her with me. I barely noticed her." He had mentioned her again. Was that really necessary?

"May I ask if you have a girlfriend?"

"Not at the moment. I work until midnight. There's little time after that."

"And when you finish work, do you go home right away?"

"Why did you ask if I have a girlfriend? Whether I have one or not doesn't mean anything, it's not a sign of anything. The person who did that was sick!" He'd planned to stay calm; and above all, he'd planned to say the same as the last time without going into detail. He imagines that details might give him away.

"Do you go home from the copy shop via the shortest route?"

"Yes, I'm very tired after work."

"You never take the tram?"

"Never. In the copy shop, I have to stand a lot, so—"

"You prefer to walk. On this side of the street?"

"Yes. What's this all about? What do you mean by that?"

"Do you play pool?"

"Did Paolo say that? Have you spoken to Paolo? Do you believe him?"

"You don't have a girlfriend at the moment, but perhaps you have friends?"

"I meet people at the rowing club, at work of course, and when I play pool . . ."

"I mean real friends. Who could testify where you were at a given time, for example."

"Would it bother you if I ordered another beer?"

"No."

"It's just because something like this has never happened to me before."

"Order what you like, it's on me." Lieutenant Gobin raises his hand.

The waitress comes, pulling out her notepad with a flick.

"The young man would like another beer."

"A beer. And you?"

"Nothing for the moment, thank you."

After Fabian takes a few big gulps, their eyes meet again, and he doesn't look away. From that moment on, something changes. Suddenly, Fabian is determined to talk. What's more, he feels like having a longer conversation with this man in the old-fashioned suit. Why? Wasn't he anxious a moment ago that he'd already revealed too much? Hasn't he heard often enough that he is not obliged to say anything without a lawyer? Didn't his class at university discuss privacy, surveillance, and questionable practices of the state? Why does this suddenly no longer count?

"You speak German very well, lieutenant."

"Gobin."

"Is Gobin a common Italian name?"

"My grandparents came from Belgium, right on the German border, and that's where I grew up, because my parents first had to get settled over in Italy and make a living."

"In Italy."

"Correct. First in Catania, later in Naples. Anyway, I was

often in Germany, and my oldest daughter's husband . . . well."

"You have a daughter?"

"Four daughters." Again, a brief smile. "Have you ever been to Naples?"

"No. And in Naples you're something like an inspector?"

"If an Italian is killed or suddenly disappears overseas, or someone abroad has the kind of difficulties that can't be solved unaided, they send me to fix things. In this case, there's also a political aspect."

"Because of the woman on Mariannenplatz . . . You don't look like the inspectors here in Germany."

"Do you know any?"

"Well, only from the TV—but I'm sure that even the real ones don't wear old-fashioned brown suits, turquoise silk shirts, or hats like yours. And definitely not as many gold chains and rings."

"Gifts from my wife and daughters."

"So what exactly do you want from me?"

"I'm here because a politician was attacked and a young woman was killed who was probably also Italian. Do you happen to remember what she was wearing?"

"What she was wearing?"

"You've already said twice that you saw her, right? So now I'm asking you what she was wearing."

Lieutenant Gobin knows the answer, because he has already spoken to the two women who found the deceased. During that conversation, they had been standing in front of the park bench where the dead woman had been found sitting as if asleep. Behind the bench there was a shallow kiddie pool made of concrete, where children were playing. Mothers and several fathers were sitting on nearby benches.

"Just tell me how everything was," he had said to the witnesses.

"How what was?"

"Well, why did you both think there was something wrong with her? Dozens of people had passed her all day long. A few had even sat down next to her. We have established that she must have already been dead on the bench the night before."

"Well, her arm was hanging down and she was sitting all crooked. That's why."

"Her head was bent forward, and at first we thought she'd fallen asleep. You couldn't see her face because of her hat."

"At first we thought she might be sick."

"So we went over and tried to speak to her."

"Her arm. You could see the veins so clearly. But no blood."

"We wanted to keep going but then we thought it might be better to wake her up. It was hot on Monday and we thought she had heat stroke . . ."

"Because of the way she was sitting there, the way she looked."

"When she didn't say anything, I pushed her hat up a bit. I won't ever forget that. That will stay with me for the rest of my life."

"At first, we didn't move. Then the shock hit us full on and we started screaming. But there was no blood on her clothes."

Lieutenant Gobin had given the witnesses plenty of time because they needed to talk. He'd guessed from their appearances that they were hairdressers. They had almost identical cuts: jet-black hair with purple and turquoise highlights. Their eyelashes were long and very dark. At over eighty-five degrees in the shade, their makeup was on the heavy side. So you can imagine what they looked like, upset, sweating, and burying their faces in their hands as they gave their report.

* * *

"What was her name?" Fabian now asks, shocked at his own question. "Excuse me. I'm talking too much."

"She wasn't carrying ID."

"Then why do you think she was Italian? In some films, they claim that you can determine where someone is from by taking hair samples."

"We checked where she had bought her clothes. Everything came from Neapolitan shops. She had pierced ears . . . When you saw the young woman, was she wearing jewelry?"

Why did he immediately think this was the reason she had been murdered?

"I don't know whether she was wearing jewelry. It was just after midnight when I saw her."

"Did you walk on this side of the street? Like always?"

"I don't know anything about jewelry. I don't do things like that—gawk at women. I think you can go so far. It's fine to look for just a second. Two or three seconds even, if they don't notice . . . I don't judge them by their looks either. I sometimes imagine how it must be for women to be constantly gawked at. I have three sisters. Maybe that's why I look at women differently from other men."

"And how did you notice her if you don't look at women?"

"She was beautiful. I did think: *That's what you call a classic profile.* Slender. Firm skin. Very steep bridge of the nose. Almost a bit too sharp. An Italian, I thought. She wore distinctive clothing. Did she still have on the white hat when she was found? She was holding a white hat with a wide brim in her lap, like the ones you sometimes see in old English paintings. Yes, now that I think about it, I noticed it. But I did not do anything to her. I just passed her by. I would swear to that, if necessary. She was sitting in the tram shelter over there when I saw her."

"How could you have seen her? If, as you say, you walk from the copy shop to your apartment, and if, as you say, you take the shortest route when you're tired after work, and if, as you say, you walk on this side of the street, then you would walk behind the tram shelter. So how would you be able to describe her face, or a hat that she had on her lap?"

"No, it wasn't like that. I was on the other side of the street because I had gone to buy a beer over at the late-night store. They know me, they'll confirm that. And then I crossed the street, and that's when I saw her. That was the moment . . ." Fabian nods, as if he's reliving every detail before his eyes.

"And who's Paolo?"

"What do you mean?"

"You mentioned his name earlier."

"Oh, him. I met him a few times by the pool table and we had a drink."

"Did you tell him about your meeting with the young woman?"

"It wasn't a meeting."

"Did you tell Paolo about it?"

Fabian thinks back. "Maybe. Because I thought she was Italian, that's why. And Paolo's also Italian."

"And Paolo knows your name?"

"I guess so. We sometimes talk when we're playing pool, so I suppose I've told him my name."

"Where does Paolo live and what's his last name?"

"I don't know."

"But he knows where you live."

"Did Paolo . . . ? I was wondering how the police came up with my name."

"Thank you for your help," says Lieutenant Gobin, asking for the bill.

"Women who look like that," Fabian adds quickly, "are bound to receive compliments. And they don't always want them, right? They're not trying to provoke anyone, they just want to look young, pretty, and fashionable. And sometimes they are so caught up in themselves that they ignore people."

It's eleven o'clock at night. Seven hours have passed since their conversation. Inspector Rotter has made inquiries, and that's how Lieutenant Gobin now knows that Fabian has no criminal record and really did complete his master's degree a month ago.

He also has a better photo of the dead girl. Berlin police specialists have edited it so that she looks as if she's alive. Lieutenant Gobin has also been to the copy shop and talked to the owner of the late-night store, who confirmed that Fabian buys a bottle of beer there every night.

"Just one, never more than one?"

"Just one."

That was the case on Sunday too.

And shortly before midnight, Lieutenant Gobin returns to the place where he and Fabian had their conversation. Only this time, he doesn't sit down at one of the tables in front, he goes into the back. And as so often in Berlin, at least in some of the old buildings, the room he enters is dark and much larger than you'd think from the outside. The only light is above the pool tables and its halo is sharply defined.

Lieutenant Gobin stands right in front of the wall. The people in the room are little more than shadows. Only the upper bodies of those bending over the tables during the game can really be seen. As he watches the players, Lieutenant Gobin hears music that is more his generation's taste. One particular song makes him think of his wife Maria. They had been lying in a sandy hollow by the sea that smelled of tar and diesel. From there they'd had a spectacular view over the bay of Naples. That was thirty-one years ago. Lieutenant Gobin has just worked this out based on the age of his oldest daughter. Hadn't they heard the same song at the time some distance away, and hadn't it sometimes sounded louder, and then quieter, as if the wind were wafting the sounds over to them in waves? Memories of this kind go through the lieutenant's mind as he watches the players.

At some point, he pushes himself off the wall, strolls from table to table, and plays a few rounds of pool. As he plays, his torso dips into the light; his brown hat and gloves lie on the edge of the table. No one touches them or takes them away.

Nearly two hours pass until he notices a man's voice which, at some distance from the tables, moves across the room, exchanging a few brief words with players here and there. The man is dressed like many—black pants, black jacket, and a baseball cap. His Italian accent is unmistakable, but there's something odd about his name because sometimes he's called Paolo, sometimes Lorenzo, occasionally Leonardo or even Francesco. A young guy who hands him a parcel refers to him as Matteo to another person not long afterward. When he leaves the poolroom, the lieutenant follows him.

The street is still lively and you might even say that the light is blue: and in this blue light there are colorful clusters of flickering candles and lanterns, and people too, probably from all over the world. Some sit at tables and are served by Indian, Syrian, or Thai women. A tram struggles through the crowds, ringing its bell over and over again, sounding almost angry. The cars are barely moving forward. The drivers' faces—you had to have seen them—are what must be German faces. They look focused, patient, almost indifferent, because this is what they are used to.

After taking in these impressions for a few seconds, Lieutenant Gobin puts on his hat and follows Paolo, or whatever his mother really named him. He sees many young faces at the tables, some with beautiful eyes. She would have fit in at any one of these tables, she would have been quite at home and not have stood out, not even with her unusual hat. And maybe she sat here—just there. Or there, on the other side of the street. Or she maybe she did what the groups at the edge of the square are now doing—standing around and drinking beer while their dogs wait.

Just as Lieutenant Gobin has reached this stage in his reflections, the Italian with the many names enters a restaurant. The illuminated sign over the door says *Linzer Hof*.

How beautiful everything is in here. The interior of the Linzer Hof is all natural, all honey-stained wood for the shoulder-high wall-to-wall paneling, and the tables and chairs too. A few pairs of antlers and paintings of hunting scenes hang among scythes, sickles, pitchforks, and wooden rakes. These are complemented by earthenware jugs that stand on the broad cornice above the paneling. Young Thai women in rustic clothing serve the guests with light variations of Austrian cuisine, but there is also a fully stocked bar with rows of bottles in front of a large mirror. Lieutenant Gobin watches the Italian talking to the man behind the bar. During their chat, the name Matteo comes up twice. Here too he is handed a parcel.

Lieutenant Gobin beckons to the only waitress who is not Asian and who he assumes to be the supervisor. He shows her his ID and the photo of the dead girl.

She looks at the picture for a long time. "She's the one in the pictures all over the streets that—" She stops abruptly, gives Lieutenant Gobin back the photograph, and points to the man behind the bar. "Talk to Draško."

Lieutenant Gobin immediately turns around and looks out of the large window onto the street. The Italian with many names has disappeared.

"Ask Draško," the waitress repeats, "he's our manager, he knew her. We aren't allowed to give any information like that."

Lieutenant Gobin decides not to pursue the Italian and goes over to the bar. There he smiles pleasantly at the stocky man, showing his teeth a little. Then he hands Draško the photo. He in turn barely glances at it, peering at Lieutenant Gobin with amusement instead. "And who are you? Her father? Did she run away from some backwater dump? There are lots of people like her around here. But I've never seen their dads come looking for them. Which village are you from?"

"First take a look at the picture, then we'll talk," Lieutenant Gobin says. "And please tell me who the young man was to whom you just gave the package."

Draško does not want to play ball. He isn't rattled by a stranger who looks like a peasant with a penchant for cheap jewelry. Rather than helping, rather than taking a good look at the photo, he says something that doesn't have anything to do with the matter at hand: "Hey, bro, maybe you've seen too many seventies films."

Lieutenant Gobin goes behind the bar and shows him his ID. Draško shoves him backward.

Two minutes later, they are in a room where the Vietnamese chefs take their breaks and relax. Draško is sitting on a low stool and massaging his right ear. Now he's talking, but what he's saying is not pleasant. Lieutenant Gobin is acquainted with such situations: some people need to let off steam first before their reason kicks in. But Draško is not the kind of man who calms down like that: in his case, it's exactly the other way around. He gets worked up when he talks, pumps himself up. So Lieutenant Gobin takes his gloves out of his jacket pocket and pulls them on.

Draško is worked up enough now. He stands up and rams his fist into the lieutenant's guts.

Then a great deal happens, one thing after another, and it all takes its time. When Lieutenant Gobin returns to the dining room, he waves the waitress over.

"Where's Draško?" she asks before the lieutenant manages to speak.

The lieutenant slips his gloves into his pocket. "In the break room, resting."

"Did he get violent?"

"Emotional. Maybe now you can tell me something about the woman in the photo?"

"She was wearing a long white skirt that went down to her calves, ballerina pumps, and a blouse with thin stitching in blue and red. The most noticeable thing about her was her hat. It was like the ones people used to wear at horse races. She came three times. Every other day. She was looking for work and wasn't put off as easily as most. The very first time she was here, she said that she had worked on the outskirts of Naples in a restaurant owned by her parents. So she had experience, she spoke good German and was good-looking. I don't know why Draško didn't hire her."

"Did she have a purse or something like that?"

"A small bag made of white tulle. I'd guess that she'd made her clothes herself and that she wasn't from a city. The necklace you're wearing around your neck—what figure is that?"

"The Archangel Michael, patron saint of policemen."

"Are you religious?"

"That package that Draško handed over to the young man . . . ?"

"Flyers. Matteo distributes them for us. For us and for various other restaurants."

"And is his name really Matteo?"

She shrugs.

"Does he work for an agency, or does he do it privately?"

"He works for Flyers—their office is nearby, over on Simplonstrasse."

"Thank you. And if Mr. Draško wants to complain, then please give him this card. They'll deal with the charges."

"If there are any."

"If there are any."

After leaving the restaurant, Lieutenant Gobin puts on his hat and glances around. After a while, he spots Matteo skateboarding elegantly backward along the sidewalk, distributing his flyers. The lieutenant guesses he is in his early twenties. He's also very lively and obviously clever. When he stops at a table to hand out his flyers, he often performs a little trick on his board. He says things that the lieutenant can't hear from this far away. It seems to be something funny, maybe even titillating, because many of the women at the table laugh and look at each other. By the time they're ready to reply, Matteo is already off to the next table and doing his tricks there. In this way—meanderingly, playfully, artistically—Matteo slowly makes his way toward Boxhagener Platz. There he throws the rest of his flyers in a trash can, then practices different jumps. There is nothing playful at all about how he does this; on the contrary, he never takes a break and does the same thing over and over again. After a while, the lieutenant has had enough. And he's hungry too.

Whenever he's on business in Berlin, Lieutenant Gobin stays with Inspector Horst Rotter and his wife Ingrid. This time, he has brought her earrings of two seahorses with turquoise and red stones and a matching turquoise silk scarf. Ingrid is overjoyed. The three always spend convivial evenings together and there is much laughter. Ingrid Rotter is no shrinking violet. She joins in every occasion, is usually the loudest, and opens her mouth the widest when she laughs. The procedure is always the same: first, they drink some schnapps and a few beers, then Ingrid brings in her homemade pickled cucumbers, good rye bread, and garnished meatballs, while Horst sets up his slide projector. A nice, sociable end to a long day.

The next morning, the lieutenant is the first customer in the Flyers agency. It consists of a very white air-conditioned room with two desks, behind which sit two young men in bright shirts. The room is perfectly silent. The female manager tells the lieutenant that Paolo Lorenzo Allessandro Francesco Leonardo is known in the agency under the name Matteo. She writes down the details and the long number from Lieutenant Gobin's ID card. Then she hands him the photocopy of a passport. The young Italian with the many names is called Matteo Frattini and comes from Perugia. After gaining her trust, the lieutenant finds out that Frattini does two rounds—one in Friedrichshain and one in Kreuzberg.

"Where in Kreuzberg?"

"Between Oranienstrasse and Mariannenplatz."

When Lieutenant Gobin leaves the agency and puts his hat on, his cell phone rings. "Hi, Horst. What's up?"

"Revaler Strasse 8, backyard. There's a bar called Snakes."

Horst Rotter and Lieutenant Gobin stand for just a minute in the corridor to a fifty-square-foot room. The woman is fully clothed and sits on a chair next to her bed. No blood on her clothes, although there should be some.

"Italian," Rotter says as they go downstairs. "She worked here as a dancer and lived upstairs. Been sitting there for at least two days, says our . . . Ah! Wait!"

Rotter introduces Lieutenant Gobin to a man with bright eyes. "Mr. Jankowski is the owner of the bar."

Jankowski looks depressed. "I was planning to report Viola as missing, but then I thought I'd just take a look. I don't usually go into the girls' rooms. I hope you find her ID; I have to notify her parents."

"Don't worry, we'll talk to her parents," Inspector Rotter explains in a friendly but firm manner.

This doesn't stop the man with the bright eyes from telling them about a guy in his fifties. "He had hair down to his ass, looked like he came from a different era. I saw him downstairs in the bar. Actually, we were closed, we were just airing out the place, and . . . apart from him, there was no one around. He had a baseball bat in his hand and was swinging it as if his life depended on it. The same movements, over and over again. He was totally wrapped up in himself."

"We've already received a tip-off of a possible suspect who matches that description," says Rotter. "Anonymously again. Name and address the same as last time. The informant had an Italian accent."

Lieutenant Gobin shows Jankowski the photocopy of Matteo Frattini's passport.

"Yes, he's often here, delivers flyers for me."

In the afternoon, more lines gradually start to converge. The Italians have checked up on Matteo Frattini, and he is wanted in Perugia on suspicion of several break-ins. Inspector Rotter instructs his people. Later, he and Lieutenant Gobin spend a long evening at Boxhagener Platz. Matteo Frattini doesn't show up.

"Maybe he saw me when I followed him yesterday."

"Did you have your hat on?"

"Hmm."

"Don't worry, the wheels are in motion."

Lieutenant Gobin spends the next day at Berlin Zoo. It's something he always does when he's in town. He particularly likes to see the seals and penguins, and when he does, time flies. At some point he pulls himself away from the seals, sits down on a bench, takes notes, then writes his report. When he's finished, he crosses Breitscheidplatz and goes into the KaDeWe department store, where he speaks with two sales assistants for a long time.

At eleven p.m., the lieutenant and Inspector Rotter are sitting back on Boxhagener Platz. They are talking quietly and feel the kind of tension they know from fishing trips with Maria and Ingrid up at Horst's holiday cabin in Mecklenburg-Vorpommern, when they have no luck for hours but are poised for a decent bite at any moment.

"There's always someone around," Rotter observes at about three in the morning, "someone who must have seen her murdered." There's a pause, then he adds. "I was born in Berlin . . ." He breaks off and goes silent for a while, breathing deeply. Then he talks about indifference and people who live in a world that has nothing to do with the old society and its laws and morals.

"I don't mean drug addicts or the homeless, I mean people who go to work, pay their insurance, and spend their evenings with friends in clubs. They wouldn't see you and me even if they passed us by—they wouldn't see someone being murdered right next to them." Rotter compares Berlin to a carcass swelling with maggots, always taking on new shapes.

A good old attitude from an era long past, thinks Lieutenant Gobin. He holds Rotter's hand for a while to help calm him down.

"Let's call it a night, he's not going to show up," Rotter decides when it starts to get light.

On the third day, the Italian is still missing. Even though they know Matteo's usual routes because there are many people who remember him and his jokes. Lieutenant Gobin would have liked to arrest Matteo Frattini himself. *But Horst will have to do that for me now,* he thinks. *I just hope the Germans hand him over.*

After a long final night with Horst and Ingrid, with many pickled cucumbers, sandwiches, and photos of their vacation in Thailand, it's time to say goodbye to Berlin. And it has to be said, at least once: Ingrid cuts a damn good figure with her huge Italian sunglasses in her turquoise bikini.

The next morning, Inspector Rotter drives the lieutenant to Tegel Airport. It is still early and the night has been so chilly that Rotter's well-waxed Astra is scattered with dewdrops. In just under three hours, Lieutenant Gobin will be in Naples and will see his wife, daughters, and granddaughters. And of course, he cannot return to his granddaughters empty-handed. That's why he has eight flat boxes of colorful giant candies with the sights of Berlin on the front. For his wife, the lieutenant has a small blue hat from KaDeWe, because he always brings her something from abroad when he's sent to collect people, or at least their bodies.

En route to his flight gate—a gray door, rarely used—he and Inspector Rotter stop once again and watch as a throng of young Spaniards pour out of a different gate with huge suitcases.

At the gray door, Lieutenant Gobin is inspected by a man who looks him in the eye for a long time. Next to him is a second man with a submachine gun that hangs, black and heavy, on a narrow belt. Here they say goodbye, hugging each other tightly.

"Give my regards to Ingrid and tell her that I think of her often."

"Say hello to Maria and tell her that I also think of her often, and always fondly."

Twenty minutes later, the noise outside is deafening and Lieutenant Gobin feels a stiff wind in his face. He holds on tightly to his hat so that it doesn't get blown away.

The wind is coming from the four propellers of the C-130 Hercules, because Lieutenant Gobin is standing at an angle on the tarmac behind an Italian Air Force aircraft and checking that the coffins are properly loaded.

This is part of his mission: to bring the two women home. Next to Lieutenant Gobin stands a darkly dressed staff member of the Italian embassy. A man without a hat. His hair is completely disheveled, his jacket, his trouser legs, even his red tie flutter wildly.

Lieutenant Gobin has accomplished his mission. He realized that Fabian was a young, insecure man who had been denounced by the culprit. Fabian had been wearing jeans and an olive T-shirt with the name of a band in odd, spiky letters. Or had he? What had his face looked like? His hair? The lieutenant finds it difficult to remember.

"Fabian and Matteo are like the light and dark side of a coin," he had said to Inspector Rotter when they said goodbye. "The one is as unobtrusive as the other is conspicuous."

Now, as Lieutenant Gobin climbs the ramp of the C-130 Hercules, over the rib-like struts of the fuselage, he sees two officers from the Italian armed forces. In their uniforms, with their caps pulled down low over their faces, they are as similar as two peas in a pod. A third man is handing out the photocopied papers of their mission for the return flight. And at that moment in his mind's eye, Lieutenant Gobin sees the copy shop on Warschauer Strasse, where Fabian was known as Fabian and a few people backed up some of his statements. It had been so obvious. All he had needed to do was ask the employees if the copy shop could print leaflets; he should have asked himself why Matteo was so conspicuously dressed and so extroverted. But above all, he should have asked himself why the guy had suddenly disappeared without a trace.

So Inspector Rotter has to pick up Lieutenant Gobin again and immediately disagrees with him three times, steering the wheel of the Astra with his left hand.

"Yes, Horst. This Fabian guy incriminated himself. Either he wanted to lead us onto the wrong track by inventing Matteo, or . . . I have never spoken to such a willing witness. He totally delivered himself into our hands with his statement."

"But you saw both of them."

"I saw both of them and thought that they were two different people."

"So he likes dressing in different ways? Standing in front of the mirror and turning himself into someone else? Any idea where he might be?"

"Johannesburg. He is one of those boys who looks up to his father. He told me everything I need to know to convict him."

"When are you flying?"

"As soon as possible."

* * *

When Fabian leaves the station in Giessen, he hears his name being called. First his heart leaps for joy, thinking it is the Italian lieutenant. But then he sees that it is just two women running across the street.

"Fabian! When did you get back?"

He points to his wheeled suitcase. He tries hard to remember their names.

"Are you coming to the concert tonight? Gegenstrom is playing in its old lineup, and the Boxhamsters are probably going to be on stage too . . ."

Had he already planned to visit his father at that point? They had often talked about it. They would explore the country together like they had done in the past, and see many new faces. Yes, the plan had probably been fixed in his mind for a long time.

On the plane to Johannesburg the next day, the stewardess forgets to put down Fabian's tray, but he takes the food from her with a forgiving smile. The smile remains on his face, because his last thought, before falling asleep like a protected child, is the Italian lieutenant.

OVERTIME

BY MIRON ZOWNIR

Kreuzberg

1.

It was the first warm day of spring, but the long-awaited sun bothered Tom more than the gray winter tristesse of the past few months. Everything was brighter, more colorful, and louder, while his nervous system was still set to the dark, monochrome, lower frequencies of winter. As nature revived itself in the backyard of his foul-smelling apartment block in Wedding, the rat holes multiplied in the neglected patch of wasteland that no one was responsible for, and the piled-up garbage spilling out of the dumpsters crushed the last few flowering crocuses. The first newborn sparrows dove in high spirits from their nest under the roof, only to smack brutally onto the bikes or dumpsters, losing their lives before they had even begun. None of them had yet managed to reach the courtyard wall of the neighboring building. Only the smallest and weakest one, who was still cowering and trembling in the nest in fear of his maiden flight, was still in the race. It was good that he hadn't imitated his kamikaze siblings. *Stay cool, take your time, don't forget that you have wings, you're not made of stone,* Tom would have liked to encourage him. Who wouldn't have wished the little sparrow luck? Too many, he thought.

Tom had become a misanthrope. Not a people-hater, but someone who was always ready to assume the worst. Nature's cruelty was nothing compared to the malice he had experienced and come to expect from his fellow human beings.

He wouldn't wish eternal life on anyone. An immortal person—what a pain in the ass he would be. In fact, no one really believed in the metaphysical consolation of infinite life when faced with imminent death. And there were enough murderers who legitimized their crimes with moral lies, supernatural fabrications, or God-given missions. The death penalty was still widespread, and there were more terrorists, gunmen, politicians, and suicide pilots than ever who annihilated people in cold-blooded, smart, and nasty ways.

Looking hesitantly out of the window, he saw the trembling chick teetering on the brink of the nest. Its pitiful chirping and the hysterical, uncoordinated flapping of its wings gave Tom no reason to be optimistic about its chances of survival. Betting on the chick making it was bound to be a loss, but he would have bet on it anyway. He always made bad bets and was not a good loser.

"Close the window, Tom. I'm cold."

"Sorry, honey." He closed the window and sat down on the bed next to her. "Don't you want to get up? I'll make you breakfast."

Her blue, dejected eyes stared into space. "No thanks, I'm not hungry."

"Then let's go for a walk. It's a beautiful day."

"Could you pull the curtain, please?"

"You can't stay in bed all the time, honey."

"Why not?"

"It's depressing. Let's do something."

"I'm not in the mood. I'm sick."

"Because you swallow too many pills, Lucia."

"You help yourself to them too."

"That's not true."

"Yes, it is."

"Mind if I play Mozart?"

"I don't care. But take the stereo into the kitchen and close the door."

"All right," Tom scowled. He'd already gone off the idea of Mozart but made one last try. "We could go for a swim . . ."

She turned away from him and stared at the wall. Tom took the ashtray from the bedside table, counted the butts, then lit one.

"You're going to kill yourself with your fucking smoking."

"You smoke yourself."

He went over to the window and pulled the curtains closed. There was no point in making her suffer. Perhaps she'd have a better day tomorrow.

Life had become a drag since Lucia had gotten sick. Drag wasn't the right word; fragile was more accurate, or precarious in a sad kind of way. Between them lay a gap that nothing could bridge, caused by the pharmaceuticals she took. Every gesture, every glance, every emotion that went beyond an everyday reflex disappeared in a twilight state of isolation, which both of them felt and neither could express. Years of mutual helplessness had secluded Lucia and weakened Tom. While Lucia had grown harder in her seclusion, Tom's urge to come to grips with his life had slowly slipped away.

Now he just muddled through and had reached the point where he would have gambled away everything he had. Because what was everything if you'd already lost what was most important to you?

He went into the kitchen, took the vodka out of the freezer, and stared at it, unsure. Smoking, drinking, and silence—because you couldn't share your life anymore. His wife was indifferent to him and he hated his job. He hadn't painted in years and had destroyed all his pictures except for a sole portrait of Lucia. It hung in a battered frame above the kitchen table, hiding an ugly water stain. It wasn't one of his strongest paintings from his early years at art college, but it reminded him of a time when they had both still been happy. He had already thrown it out of the window several times but had always gone down to collect it again. It had survived rain, pigeon shit, and footprints. In a dadaistic way, these had all added to its artistic quality. But Tom was through with art. He was over and done with it. Had he not mistakenly believed in his talent many years ago, he would have saved himself a lot of trouble.

Two pigeons were fucking on the windowsill and he watched them absentmindedly. Two young crows on a nearby TV antenna also watched them, and by their snooty expressions it was clear that neither thought much of the pigeons' flagrant behavior. Tom had bummed two tranquilizers off Lucia and, draining half the vodka bottle, he peered listlessly out of the window. Lucia was still in bed, just waiting for him to leave the apartment. She only ventured once to the door, to tell him that he had smoked her last cigarette. But his mood had soured and he gave her the cold shoulder. His repertoire of conciliatory gestures was all used up.

When the phone rang, he had just killed the first spring fly. Or the last winter one. It lay drowned in a pool of its own blood. *But bugs don't have blood*, he reflected in a moment of confusion. Tom let the phone ring until the caller gave up. Then he refilled his glass. He had plenty of time to kill before his shift at Kinski began.

2.

Herbie ordered a drink at the bar and sat down at a table.

He was in his midfifties, divorced, not in very good shape, and expected nothing more from life except perhaps that it would go steadily downhill. Heading his way was a future full of health problems, money worries, inflation, and a lack of independence. He had no funds whatsoever for a decent retirement or nursing care.

He sipped listlessly at his drink and rubbed his eyes. Morning had burst in too suddenly on his drowsy, semiconscious state, and the weak spring sun bathed the wasteland on the other side of the bar's dirty windows in a terrible, ghostly light. Although he kept his eyes closed, he could sense every filthy puddle and see every wasted body, all the way down to its reeking, alcohol-clogged pores. The noise level was a sign that there wasn't much going on. The times when hookers trawled through the Kinski were over, and the pedophile curb-crawlers from Kurfürstenstrasse no longer showed up here either. Even when he'd been a cop, the feds had kept an eye on the joint and he'd made the occasional catch.

But since raids had picked up, the place had turned into a graveyard. The cheerless atmosphere only underlined his own emotional state. He found it hard to let time drift like this and had already started to feel bad about the money he'd spent on drink. The end of the month was nearing and the last cents he kept aside for entertainment were already spent. Though he always consumed the cheapest booze, he could no longer afford to get smashed because in the days that followed, he would be shot to pieces by his bottomless arsenal of frustration. After every hangover he ended up more depressed than before. He was just looking for a convincing excuse to tear himself away from the dreary bar and was glancing around, uninspired, at the dirty tables, unoccupied except for a Turkish drag queen, a quarreling couple, and a wasted punk, when he caught sight of a better-dressed guy, his leg in a cast; the sight felt like a punch in the gut.

Herbie almost didn't recognize him. His face looked firmer and younger than he remembered. It no longer resembled a runny pancake marked with the dirty prints of an excessive past. He no longer looked sleazy, washed out, or repulsive. His entire personality had been removed with plastic surgery and a neutral facade stood in its place, behind which he probably still sought out potential victims with the same vigor and malice, still up to his old tricks.

Back when he was a cop, Herbie had always despised this guy. But now, in his steady downhill state, he realized he was envious as well as angry, which almost made him ashamed.

He must have stared at him for a long time because the guy with the cast seemed to feel his eyes on him. At any rate, Herbie noticed the guy was getting restless. He saw him reach for his crutch, preparing to hobble away without finishing his beer. But before he could heave himself to his feet, Herbie planted himself three paces in front of him.

"What's the hurry, Pat?"

"I don't like this joint anymore."

"You've gotten fussier."

"I was always fussier than you."

"What did you do to your face?"

"I shaved this morning."

Herbie sat down beside him. He was still holding his drink, which he kept a hand on after setting it down. Just in case. "Looks more like a makeover. How much does a facelift like that cost?"

"You want to treat yourself to one too?"

"Can't help thinking you have me to thank for your new look."

"Thanks, Dad."

"Wipe that grin off your face—you know exactly what I'm talking about."

"Was I grinning?" Pat asked.

Herbie felt his bile rising. "You've been gone a long time," he grunted.

"I was sick of Berlin."

"But now you're back. And I bet a lot of people are sick of you, Pat."

"I only know one—you."

"Why is that?"

"Because you haven't learned a thing. You're still as pig-headed and opinionated as ever."

"You mean grudging. We have a score to settle."

"I don't owe you a thing," said Pat. "Not a cent."

"Is your phony, shitty life worth so little to you?" hissed Herbie.

Pat looked straight at him for the first time. His mouse-gray eyes were strangely vacant. "What is it with you?" he asked. "How many years have you got left until you're too shaky and gaga to wipe your own ass?"

Not many, thought Herbie. He had grown tired and fat. He had drunk too much and exercised too little. He had wasted his energy on things that he hated. Pat, by comparison, was an Adonis. Younger, more laid-back, and more predisposed to violence, despite his leg being in a cast. But he had screwed Herbie out of a deal that was meant to bring in fifty thousand bucks.

"What did you do with the dough?" Herbie asked.

"Nothing. He took it off me."

"Who!"

"Your fucking cop friend."

"Mike?"

"It was a setup."

"By who?"

Pat leaned forward. He lost his balance slightly and had to lean on the table. "After all these years, you must know by now who screwed you over."

"You," said Herbie. "Maybe *you* tipped Mike off and split the cash."

"Me, share with a cop?"

"I'm a cop too."

"Not anymore," said Pat. "I've made inquiries. To my knowledge, you're a night watchman."

"I'm with a security firm," Herbie lied. Again, he felt the need to hurt Pat. How come the scumbag had made inquiries about him? Herbie had looked for him everywhere for years and hadn't even realized that he was back. He felt a blush rising to his face. It meant that he was losing his touch. Since Pat had vanished, he had been on a nonstop downward slide. He still hadn't fully settled his debts from the dope deal and the Turkish mafia was after his ass. He blamed Pat for his failures, whether he'd been screwed by him or ripped off by someone else.

Pat finished off his beer and leaned his bulked-up torso across the dirty table. "Listen," he said, "I can see that you're bent out of shape. You've lost your old lady and your job, you look like shit, and you're bitter—and you're taking it out on me."

"Yeah, who else? You tricked me."

"Listen to you, man! You're blathering on about the past. I didn't do anything. We were both fucked over."

"Did you pimp yourself up like this because you like being fucked in the ass?"

Pat stayed calm. It was incredible how calm he stayed. He used to be a bundle of nerves, easily provoked.

Herbie swatted a fly away with his elbow. "What did you do with the dough?" he asked.

"Nothing."

"You're not going to get away with it. You'll have to come up with something better than that."

Pat looked at him impassively. In silence.

"What's up?" asked Herbie. "Cat got your tongue?"

"I've said enough."

Herbie reached into his jacket, but Pat was faster.

"Drop it, Herbie. I don't like shooting in public."

His piece was hidden under the table, though Herbie knew it was aimed at his genitals.

"I asked you what you did with the dough," said Herbie, pulling his hand out of his jacket. He was only bluffing anyway.

"Do you really want to know?"

"Cut to the chase!"

"I blew it."

"On your fucking asswipe of a fuckface."

"Among other things."

"And Mike?"

"I made up the thing with Mike."

"And you just go telling me this?"

"Why not? I even cheated on you with your old lady and fucked your daughter."

"You're lying!" Herbie shouted so loudly that the bartender and a few other patrons sat up.

"Maybe," said Pat, cold as ice. He pulled a business card out of his jacket and threw it carelessly on the table. "When you've found out the truth, you can call me or come by."

"I'll come by just to kill you."

"Shhh, not so loud, Herbie, baby. Otherwise, people will think you're a real killer. I just wanted to offer you a job."

"You want to hire me?"

"You can clean the shithouses in my betting shop."

Helplessly, Herbie watched Pat as he turned away and walked out. He had a good posture, a firm ass, and a confident if limping gait, like a well-off faggot with his leg in a cast. There wasn't a trace of the slimy toad he used to be. *I should never have handed in my gun*, he thought bleakly. *I need to get myself a new one and blow his brains out.*

Tom came over and wiped down the table. "What's going on?" he asked. "Did that guy just threaten you with a gun?"

"Did you see a gun?" Herbie asked.

"All the same to me," said Tom. "My shift's over for tonight."

Herbie followed him over to the bar and sat down on a stool. "Two more drinks, on me."

"Only shots. 'Cause like I said, I'm wrapping things up here for the night," Tom said.

"No problem," Herbie replied. "Wanna earn a hundred bucks?"

"What for?"

"I need a driver."

"Why don't you take a cab?"

"Two hundred bucks if you don't ask any questions."

Tom knew about these kinds of offers. Some shady fucking deal. Or maybe not. Anything was possible. But he was dog-tired and too drunk for speculation. He poured Herbie and himself two more shots.

"Three hundred bucks just for driving. If someone points a fucking gun in your direction, I'll look away. And if he kills you, I'm not going to the cops. I'm staying neutral, I don't know anyone, and I'm not getting involved. I'm just the driver, that's all."

3.

The car radio was playing Bach's *Well-Tempered Clavier* and Tom was humming along. Glenn Gould's monotonous plinking was a stark contrast to Herbie's edginess. But Tom stayed calm. Compared to Lucia's griping, Herbie's whining went right over his head. He drove down Skalitzer Strasse alongside the elevated subway tracks and felt pleasantly sleepy. At this time in the morning, nothing was going on. You could have cruised the streets blindfolded.

"Turn off the fucking radio," Herbie said. "I can't concentrate."

"Relax." Tom turned down the radio.

"Do you always listen to this kind of shit?"

"Yeah, mostly, preferably Mozart."

"I don't like any kind of music. Not even the hits."

"I understand," said Tom. "Hits get on your tits."

"What do you mean?"

"Never mind," said Tom.

Herbie gave him a dismissive look. "Do you want to know what gets on my tits?"

"No."

"Listen—"

"I said no, I'd rather listen to Bach."

"Sounds like church music," grunted Herbie.

Probably is too, Tom thought. He would have preferred silence, but Herbie couldn't keep his mouth shut.

"Your car is a piece of crap. Can't even stretch out my legs."

"Sorry, this is all I can afford."

"You haven't made it very far for your age," growled Herbie.

"Maybe not." Tom knew that himself. He really didn't have much to show for his thirty-five years. But what was it to this fat-ass loser? Nothing, a big fat zero, he thought. He hated it when people were rude.

At a red light on Kotti, Herbie got out for the third time. "Drive around the traffic circle until I get back," he panted through the open door.

"Okay," said Tom.

After five or six red lights and several rounds at a snail's pace, Tom eventually got fed up and parked between the library and supermarket on the corner of Adalbertstrasse. He bought cigarettes at a Turkish kiosk and when he came back, Herbie was sitting in the car. He looked even paler and more wretched than before.

"I told you to drive, not stop."

"I was only buying cigarettes."

"Take the freeway, we're going to Innsbrucker Platz."

Tom drove back along the Skalitzer Strasse alongside the elevated train tracks. This time in the opposite direction.

"Take a left on Mehringdamm," barked Herbie.

"I know the route."

"Every loser has a GPS except you."

You don't even have a car, Tom thought. But he kept his mouth shut. The morning sun was behind them, and he had already spotted a starling and two blackbirds. On the radio, a despotic violin concerto by Paganini was playing, but Herbie didn't complain anymore. The nerve-racking violins matched his adrenaline rush, while they now only gave Tom a headache. He made an effort to drive slowly, constantly looking at the speedometer. He still had a skinful and was not in the mood for hassle from the cops.

"Park in front of the Greek," Herbie blurted out. "If I'm not back in five minutes, call this number."

Ten minutes later, Tom took Herbie's business card out of his pocket. He had put it away carelessly, not expecting to need it. He called the number from his cell phone, but no one answered. As he was about to drive away, Herbie came panting toward him.

"That bastard has vanished into thin air," he said.

Probably better that way, Tom thought.

Herbie sank into the car seat. He stared dully through the windshield at a billboard from last summer, or maybe the one before, with a young girl in a bikini licking an ice cream cone.

"If you want ice cream, I can jump out quickly," Tom said. "What?"

"I'll get two Magnums. How does that sound?"

"Fucking stupid. Drive."

The next stop was the longest. Exhausted, Tom had dozed off by the time Herbie came back. By now, the light was so bright that he had to squint to see. Herbie produced a pair of sunglasses from his jacket pocket, reminding Tom when he pulled them on of a fat, disagreeable actor from his childhood: the classic villain who could only be imposed on the audience as long as he was eliminated later on.

"What's up?" asked Herbie. "Don't you like the way I look, or what?"

"Huh? It doesn't fuckin' matter to me how you look. I'm just tired."

"Don't flake out," said Herbie.

"I'm not flaking out," said Tom.

They took the freeway to Neukölln. Herbie had switched back to silent mode, and Tom could concentrate fully on driving. A huge flock of migratory birds flew eastward above them and, as always, he felt a longing to fly away too—to Alaska, and from there as a stowaway on a ship to LA. He would paint the last empty walls on Skid Row, celebrate his long-awaited comeback as a street artist, and sleep in the gutter in front of Lucia's portrait. That was just about all the optimism he could muster in his dreams.

At Hermannplatz he turned right and drove southeast at a leisurely pace along Sonnenallee. He had long since lost sight of the migratory birds. There were mostly Turks on the street, veiled women, Arabs, a few black people, and here and there a bum. Early risers and people with no place to sleep. Late-night revelers leaving lousy dive bars, torture basements for techno freaks, and sleazy fetish clubs. Egomaniac masochists and sadistic gluttons. God-worshippers and -haters. Ravers and cynics. The dull and the sick. The virtuous and the players.

The next address was a betting shop on Flughafenstrasse. Still closed.

"Turn off the engine," said Herbie.

Tom obliged and lit a cigarette. The bookie joint was twenty yards from the road behind a huge parking lot, between an Aldi supermarket and an electronics store, both of which were also closed. On weekdays you wouldn't notice it tucked behind the parked cars. But right now, the parking lot was an empty space. And there wasn't much going on in the street either. A strange bookie, for sure, one that reeked of money laundering.

"Do you want one?"

Herbie wordlessly took a cigarette from him. He leaned far back into his seat, keeping an eye on the entrance.

He's waiting for him, Tom thought. *As calm and cold as a sniper*. It seemed that Herbie had become more self-confident since their last stop. As if he had snorted some speed or gotten hold of a gun.

"I hope you're not going to pull any shit," Tom said. "You're not going to kill anyone, right?"

"Why would I want to kill anyone? I'm a cop."

"You're a cop?"

"No questions, damn it. You fucking got it?"

Tom was rattled. He had taken Herbie to be a crazy coward who would eventually give up. If Herbie wasn't really a cop and just thought he was one, his obsession would stop at nothing. And if he was a cop on some psycho trip, he was even more dangerous.

Tom felt the sweat running down his neck. The radio station was playing Strauss's *Death and Transfiguration*—deep, gloomy, merciless music, like the soundtrack to a massacre. *Zarathustra* or *Till Eulenspiegel* would have been preferable.

"I had a psychotic episode once too," he began, unsettled. "You lose track of things, fight windmills, make dumb mistakes."

Herbie angrily pulled out a gun from inside his jacket. "You think I'm a lunatic?"

"No, but . . ."

"What?"

"I was just talking about myself."

"Shut up, here he comes. Not a fucking peep, or I'll kill you both."

Now Tom saw him too. The guy with his leg in a cast who had been in the bar the night before. Pat limped nonchalantly across the parking lot. Herbie took off the safety catch with a sober click. Then he lowered the window. In the old Ford, everything still worked manually without central locking and other gimmicks. A glance at the dashboard told Tom it was almost eight. A totally ordinary Sunday morning in fucking Neukölln. In half an hour, the first Christians would be on their way to morning Mass. The church lay diagonally across from them. *None of this has anything to do with me*, he thought. *It's not what I signed up for. If he shoots out of the car, I'll let him get busted.* Although Herbie had turned his back to him, Tom made no attempt to stop him. *If he gets out, I'll drive off without him.* Everything was under control.

Pat was just a few meters from the entrance. *He'll never hit him from here. If he doesn't do it now, it'll be too late.* Tom was neither disappointed nor relieved. He was just watching as a neutral observer.

With a sudden movement, Herbie took the key from the ignition and got out.

"Damn it!" Tom yelled.

The driver's door jammed and he rammed it open with his shoulder. It hurt like hell, but he was too angry to feel any pain. *This bastard is making me an accomplice to murder. My life and a damn long prison sentence for three hundred euros.* The fat-ass moved surprisingly swiftly and was soon too far away to be stopped. The guy with his leg in a cast was just unlocking the door of the bookie joint. He noticed Herbie and pulled his gun. But Herbie was faster. Tom counted three shots, all of which missed their mark. Then more shots, one of which grazed the leg-cast guy; and then a direct hit, which made Pat flop down in the doorway. But at the last moment he had managed to open the door, and shot back several times.

Herbie staggered toward the entrance like a wounded bear. Blood dripped from his jacket sleeve onto the sidewalk. He slumped to his knees and slid forward. His Walther PPK hung limply in his hand: too weak to shoot, and too pissed off to drop it. Tom could have overpowered him now. But what

for? Two assholes messing each other up made two fewer assholes in this fucking world.

4.

Tom locked the door from the inside. Apart from the death
rattles and the moaning, it was pleasantly peaceful. They were
so messed up that they couldn't even blow their own brains
out. Pat's gun was out of reach under a table. Herbie's was still
clenched in his fist. Tom had to step on his arm until he let go.
Then he kicked it in the direction of the other weapon. Outside, the first churchgoers were passing, enjoying the spring
sunshine. A yapping dog ran across the parking lot, going wild
for Herbie's blood. Tom dragged the two injured men into the
back where they could not be seen from the outside, each in
a separate room to be safe. He had beaten Pat unconscious
with his own crutch and kicked Herbie in the wound between
his ribs until he fainted as well. But they would wake up, and
then he would have to get them to fall asleep again. This time
permanently.

Tom went into the bathroom and opened a tap. Pulling
his head from the sink, he realized that he had been splash-
ing himself for the past five minutes. He felt fresher but still
groggy. He had pretty much used up all his strength but knew
that the worst was still to come. There was no turning back
now. He had gotten mixed up in this whole thing, and now he
didn't care how it would end.

Next door the situation hadn't changed. Pat was still
knocked out. The blood trickling from his ears for some
reason reminded Tom of a Christmas tune. He hummed it
to cheer Pat up. He would have bet that Pat had an ear for
music. *Brave Pat*, Tom thought. Pat coughed up blood, but it
wasn't a big deal.

"Everything okay?" Tom asked. He felt Pat watching him. Was that possible when someone was unconscious? "Can I ask you a few questions?"

No reaction.

"What's it like to die? Or aren't you dying yet?"

Nothing.

"I'm not afraid of death. Are you, Pat?"

Tom took another step toward him and looked at the broken crutch. He picked up a sharp, three-inch-long sliver of aluminum and decided to ram it in Pat's solar plexus at the next opportunity.

Time to look after Herbie, Tom thought with a tinge of sadness. He had taken a liking to the fat-ass.

Without medical help he would bleed to death faster than Pat. Tom was not a monster. Herbie needed help, and Tom was ready to curb his suffering. With his leg in plaster and the severe gunshot wound, Pat was in no state to run away. He could wait. Before anyone showed up, Tom would have to take care of everything. If they turned up early, he would need to rethink his plan.

Tom went over to Herbie in the next room. His fat figure hung limply in his cheap, soiled, off-the-rack suit. There was blood everywhere. Even his eyes seemed to be bleeding. Bloody tears like in a Shakespearean drama. Not a bad ending for a cop.

Tom tried to coax a last conversation out of him. Herbie was sure to have plenty to say. He had probably learned a lot since getting shot.

Tom sat down carefully on the side where Herbie was spilling less blood. "You hanging in there still?"

"Nope. Not really."

"How does it feel, Herbie? Can you see the tunnel?"

"What fucking tunnel, man?"

"Some see clouds. Others, angels. Basically, everyone just sees what they want to see, even though we're all blind when it comes down to it. You're staring at your inner self, mad with pain, and can't understand anything. Priests, though, they'll try to persuade you that you're seeing God. Can you see God, Herbie?"

"Damn it," grunted Herbie.

"Such an apocalyptic word," Tom said. "You don't believe in hell, do you?"

"Damn it, I'm dying."

"I know," said Tom. "But death is overrated."

Herbie cursed him with a long tirade that became more and more incomprehensible. A staccato groan as if from another species.

"I know what you mean," said Tom.

He would have liked to play the *Requiem* and convert Herbie to Mozart as a fond farewell. The way others found Christ just before they abdicated. He pulled the car keys out of Herbie's jacket pocket and stowed them away. In his other jacket pocket, he found three bloodstained hundred-euro bills. But Tom was no Judas.

High time to get to work, he thought. But work was too weak a word. He was looking for an equivalent from the opera, but opera bored him. "Finale: Presto!" was his favorite. Herbie would have liked it too. Although Herbie knew nothing about music.

Tom turned to him one last time. The poor guy looked pathetic. Huge bloodshot drunkard eyes. Sagging face. No composure whatsoever. More horror than anger. Too much fear. Too much blood. Too much pain.

Drive away, thought Tom. *They're both going to die anyway.*

But thoughts were free and you could always change your mind.

5.

When he got back to his apartment, he was glad he hadn't left anything half done. And no fingerprints either. He had taken his time and removed all traces. It was an immaculate job, no need for the cleaning woman to come. If she had turned up, he would have had to kill her. What other options did he have?

But two bodies were enough. Lucia was probably still asleep, he wasn't sure. He went quietly over to the door and peered through the keyhole. He couldn't see the bed, but in the room, not a thing was stirring. There was barely a glimmer of light coming through the closed curtains. It was as quiet as if Lucia had moved out and left him. She had announced it often enough, but now the thought left him strangely cold. Maybe he would start painting again, with her gone. He was through with art, though maybe it would be better to be through with Lucia.

He took a long shower, washed thoroughly, and went back into the kitchen. He turned on the radio but couldn't find a decent station. The classical stations he listened to in the car sounded like a miserable cacophony in his apartment. He turned off the radio and felt pleasantly empty. He went over a few questions that were on his mind, but not ones he felt he had to find answers to. He had risked his life and broken the biggest taboo. He had proved nothing and hadn't wanted to prove anything. It was basically like the beginning of spring. You got carried away by its sudden energy, got used to it quickly, and then missed winter before spring had really begun. Winter made no demands or promises, and you were reconciled to the cold and bleakness that faced us all sooner or later.

His energy was all used up; he decided to feed the sparrows. As he rummaged around in a drawer for the birdseed, he realized that he was naked.

He was about to go back to the bathroom and get a towel when Lucia came in. For the first time in a long while, she was wearing makeup and a pretty floral dress.

She beamed at him, seeming not to notice his nakedness. "Hi, honey. How was work?"

"Like always."

"Did you do overtime? Or were you with your new girlfriend?"

"I don't have a new girlfriend."

"How sweet, then I'm the only one."

"How many pills have you taken?"

"Just the usual number. How come?"

"Just asking."

Lucia took Tom's half-smoked cigarette from the ashtray and finished it.

"I thought we could go to Wannsee today."

"Why Wannsee?"

"I dreamed about it," Lucia said. "We were on a boat and the sun was shining beautifully above us. Suddenly the sky darkened and a huge flock of crows swooped down. The boat sank and you saved me. Great, huh?"

"Sure," said Tom. *Great reason to go to Wannsee,* he thought bitterly. *I haven't been your hero in ages.* "I'll just put something on."

"Should I make breakfast?"

"If there's anything in the fridge."

"I'll find something," said Lucia. "I'm starved."

Tom went into the bedroom, pulled back the curtains, and opened the window. On the gutter above the nest sat the little sparrow, peeping his lungs out with pleasure at having over- come his fear.

The little bird did it, Tom thought. *That's one bet I would've won.*

VALVERDE

BY UTE COHEN

Grunewald

He sat behind the rhododendron shrub and waited for the shrill echo of her voice to fade. It went right through him and he couldn't bear it anymore. The only comforting part was that she trembled at the sight of him; he awakened something archaic in her, which she herself had no idea was there. Madame was the ringleader: she was affected, babbling with a terrible accent in what she imagined to be French. Her blue-marbled bare feet tested the temperature of the wet grass before she sat down in the covered wicker beach chair. An import from Sylt, just like the bubbly, which she deposited on a wooden table in a bucket filled with ice. With crossed arms, she squinted at the sun, seeming to have forgotten him for a moment. The wind blew the smell of fried chicken over to him. He wondered how she could eat that disgusting food. Putrid meat pumped with chemicals that her Thai housekeeper fried in peanut oil, dabbed with a paper towel, and drizzled with a disgustingly sweet soy sauce. One morning, when Madame was still asleep, the housekeeper had given him a piece to taste. Somehow, in her esoteric-Asian simplicity, she believed that doing him good would bring her happiness. But if he now had to take care of the domestics as well, he wouldn't get a thing done. He had set himself clear priorities. At the top of the list were the Big Five, and this Asian chow wasn't going to get in his way. He lay in the grass, hidden by the leathery leaves of the shrub.

Madame unfolded the footrest of the beach chair and looked at her toenails, which were painted the same garish pink as the rhododendron flowers. *Back to nature*, she probably thought to herself, feeling proud that she was so in touch with the living world. He hated himself for being able to smell her thoughts like a damned dog that would lick her ass for a fucking treat. He was careful not to make the slightest sound. He wouldn't be able to take her voice a second time.

Valverde. He wondered how she'd come up with that stupid name. Here they were, in the middle of snobbish Grunewald, beside Charlottengrad, Little Russia, and there was nothing even remotely fucking valley-like about it. He squinted and forced himself to think clearly again and, above all, to expel from his mind the fake proletarian slang used by spoiled Grunewald brats and their champagne-sipping tennis moms. *Valverde*. Maybe they were thinking of that character Valmont, who had at least managed to pull off a halfway decent deflowering and had driven that aristocratic mishpachah to the brink of madness with his intrigues. This lot certainly didn't underestimate his intelligence, and the fact that he was still considered eligible for *liaisons dangereuses* even flattered him a little. He had to be disciplined—after all, he knew his weaknesses. As much as he liked to seduce others, he wasn't immune to sweet talk and flattery. *Valverde*. He let the sound of his name sail past his ears and dozed in the springtime sun until a cocky bee woke him with its buzzing.

Madame was now sitting in the barbecue area which was done up with terra-cotta tiles, while next to her sat a brunette in her midforties, her head bowed over a portfolio. Behind her stood a blonde, who was fanning herself with a brochure. "We could get rid of the clichés about Russians by turning it into an art project," said the brunette, and stuck a pencil behind her ear. The blonde, whom he called White Russian due to her fondness for vodka with milk, cooed affirmatively and made a circular motion on her temple with her index finger while she knocked back her drink of choice with the other hand. Madame's expression remained unchanged, though he sensed that she was suppressing a mocking smile. If the old bag had anything going for her, it was how well she understood the inscrutable emotions going on behind these grotesque masks.

He pricked his ears and eagerly awaited the next episode of this Grunewald soap. Last week (he couldn't bear more than one episode a week), they'd been talking about the physical assets of the personal trainer, whose endless stamina was unfortunately being overstrained by the newcomers in Hilde-Ephraim-Strasse. He had made a mental note of the name and incorporated it into the "Pentagram of Decadence," which he'd invented a few months ago. But the brunette and her photo project wouldn't fit into this constellation. She waved her arms, talking about a movie in which a Russian mafioso falls in love with a nurse. "Then we paint the tattoos on Irina's body," she said, "and copy the poses from *Eastern Promises* down to the last detail."

Cronenberg, he thought. It turned him on the way she rhapsodized with a slight lisp to the other two about a Danish actor whose selfless, criminal energy she admired. At last, someone who seemed to understand him; someone who could handle contradictions, who understood that not all crimes and not all victims were the same.

Madame opened her laptop and pointed with a contrived "Voilà" to the screen. "That was my project in Moscow radical urban impressionism. It was groundbreaking," she said in a voice that could break glass, which made him wonder whether he should ask for hazard pay after all, especially for his hearing.

"Fuck!" he yelled, and slapped his bicep. The bee had stung him. At least it was going to die now, the lousy creature. He sucked the poison and stinger from his blood and spat it into the flower bed. The snake tattoo on his arm swelled up, as if it wanted to spew hellfire at the entire deceitful lot of them. *Keep calm*, he told himself, stepping out from behind the bush with a smile. They stared at him with blatant greed, as if they hadn't been laid properly in months despite the personal trainer. The other three were now sitting in beach chairs: Rosita Esteban, the Mexican, and Ruth, a retired teacher and bottle-redhead who seemed at first glance to have strayed randomly into the group but in fact was a sly old dog. In a deck chair, her perfectly toned body sheathed in a dark-blue stretch bondage dress, was Nermina. She ran her tongue over her lips and flicked the ash of her Gauloises Blonde onto the manicured lawn. "Valverde, a glass of champagne for you too?" she asked, winking lewdly behind her sunglasses.

He had no desire to consort with the gang. Besides, it would be a strategic mistake. One glance at Madame was enough. With her eyebrows raised and the corners of her mouth rigid, she pressed a fifty-euro bill into his hand and indicated the way out with a slight toss of her head. He tipped his cap lightly and silently left the garden. In the car, he lit a cigarette and kicked the driver's door, cursing because the damn wreck wouldn't start yet again. When the engine finally purred, he threw his ciggy out of the window and stepped on the gas. He waited until he was on Königsallee before he turned up the radio, flicking channels between Energy, Jazz, and Flux, where he got sucked into "Emotional Rescue" by the Stones. He snapped his fingers and sang in falsetto: *"Nothing I can do to change your mind?"* He laughed and wondered if he should eat a curried sausage on the Ku'damm near Bier's, but then thought better of it. He allowed himself the luxury of this capriciousness because in all other ways, he was as reliable and synchronized as a QuikTrak lawnmower. He himself couldn't explain why he had taken on all this shit. There was no objective reason for it. It wasn't like boy racers had mowed down his kids on Ku'damm. Hell, he didn't even have kids. He couldn't say that he had been sent by some political power, or that the red-red-green coalition had kicked his ass and given him a justice mission. It was just his damn moralizing conscience, which gnawed at his heart like a rat. The day when Rosita Esteban had washed her children's eyes out with soap, then stuffed toilet paper into their mouths before making them stand next to the dumpster, because they had been cursing, had, of course, been a turning point. He would have liked nothing better than to grab Rosita by the throat, pull her by the hair out of her toy villa, and throw her into the waste-incineration plant. Instead, he had stayed calm and listened to his heart—that megalomaniac moralist rat. He had to take them *all* down.

At home in his winged armchair, a relic from his recently deceased neighbor, he thought over his plan. He put aside de Sade and cut himself a slice of black sausage, which he'd fried with lots of onions in goose fat (one of his specialties). How grateful he was for his last jail term. Where else would he have discovered the old Frenchman, if not in the prison yard? (From a philosophy professor who had marched into his wife's office and pumped her with nine shots, five of them fatal.) From that day on, he knew that all the talk about virtue was only lame bullshit made up by cowards. Evil could not be eliminated, only outsmarted. His goal was to have a successful criminal career, so as not to be thrown to the lions. However, he had to prevent the worst evils, limit the harm people inflicted on each other. He skewered a piece of sausage on his fork, happy that it had ended up crispy and juicy at the same time. He dozed for a while and then went to the bathroom. Standing in front of the mirror, his hands resting on the washbasin, he fished out a peppercorn from between his front teeth with his tongue. He spat it into the sink, took out his dentures, and put them in a pink plastic container, not without an admiring look at their sparkling white appearance. Then he lay down on his bed and waited for the devil, or whoever, to suck the thoughts from his brain.

Over breakfast of three fried eggs, a green smoothie—he had to use that thing Madame had given him somehow—and black coffee, he began drawing the pentagram. The article in the *Morning Post* had been the last straw: "Fraudulent Real-Estate Agents—Bankruptcy, Bad Luck, and Suicide."

He scrunched his foot into the discarded newspaper on the floor as if it were a disgusting insect and sketched his pentagram on a paper napkin stained with curry sauce. Five names and their crimes. Madame formed the highest spike: a straw woman who covered up the corruption of her sleazy slumlord husband and who had more Louboutins than sense. Red soles on her shoes, perhaps from the pools of blood left behind by her victims on the asphalt? Actually, what did he care about these fake Italian slumlord types? They wove their net into a system, and systems pissed him off as much as ideologies. If it hadn't been for that little kid from the sixth floor . . . He wiped the grease off his lips with the back of his hand, tapped his pencil on the table, and concentrated.

The next spike: Rosita Esteban, that Mexican slut who strutted in stilettos all over that pussy of a husband until he lay prostrate on the sofa, *The Secret* blasting through his headphones, incapable of protecting even his children. He stabbed a hole in the pot-bellied *b* with the tip of the pencil and drew the tip of the third spike: White Russian. He had seen with his own eyes how she'd stirred Cytotec into the milk of her pregnant rival, a Serbian girl who had crawled out of some shithole and landed in the bed of the distillery mogul, and soon that ill-gotten bastard was taken care of!

Speaking of unpleasantness, he was amazed at how it all fit together. The next spike was for Ruth—harmless Ruth with her worn-out shoes, her collection of condos, including the one with the listed garden—who had rammed a stick into her neighbors' labradoodle's ass until it had croaked miserably. Valverde had just mowed the lawn and was checking the blades when she had picked up the stick from a pile of leaves, sharpened the end with the kitchen knife, and pushed it into the poor animal's anus. It would be easy for him to eliminate her. *Torture never stops!* Zappa would have patted him on the back.

And last but not least, Nermina, that piece of vermin. It was fucked up how often she had given her gullible old man the clap and then blamed him for it. It was only when her hubby groveled for forgiveness that she showed mercy, had him buy her a few rocks from Bulgari, only to hop in the sack with some bartender or odd-jobber from one of her clubs. Valverde couldn't work out why the others didn't get sick of hearing her fuck sagas over and over again. He wrinkled his nose and moved the corners of his mouth down in contempt. He mustn't get sentimental. Being promoted to avenger of cuckolded Grunewald senior citizens was not a job he could take on. He braided the mini pigtail growing from his chin, which he had to put up with until the last drug tests had been done, and pulled on his army jacket.

The skies over Berlin were merciless. The rain drizzled like stinking discharge onto his bald crown. Shoulders hunched, he lurched to his car and drove back to the hell of Grunewald.

"Should I turn on the sauna?" she asked, reaching for her champagne glass. His cock slunk away like a snake flung into the bushes.

"No, leave it," he said, patting the bedclothes jovially. "Pussycat," he added. She liked it when he treated her like a pet and enjoyed punishing him at the next available opportunity in front of her friends.

"Valverde, you've done the edge of the lawn really shoddily, and the hedge looks like Edward Scissorhands has had a go at it," she would say with a brazen wink. Sometimes he felt like cutting her throat with a blade.

She pulled the thong over her hips, some bondage affair with gold rings and leather straps, and sat on a stool in front of a mirror dresser. Skeptically, she eyed the sweep of her eyebrows. "Are you coming to Anja's birthday party next week?" she asked. "You could help the bartender, and we," at this, she spread her legs and slid the thong to one side, "we can slip off to the master bedroom." She shook her blond mane. With her back curved and her ass stretched up in the air, she crawled toward him, purring. She wasn't beneath trying any kind of stunt and thought it was the ultimate in sexiness to play a big cat.

He rubbed his cock, pulled on a rubber, and waited for her to straddle him. It wasn't so bad, he thought, and afterward she was bound to offer him a joint and tell him the gossip. Actually, she didn't have much in common with the other four, except for her insatiable greed, which was manifested in her sex addiction: the others were compulsive torturers, gluttons, or alcoholics. He felt a small spark of pity. Somehow it was a waste that such a hot piece of ass should wither away at home. He tenderly stroked her back.

"I just want to make one thing clear," she said. "You're going to man the bar!" She blinked at him with her green eyes. "*Roarrr!*"

Another one of those fags, he thought, loosening the tie around his neck that had been fastened too tightly by a waitress. The bartender straightened his upper body, bent his knees slightly, and shook the cocktail shaker in an affected pose. Old Böhlke himself was standing at the bar, roasting a bullock tenderloin, while the Asian housekeepers arranged the African buffet. Madame's voice trilled from the upper floor, complaining about the champagne: "Veuve Clicquot! When you know that the CEO of Chateau Berlin only drinks Roederer Cristal!"

Valverde polished a glass with a linen cloth and squinted over at Nermina. She was engrossed in conversation with the brunette artist, whose four kids had demolished the buffet and were now lounging with mango *maracuja* cocktails on Fatboys on the lawn. He wondered how she made ends meet with so many kids. Russian satire was hardly a lucrative source of income.

"Valverde, two Moscow mules!" The fat man propped his arms on the bar and pulled out two cigars from a leather case. "Romeo y Julieta," he said, cutting the cigars. "Brought to me by Dmitri last week." He patted the other man on the shoulder, a tall blond guy with a well-toned body under his tailored suit, and said, "Thanks, dear fellow! The Riva model is fantastic!"

"Just wait till you see what's on Lake Como," the blond guy answered, exhaling cigar smoke.

"And there she is, the queen of the evening."

Madame was standing next to them, a glass in her hand, her lips drawn into a thin smile. "Please excuse us for a moment, Mario," she said, and pulled Monsieur over to the piano. She whispered something in his ear, screwing her left hand into a fist, and turned abruptly in Ruth's direction. She greeted Ruth exuberantly, while Monsieur, his back bent, made a last attempt to hold her back. With a dismissive wave of his hand, he finally gave up and returned to the bar.

"I have a few things to fix," he said vaguely, knocking back his vodka in one go.

Valverde looked at him pityingly. *What an idiot!* Letting himself be bossed around by that tyrant and making a fool of himself. He failed to understand how these businessmen, who had snared half of Berlin in their sham real-estate web, could kowtow to their money-grabbing wives. Tomorrow Monsieur would surprise her again with a short trip to the Côte or to Sylt, just so she could complain about the crowds and how stressful it was. Fuck, if Ruth started her 1968 schtick along with her commune stories, he'd spill frying fat all over her shoes. One of his pet hates was when these women, who could all afford yachts, came on all modest and sashayed about in red shoes talking about their Maoist past.

"Valverde!"

He placed a cocktail on the bar, which the White Russian snapped up immediately. With a wink, she dropped into a lounge chair and leaned back with her eyes closed, as if having one of her intoxicating yoga highs, while her financier was probably thrusting his cock into another anorexic Ku'damm street girl, until he would eventually force himself to show up here with an air of innocence. Hopefully she wouldn't ram her high heels in his face when one of her friends reported her husband's latest sexual escapades, like she had done the last time. He slipped on black latex gloves, sliced a cucumber, and opened a bottle of Lillet. The French were back in fashion! Hugos had been put on ice a long time ago. He laughed at his own stupid joke and granted himself an aquavit.

"Well, the staff are enjoying themselves." Rosita Esteban stood in front of him in her off-the-shoulder gown and straightened hair, an uneven swelling on her forehead. The Botox injection had probably not spread properly. "Champagne, please!" she said, and clacked her red-lacquered nails on the bar top. She took the glass with her fingertips and brought it to her mouth. "Herbert," she said, pushing her husband hard in the back toward a woman who was barely able to suppress her obvious boredom. Her other half stole a glance at his watch, TAG Heuer or some other nautical bullshit. "Herbert," Rosita Esteban began again, "feels great since he's been reading *The Secret*. We're living life in the fast lane. Happiness, money, love. Every night he listens to a chapter and goes to sleep with the recipe for success in his ears."

And you lock your kids down in the basement until they scratch at the door with thirst, he thought, and smiled at her. No doubt, he would have to destroy them all in one go. He poured another aquavit and wondered how he would immortalize all five on his body. The tattoo would have to be very special. Maybe five intertwined snakes?

"Valverde." The sound of the brunette's voice was enchanting. "Thanks for the wonderful service," she said, smiling at him. "Children, come on," she called, and then addressing Madame, "I have to get up early tomorrow. Work calls. Thank you so much for the recommendation. If you think of anyone else who needs tutoring—"

"Oh what a shaaaaame," Madame trilled, "you're so welcome! I'm rising early tomorrow too, for my tennis class."

The brunette smiled and picked up the youngest child before leaving the garden through the side entrance.

Over the next two hours he served cocktails at top speed and wiped lipstick stains off the crystal glasses. When he went into the living room at around two o'clock in the morning, they were all sitting on the sofas, summing up the evening. Madame was complaining about the outrageous brats who had wolfed down every last crumb of the chocolate cake. "Absolutely no control over her kids! No wonder her husband left her."

White Russian nodded, straightening a line of coke on the glass table with the back of a narrow comb.

"But she is sweet. Did you see the tits?" Nermina asked, looking provocatively in his direction.

Rosita Esteban chewed on her sunglasses, lost in thought, and muttered, bored, "Oh, come on!" She straightened her back and said, "Sure. Zero ambition, that one. I have to get going. Visions, what we need are visions." She looked at Madame and added, "I think we could use her. She can expand the network downward, stabilize it."

Ruth nodded. "Where there's muck, there's brass." The others looked at her in surprise. "Don't stare at me like that! Business and revolutions are not mutually exclusive. We learned that in Bavaria in seventh grade."

"And *I* always thought that the revolution devours its children," said White Russian, shaking her head and rubbing her nose. They laughed.

"Will you bring us some more pretzel sticks, Valverde?" Madame asked. "I'm feeling so retro today."

* * *

Throat lozenges, ibuprofen, Zopiclone, Zyrtec, the blue pills. He took the brown vial out of the cupboard, on which some-one had stuck a cross with a red Band-Aid a long time ago, and narrowed his eyes. *Psychopax* was written in pink letters on the label. His first thought was to hurl the thing into the trash. It reminded him of the time when she was still around to breathe a kiss on his mouth in the morning, when the room was fragrant from the smell of her hair, like freshly cut grass. He put the vial back in the metal cupboard almost tenderly, next to a stack of benzodiazepines in various dosages. He clung tightly to the edge of the sink and took a deep breath. He'd certainly need that stuff. But now he needed the damn amoxicillin. Why had he been dumb enough to let Nermina give him a blow job? And then, of course, she'd wanted her reward. He liked her taste. Actually, it was hard to resist. Or rather, he hadn't thought about it for a second. There were two packs left. That should be enough. He pushed two tablets out of the strip and swallowed them with a handful of water from the tap. For that alone she deserved a thrashing. Who knows where she'd picked up that shit again! He opened his fly and peed in the toilet bowl, not without grimacing in pain. Hopefully it wasn't something worse. He sprayed the toilet with Lysol and carefully wiped it with a sponge.

Then he ambled into the kitchen and tossed lettuce, a ba-nana, and two carrots into the smoothie blender. The steady whir brought clarity to his thoughts. Nermina had let slip that they wanted to use the brunette for real-estate transactions that were too hot for them to deal with personally. They already had a notary, an old acquaintance with a law firm on Hohenzollerndamm. "Wears gold-rimmed glasses," she'd said, "an old West Berliner, you know the kind." He didn't know, and it didn't interest him in the slightest who played what part in this gory business. But what had gotten to him was the fact that they wanted to drag this woman and her kids into their shit. Her smile. Sweet and red like cherries. His likeness was reflected in the windowpane, his expression strange and meek. He wiped over it agitatedly with a dish towel. Then he drank a big gulp of juice, grabbed a piece of salami from the fridge, and sat down in his armchair. On the radio, "Night Train" by James Brown was playing. He closed his eyes and let places pass by his mind's eye. Miami, Florida; Atlanta, Georgia. At some point he would get there, across the Atlantic, drive down Route 66, and chase alligators in the New York subway.

A fire truck siren made him start. He rubbed his eyes and looked at the clock. Still plenty of time. He loosened his shoulders and tapped his knuckles against his teeth. Firm. Nermina knew about his dentures. It turned her on, she said. She would have liked it even better if he had gold teeth like Jaws from James Bond. She was definitely off her fucking rocker and he felt almost sorry for her.

He took the notepad from the side table and read through the shopping list. He struggled over the size of the brush. Cable ties were still among the supplies he needed. He first had to test the gold-foil washi tape. There was no way he could take any chances.

At Halensee he parked the car directly outside the hardware store. He took a shopping cart and decided to have a stroll through the garden section. A sleepy saleswoman was trundling some potted plants through the corridors on a trolley. Pansies, dark purple and yellow, gleamed next to a stack of bark mulch. For a moment he hesitated, then decided on the balcony arrangement: Tyrolean hanging carnations, petunias, and million bells. *Just don't get sentimental*, he thought, taking the escalator to the ground floor, where he ordered a double espresso in the bakery. She would have certainly chosen the lilac pansies. He shooed the thought away with a bite into the cookie the shop assistant had put on his saucer, then paid and went back to the packaging department. He selected two types of gold tapes and tested them for tensile strength. His decided on the high-gloss, extremely durable sort. Then he strolled into the paint section and headed for gold paints and varnishes. Ecological, water-soluble. The chemical industry had clearly made progress. He picked up a pot of Maya Gold Decor but put it back on the shelf as it wasn't suitable, then opted for BOND-age Brilliance. At the cash register, he pulled a crisp fifty out of his wallet, complimenting the cashier on her butterfly tattoo, even though it made him want to barf. He was exhilarated: adrenaline was rushing through his veins, closely followed by endorphins. Then he headed downtown and bought two scoops of lemon sorbet and a scoop of mocha at the ice cream parlor. The taste reminded him of Sorrento when they had sat high on the rock, eating *gelato al limon*, and in their minds, Caruso sang, "*Te voglio bene assaje.*" Did he actually wipe a tear from his eyes? They deserved nothing less, those corrupt creatures to whom love meant nothing.

He could not properly decipher the drawing. The brunette had left it lying on the dining room table after the last discussion about her art project. He was sure that they would never get it underway. The bitching was in full swing. Which camera? Should Madame take the photos or should they hire a pro? Which network should they use? Where would they exhibit? After all, they were not allowed to jeopardize the main business. The director of the Chateau Berlin was definitely out of the question because, in his cock-driven stupidity, he'd set his mind on marrying that teenage escort girl. And anyway, he hadn't quite understood the project. The drawings contradicted each other. At some point, they would drive the brunette and her kids mad or make her a scapegoat when the Russian community were at their throats. Exposing the decadence of Russian women with kitsch photography? Was there ever a more stupid idea? They themselves were the very spearhead of decadence!

Once again, he studied the drawing in detail. A rococo structure of flesh and blood, that's how he imagined it. De Sade would love his idea. Classical and in gold, like their faucets, very Grunewald. He clapped his hands, rolled up the drawing, and grabbed the plastic bag from the bathroom.

Nermina had persuaded them. Somehow, he had managed to get her thinking about a weekend free of radiation and toxins. The colors could not have complemented each other any better. The black cube, which one of their star architects had planted in the Uckermark landscape, along with a sculpture of Berlin's bear mascot, was the perfect setting, not to mention the logistics and timing.

The gravel crunched underfoot as he walked from the parking lot to the main entrance. They had certainly heard him coming and were happy for the change. He rang the bell. Nermina opened the door and tweaked him between the legs by way of greeting. One, two bottles of champagne? He took off his military jacket and followed her into the living room. The image that presented itself to him seemed like a cheap copy of a Newton photo. In purple negligees, Ruth and Madame were lolling in front of the roaring open fire, while Rosita Esteban was eating the remains of a roast chicken. White Russian was standing on a wooden table and dancing in an emerald gown to a schmaltzy song. *"Love is in the air,"* she slurred, and tried to stick the stem of her cocktail glass into her bra. When she saw him, she stumbled and almost fell off the table.

Nermina, laughing, propped her up. "I thought a little backup wouldn't do us any harm. Will you freshen our drinks, Valverde?" she said, winking.

He greeted them with a friendly smile and went into the kitchen. He knew the house. Nermina had once taken him there when her husband was on a business trip or screwing around. Without the blue pills, he could not have survived that weekend.

He mixed the cocktails and brought them into the living room on an Oriental brass tray. Nermina grabbed a glass and danced over to the fireplace. She pulled the cucumber slice out of the glass and sucked on it. Then she raised a toast: "To us, girls! The Grunewald Quintet! Cheers!" She lifted her glass. "So, how about it? *Cul sec!* Down in one!" She emptied her glass in one gulp. Ruth hesitated for a moment, but eventually did the same.

Rosita Esteban was the heaviest. She didn't make a peep. The dose was enough. He pulled her to the wall with both hands and leaned her back against a sideboard. Then he took toilet paper from the plastic bag and stuffed it in her mouth. He looked around the room, pulled up a chair with pointed, tapering legs, and turned it over. He picked up Ruth from the floor—she was lighter than she seemed—lifted her skirt, and positioned her on the chair leg next to Rosita Esteban. When he tugged off White Russian's high heel and drilled into her eye, he had to pause for a moment. Fluid and tissue dripped from her eye socket. With a roll of paper towels, he dried the spot and smoothed the wound. He spared Nermina. He kissed her between the legs one more time and draped her over the other three, her back sagging. Madame's turn came last. He opened her purse, pulled out a bundle of bills, tucked them firmly into her hair, and dropped a lit match onto her mane, which then caught fire. When her scalp blackened, he extinguished her head with tonic water and leaned her back-to-back with Nermina. He pulled out a folded sheet from the breast pocket of his shirt and put on his reading glasses. He took a few steps back and compared his work to the drawing. She would be proud of him. He nodded benevolently and began wrapping the golden tape around the quintet. For a moment he thought he heard a faint whimper as he touched Rosita Esteban's leg. He listened until the last sound died away, and no trace of breath could be felt whatsoever, then quickened his movements, diligently checking that the overall expression of his work was preserved. Then he opened the paint pot and dipped a thick brush into it. In large, even strokes he began to apply the golden paint to the quintet. He took his time, refining Nermina's breast and décolleté and making corrections to White Russian's eye socket.

It was already dawn by the time he sat on the leather sofa and made a toast to her health.

When he heard the first lark, he closed the door behind him and drove back to Grunewald.

Nervously, he tugged at his goatee and straightened his back. The bell made no sound. He pushed down the handle of the garden gate, which was still unlocked, and knocked on the glass front door. She blinked from behind the curtain of the kitchen window, pushed a strand of hair behind her ear, and opened the door with a toy car in her hand.

"Valverde," she said.

"Lemon?" he asked, holding an ice cream out toward her.

PART III

Berlin Scenes

HEINRICHPLATZ BLUES

BY JOHANNES GROSCHUPF
SO 36

The nights on Heinrichplatz are not the same as they were when Nick was around. In Roses, they still drink until seven in the morning while the taxi waits in front of the door. And at the Rock 'n' Roll Hostel, the boss still sleeps on the pool table when she doesn't make it home. But no one covers her with a blanket. Nick covered her that night two years ago when neither of them managed to make it back to her apartment, but it was nice on that green cloth too. The balls rumbled in the belly of the table as the two of them found some things in common. When Nick left, he draped a coat over her shoulders so that she could keep on sleeping.

Now he's gone. Nick disappeared from one day to the next. At first we didn't think anything of it, because he often wasn't traceable for days on end. He just isn't picking up his cell phone anymore. We've left a voice message, sent a text, and called half an hour later just to be on the safe side. But Nick doesn't call back. He doesn't show his face anywhere.

We comb Heinrichplatz, loitering for a while at the bar of the Bateau; we check in the Taqueria, where he sometimes goes when he wants to read the newspaper in peace. Some of us casually drop into Schmitz Katze, but the billiard room is empty and Steffi at the bar shakes her head: "Simona already asked about him."

We don't want to be pushy; a man sometimes needs his

space, so we don't go by his apartment on Oranienstrasse very often. Nick lives above the betting shop. In the summer he would often sit at the window, smoking a joint and looking down at the crush of pedestrians, motorists, cyclists, drunkards, gamblers, and hipster tourists from Barcelona and Brooklyn. Nick was the secret king of the neighborhood. Now no one sits there. The curtains blow in the breeze and at night the room is dark. It's been like that for four or five days now, but nights are the worst. We even stopped by Rote Rose where the really dire cases end up. Just to be sure. We're starting to worry, after all. Nick is nowhere. We're all still pinning our hopes on Sunday.

Because Sunday is bingo night at Claudi's Eckkneipe bar on the corner of Mariannenplatz. Chalked on the blackboard outside it says: *Futschi cocktails Tuesdays and Sundays €1*. But people don't come on Sunday just because the Futschis are cheaper. On Sunday they come to devote themselves to the ritual of bingo. It's a must, like Sunday Mass. The music is turned off and the darts trophies shimmer unnoticed all to themselves. Jay-Jay stands at the counter and spins the drum with the numbers. The high priest of bingo rules the roost. Nick came every Sunday, without fail. After his shift at the Bateau or after soccer or whatever, Nick always turned up at Claudi's on a Sunday. And when he came in, there were pecks on cheeks all around.

"Morning, Claudi."

"Why morning? It's already evening."

Then Nick would give her a wink and send his greetings over to the regulars' table in the corner: "Good evening, ladies!"

Yes, no doubt he has manners. And in return, they would have brushed their hair and put on their best blouses. It was

Sunday, after all. Here, at the regulars' table, is the family: Renate with her pink jacket, Sigrid in her wheelchair, the plastic bag with her purse hanging on the back. Nick winked at them too, as if it might lead to something later on. But what? Well, something nice. The ladies at the table would have said nothing, of course. Just raised their hands to return his greeting. They know what's appropriate. They don't want to jump the line.

Nick is irresistible, we all agree on that. He's charming, he makes us laugh, and if you need someone for the night, Nick is available. For him, it goes without saying that a night at the club ends in bed with a shared breakfast and perhaps an encore if the interest is there. He has time on his hands. He has nothing else to do with his life. We appreciate that.

We like his smile. His eyebrows. His physique. He was once an athlete, has a flat stomach, muscles in the right places, and is otherwise well equipped. His skin is legendary. No tattoos—Nick has no need for them. His skin speaks for itself, it feels like a fresh peach. It smells of the early-morning hours on a Greek island. Nick takes his time and lets us take ours, kisses us with abandon in the places where it's best to be kissed, and what's more: Nick knows how to massage.

Who was the first one to find out? Zazie once dropped a hint to that effect. Even though there's never really been anything between Nick and her. Only once, years ago—and we're talking years. After a gymnastics tournament, he massaged her on a mat in the equipment room. She was fifteen at the time. "I came twice without him actually doing anything—he was just massaging me," she told her friend.

That same evening, Tanja, the friend, turned up at the Bateau and stayed until the end of Nick's shift. Then they went over to Roses where they began to smooch, and then to the Rock 'n' Roll Hostel where, after a close foosball match, he accompanied her to the ladies' room because she wanted to "show him something."

The actual massage only took place the following afternoon. Tanja was impressed. She had considerable experience as far as boys went, but what Nick did, and especially how he did it, was something she had never quite experienced before.

His hand movements were gentle, never awkward. He behaved respectfully. He took the massage seriously, although she unclipped her bra early on and made obvious sounds that it felt good. Nick stayed focused, loosening her arms, flexing the muscles of her thighs, and stroking a circular line over her stomach, which she politely sucked in. But it wasn't necessary at all. She no longer felt fat, just desirable. No man had ever touched her in that way.

The next day Tanja told her best friends, Mia and Lydia, what had happened. "It was pure magic. He massages like a young god." More than two bottles of ice-cold white wine were necessary to discuss Nick's methods and compare them with the awkward techniques of other men. Now Mia and Lydia also frequented the Bateau more often when Nick was on shift. He smiled when he placed their Aperol spritz in front of them. They looked at his hands while he was serving, imagining being massaged by them at some future time.

At Claudi's, everyone has a bingo card in front of them, and most have a small pils within reach too. But not Grandma Nostitz; she just drinks Coke. There's a shot of rum in it, but only Claudi knows that. Claudi knows everything, everyone, gets pecks on the cheek all the time. But when Nick came in and kissed her on the cheek, it touched her to the core. After all, she is a woman.

"Had a hard day today," he always said. "Can you pour me a small pils?"

She would, and she'd put out some pretzel sticks too.

"Mmm, dinner," he'd say.

And she'd say, "You didn't eat again today?" If he had come over to her place, she'd have made him a sandwich. A young man like him needs some meat on his bones.

Nick always sat next to Jay-Jay, Claudi's son. His voice is breaking and he already has some dark fuzz on his upper lip, but Claudi still frequently glances at the door because she's had trouble with the DCF before. A kid in a bar at night, spinning the bingo drum and calling out numbers, is not quite the norm. The youth welfare office doesn't believe in the cathartic rite of bingo. The DCF doesn't know that Jay-Jay is no longer a child, but in fact a servant of the Lord Himself, channeling the voice of the Bingo God. "Stop flirting, please, let's go!" shouts Jay-Jay in the taproom, and everyone pricks up their ears.

Nick never stopped flirting, we all knew that. Just take his question about earrings, which came right on cue: "What kind of earrings are those you've got on?" Why do other men never ask things like that? Nick notices earrings. He asks you about them. He taps them very lightly if the opportunity arises. By then, your defenses are already down, your inner goalie is already lying flat on his back. All Nick had to do was pop the ball into the wide-open goal. Many of us have started to wear earrings just because we know that Nick will ask about them.

By the way, we're not in love with Nick, God forbid. Not a single one of us. Not really, anyway. It's more a matter of hormones. We're just following the call of nature. We share Nick between us, making arrangements without him noticing. Luna can have him on Mondays, Anna on Tuesday. Marlene's turn is every other Wednesday; Franka and Kim share Thursdays. Fridays and Saturdays aren't reserved for any of us. They're an open race, even for outsiders beyond Heinrichplatz.

And Sunday is bingo day. He has to recover now and again. It can't be easy for him. Nor for us. Because Nick almost never sticks to his appointments. Just when you've put fresh sheets on the bed and lit the unobtrusively scented candles, he calls and starts hemming and hawing that today won't work. You have no idea whether another woman has elbowed her way in, or if it's a guy thing. In such cases you have to stay cool. Being possessive with Nick is completely pointless; then he gets that look. Strokes back his hair, rolls a cigarette, and his cell hums softly, because someone else is calling.

Nick's not faithful, nor can he or should he be in the face of the endless demand. There's plenty to go around for everyone. Among his circle of friends, he's seen men making their beds in stable relationships, and then had to lie in them. But that's not his thing. And by the way, he even turned down Oliver, the millionaire he met in Kuchen Kaiser on Oranienplatz, who that very same night offered him marriage along with lifelong financial support.

So, men aren't his thing either.

On the other hand, Nick does not respond indiscriminately to any woman who makes advances. He doesn't even take up the majority of the offers. A clumsy come-on—a top unbuttoned to the belly button, lips constantly being flicked with the tip of the tongue, hair dreamily played with—is steadily ignored. That's not his style. You shouldn't come on cheap. He's not a slut.

And besides, if he's interested in a Champions League match, no matter who calls, Nick stays with his boys in the Intertank or the back room of the betting shop where we women don't have access anyway. Even for some Dortmund game or a lousy 0–0 by Union in the second division. He drinks his four or five beers, three vodkas, two slivovitzes, and whatever else comes his way and goes to bed, wanting for nothing. He doesn't listen to his voice messages and doesn't reply to romantic texts. We know that, but still give it a try anyway. No chance. Men need the company of other men, of course. We're no different. That's why it took us awhile to grasp the seriousness of the situation when Nick eventually vanished.

Because usually he was back in form soon after those soccer nights. He flirted his way through the late shift with his new colleague Luna, who had been after him for weeks. They went over to Roses after their shift, began to smooch after ten minutes, and, four hours later, stopped to go up to his apartment.

"It was the best four hours of my life," Luna said later. "Can't be topped."

Nothing did top it either. Nick immediately fell asleep, and Luna was relieved because she had her period anyway. The next day, Luna told him her complex family history, and Nick listened with interest. At least until his cell phone rang. He answered the call with an apologetic smile. "Hey, Janko, what's up? No, it's okay . . . I'm just having breakfast with Luna, but I'll be right there." His interest in her family problems, her personality, and her other charms vanished, and after a last espresso, he set her in front of his door.

Naturally, she couldn't just turn off her feelings for him overnight, especially since Nick was very attentive and charming on their shift together three days later. That evening he was wearing a red-and-white-striped tie with a black shirt. When he stood by the coffee machine and Luna walked past him, catching his crisp, tangy scent, the ground almost gave way beneath her feet. She didn't usually behave like this. She had always thought of herself as a strong, independent woman, practically born wearing Dr. Martens and with the biceps of a construction worker. But her knees were weak and her palms moist. Nick instinctively sensed what she was going through. And he saw to Luna, took her to his apartment right after their shift, to the room above the betting shop, where the curtains billowed out onto Oranienstrasse during the day.

As if in a trance, Luna climbed over the mountain of clothes, ignored the Tetra Paks of sour-smelling milk, the cereal bowls with dried-up leftovers, and avoided the sight of two used condoms hanging from the edge of his desk. The same desk was also completely covered with stacks of books, unopened letters, bongs, tobacco pouches, ashtrays, coffee cups, beer bottles, crumpled banknotes, computers, and an old-fashioned TV. Luna did not think about it too hard: she just undressed, and so did Nick after quickly rolling a joint.

He did not have the time to smoke it. Luna was in a hurry. She came the first time after two minutes and thirty-seven seconds, and the second time after seven minutes, much more intensely. It was absolutely true what the others had said about his skin. And the massage, she thought, feeling slightly dizzy, was still to come. Nick, in any case, only got around to smoking his joint half an hour later. His eyes became heavy as the excellent grass did its work. He suddenly felt incredibly tired. Luna's head lay on the left side of his chest, like so many women's heads had done in the last months and years. He had stopped counting long ago.

Of course he remembered their faces, often their names too. He could distinguish them by the way they smelled. Fiona had a slightly citrusy fragrance. Elisabetta's was of rosemary. Feli's dainty ballet feet had an odor of sweat and wooden floors. And then there was Maria, of course, who tasted so seductively of cinnamon, although he never knew why. They had only met in the summer. He thought of the woman in Lisbon with whom he had spent the night smooching, until he lost his senses of sight and hearing. But early in the morning his boys had separated the two of them because the flight back to Berlin was about to depart, and Nick had the boarding passes in his pocket.

We did not find all this out until it was already too late. Nick remains missing. We ask who saw him last, who he was with when he left the Bateau or the Elefant or the Goldene Hahn or the Trinkteufel, and which direction he set off in, and where his cell phone might be. A man does not simply vanish into thin air, just like that.

"Something's not right," says Fiona, but she says that all the time. She watches contrails in the sky above Kreuzberg and sees signs of a widespread conspiracy everywhere. She swears that Nick's disappearance has something to do with the gambling debts that are being talked about on Heinrichplatz these days. Nick and his boys. That's a story in itself. Later, we all wonder, of course, if something had happened between them, something bad? We just have to think of those crumpled banknotes on Nick's desk or in the kitchen between the plates and glasses on the draining board. But Nick could care less about money.

"Only love counts," he would say. But the fact is, says Paula, that Nick and his friends have backed a poker player with a few thousand euros. His name is Mirko. They call him "our horse." Mirko plays for them in gambling dens along Hasenheide and Hermannstrasse, as well as in medium-sized and big tournaments. Hotel costs and entry fees are covered by the donors, but they get 70 percent of Mirko's winnings. If Mirko loses early on, then the money is gone. But last fall, Mirko kept winning and moving up through the rounds. In a casino in Baden-Baden, for example, he made twenty thousand euros, and in a fat tournament in Las Vegas, he was among the last four with seventy thousand dollars in prize money. Nice for everyone. But what wasn't so nice: Mirko then ran off to Malta.

Has Nick gone after him to claim his share? Has he been beaten up by Mirko's new bodyguards, taken part in a "conversation" that involved weighted-knuckle gloves and ball crushers? Is he lying on some dusty building plot near Valletta, buzzing with flies?

"No, that's nonsense," Fiona says hastily. "But the trails in the sky have been especially strong this month. And Nick is so sensitive—perhaps he couldn't stand it here any longer."

We shake our heads and keep looking for him; we stare every day at the curtain billowing out of his window, go to Claudi's on Sunday but he doesn't show up, and the feeling of unease grows and grows. In quiet moments, we wonder how it all started.

Heinrichplatz is not a huge area. People live and drink next door to each other. People know each other. At some point, Nick arrived. And as soon as he arrived, he belonged. He couldn't go down Oranienstrasse without meeting five friends as well as several former and probably future flings. You could already spot his slanting hat from Adalbertstrasse. Then, his shoulders. The way he walked, dragging his feet slightly. His face, marked by countless boozy nights, but still clearly contoured. Ravaged, but still cute. We all agreed that Nick looked like a young Blixa Bargeld.

He was one of us, someone from the neighborhood. It's rumored that he's from Lausitzer Platz anyway. Others swear that they saw him as a little boy in the Bergmann hood, at the Marheineke market hall. Ezra claims that one night he told her about watching *Batman* cartoons in janitor Fethgenheuer's wife's living room on Sunday mornings when his parents were still asleep.

If that's true, then he must have gone to Rosegger Elementary. There is evidence to back this up. And Nick must have been a gymnast in the past. He could perform a tautly stretched handstand at seven a.m. in the Schlawinchen even after a night of partying. He mentioned the name Zimmer to two women, though he contradicted himself: a Mr. Zimmer had been his gym teacher, or rather, his coach. And his mother had had a friend named Zimmer. The names may have been coincidental, but the handstand wasn't. Nick never boasted about it at all. It wasn't about luring women's attention; he didn't need to.

It all started at Bierhimmel when he had finished school and didn't know what to do next. Bierhimmel is directly opposite the betting office and his apartment right above it. Nick just had to fall out of bed and cross the street, briefly combing his hair on the way. He took charge of the coffee machine. Who did the women and girls come to if they wanted a latte? They came to Nick—because he lovingly foamed the milk, conjured up a flower pattern or a small heart with precocious talent, and wore an open white shirt with a waistcoat. He was good-looking: strong, with dark eyebrows and very sweet eyes.

"Stop flirting, please," Jay-Jay said without fail every Sunday to the murmuring and rattling coughs of guests between rounds. Nick would always sit next to him, three boards in front of him, and on each of his boards there had to be a 36. That was his system, that was his quirk; nonetheless, he never won. Because he was so lucky in love, a just God showered him with plenty of bad luck at the bingo table. His rows regularly expired halfway through the game. He never managed more than a triple. And if a set of four numbers came up, Nick could count on it that Jay-Jay would never draw the missing number.

Grandma Nostiz usually wins, although too much excitement isn't good at her age. Her hands tremble too much to keep control of her board, so Claudi has to take charge. Jay-Jay checks the numbers, and the entire crowd in the taproom holds its breath. Jay-Jay pauses for effect, then announces, "All correct! Take your numbers off!"

Nick would take his legendary losing streak on the chin, order another small pils for himself and a round of schnapps for everyone else.

Jay-Jay would draw the next number and call it out: "N44! N44!"

Some of the guests are hard of hearing, like Jürgen for example, who has to be told the number three times before he starts scrutinizing his card.

"I don't have it," he'll eventually mutter. "Can't believe it."

"Well, you should," Herbert will say from the table on the right. "I've been living there for twenty years."

Nick rarely came to Neukölln. The neighborhood around Heinrichplatz satisfied his needs. Sometimes he went to Bastard in Reichenbergstrasse for breakfast or lunch. The women there loved him too and always promised to visit him in Bierhimmel, although they never did. When Bierhimmel was sold, the staff were also replaced. Nick ended up at Bateau.

The owner's daughter fell in love with him. He stayed there and loved her back—but not just her. It soon transpired that he was not only good at giving massages, but also at mixing cocktails. As with love, he liked to experiment with ingredients. He mixed gin and port and absinthe, added a pinch of cinnamon, a spoonful of crushed espresso beans, walnut extract, and rhubarb juice. When he stood at the counter and shook the drinks, he was the king; he had swing. His negroni took not only your breath away, and his passion-fruit pisco sour would give you the final push.

Ruben, the exact opposite of Nick, is now the bartender at the Bateau. Ruben always wears a long-suffering expression, plays table tennis in his free time, and probably sniffs old socks for kicks. We smile at him gently when we ask if he knows what's happened to Nick.

Ruben doesn't smile back. He just shrugs. As far as he is concerned, Nick can stay away for good.

"Do you want a drink?" he asks. "A beer? A spritzer?" We don't want a drink; we want Nick back.

"He's not here," says Ruben. He wears a black Adidas jacket and thinks he's cool. We know that he once asked Nick a favor, one single favor. He was interested in Naima—truly, madly, and deeply. We couldn't get our heads around it, she herself least of all. The favor Ruben asked was that Nick should keep his hands off Naima. Just her, that's all. Nick promised he would, put a paternal hand on Ruben's shoulder, and wished him the best of luck. That evening, he was out with Emilia, but he lost sight of her in the course of the night and woke up with Naima beside him, fulfilling one of Naima's long-held dreams. He wasn't together with Naima for long, just two or three days, but during that time he was wasted enough to show up with her at the Bateau twice while Ruben was polishing glasses. Since then, Nick has been on Ruben's shit list.

"Do you think he did something to Nick?" Naima asks the group. We quickly brush this off. Not Ruben. That couldn't be. But what *has* happened?

We meet at the Elefant to pool the information we have. "We have no information," says Mira, ordering a Bloody Mary to emphasize the gravity of the situation. The rest of us sip our beers or spritzers. Alfred, who spends his remaining days in the Elefant, is sitting at the back by the pool table. He has half a glass of water in front of him and wipes the surface of the pool table with his palm while talking to himself.

"He's probably dead," Jessy says, her eyes shining moistly.

"Maybe he's just gone away with his boys and forgot to tell us," says Lydia.

It's an ordinary Wednesday afternoon, just like any other. Outside, the 29 bus drives past. Baby carriages stand around while mothers tap on their smartphones. Not a cloud in the sky. On the elevated railway in Skalitzer Strasse, a subway rattles to Görlitzer Station.

"No, he's hasn't," said Maja. "I called everyone." She always calls everyone. "None of the boys knows where he is. They don't really care either."

"I have the feeling he's still here," says Franka. "I keep seeing him when I'm out. I see him standing at the bus stop. Outside the bookstore. Outside the Franken bar. Outside the Fadeninsel wool store. At Hillmann deli. But when I get closer and tug his shirt, he turns around and it's someone else. Really embarrassing." She glances guiltily at us. But it's happened to most of us too.

"The other day I saw him on the platform at Kotti when

the train was pulling away," says Fiona. "I pulled the emergency brake. But it was just a French tourist. And I had to hightail it because the subway driver was really mad."

Anna lights her fifth cigarette in a row and admits that she even sees Nick in her bedroom. "Not really *see*," she says, "but I feel his presence. It's like he wants to tell me something. When I'm sleeping, his hands lie on my shoulders. It makes me feel really good, but also totally sad." Anna has a touch of the esoteric—she likes to talk to angels, go on astral journeys, and consult tarot cards every day.

But none of that will bring Nick back. We order a round of schnapps to calm down.

"Maybe something really has happened to him," says Paula. "I climbed on a construction crane with him one night—we were both completely drunk. Going up was all right as long as you didn't look down. But then Nick decided to climb around the outside to get into the crane cab, and he was hanging in the air. And I prayed to God not to let him fall. *Dear God*, I said, *I'll never touch another drop of alcohol if you let Nick down safely*." Paula sighs and sips at her white wine. "And it turned out all right."

Mira says, "But maybe some night he'll be so drunk that he'll miss a rung and fall. It's a long way down from a crane. And there's no one to catch you."

At that moment we all hate her.

Anna brings another round and says: "Maybe he'll be back next Sunday. He's always come back so far."

That's true. At heart, Nick is no fair-weather friend. He doesn't like leaving the neighborhood, but sometimes it can't be avoided. Once a year he'd drive out to Brandenburg for the Fusion Festival and add a new wristband to his collection—фузион. Afterward, during his night shifts at the Bateau, he would play more electronic music, but he soon returned to the late 1960s rhythm and blues for which he was well-known in the neighborhood. "R&B for adults," he would say. "Woman's Gotta Have It" hardly left the turntable, as well as "Lookin' for a Love," of course, and "I'm a Midnight Mover." Etta James's "I'd Rather Go Blind." Or Moodymann's "Don't You Want My Love."

Nick didn't check the clock when he worked, but wiped the counter, polished glasses, put on "Ya Blessin' Me." When the 29 bus drove past outside, he'd nod to the driver, who'd then head into the city, past Checkpoint Charlie and Anhalter Bahnhof, and over to Wittenbergplatz and Kurfürstendamm. Nick himself did not often get out that far. Moodymann's "I'd Rather Be Lonely" drifted below the lanterns at the Bateau.

"I once went to the zoo with him," says Lydia. "And he loves photos. He goes to every photo exhibition he can. Especially if it has pictures of New York City. He went there once for ten days. Do you remember?"

As if we'd forgotten. Even though he'd given us advance warning, those ten days were an eternity. He would have liked to stay longer, but ten days later he was back in Oranienstrasse. We quizzed him about the trip, but all he said was: "Good. Everything was fine. At Employees Only down in the Village, whoever's still there at four in the morning gets a hot chicken soup at last call. We should introduce that to the Bateau. Or cucumber water, like you get in Brooklyn when you order cheap whiskey, to hide the taste."

He said something about a woman he'd met in Washington Square; she'd lived on the Upper West Side, and they had walked together through Central Park at night to get to her apartment. We weren't interested in hearing any more. Nick is pleasantly unforthcoming on the subject of his womanizing. Among ourselves, we've worked out what he's done with whom. He sometimes loses track of things.

But deep in his heart, he's a very loyal soul. In winter, he hauls stacks of coal up to his mother's apartment on the fourth floor. A good kid. He even stays for coffee and a cigarette in her kitchen and tells her an edited version of what's going on in his life. She always likes to hear what he's doing, even if he's not doing anything. She also understands when women get to be a drag. In the past, she had it similar with men.

Occasionally he's compelled to take long walks, furious hikes to the point of exhaustion that lead him far beyond the borders of Kreuzberg, all the way to Neukölln and Britz, along the canal where longboats used to deliver bricks and wood to build the city. We can't follow him on these hikes, it goes without saying. But we have always sensed when he needs to take off. In the days running up, he's noticeably short-tempered: no more smiles, he looks terrible, boozes more than is good for him, and then a little more, just out of principle.

Maybe he hasn't returned from one of his hikes . . .

Claudi says: "I don't believe that. Someone like him doesn't just get lost. He'll be back on Sunday for bingo, you'll see. The door will open and Nick will come in and say, *Hello, hello.*" She's standing at the beer tap as she says this and has a lump in her throat because she no longer believes it herself—but no one needs to know that.

"Maybe he's found the right woman. Got married," Caroline suggests, and we could all kill her for it.

"Nick and marriage? Don't make me laugh," says Anna. But she downs another tequila, just in case.

"What does that even mean, *the right woman?*" says Nina. "What does Nick need that we can't offer him?"

Mira says with shining eyes, "Love?"

"Oh, come on. Nick's an Aquarius," Anna says, true to form. "They never tie themselves down."

At bingo the next Sunday, we sit at different tables, our number cards in front of us, a Jägermeister close at hand, and the door in view. It's the saddest game in the world.

The old men sit at the bar. One says, "Where's the young guy who always used to come?"

"He's gone," says his neighbor.

"He'll be back," says Claudi, emphasizing her words, as if that'll make it more likely. She pours a small pils. Nick always took a small one so that it stayed fresh. Her gaze wanders constantly to the door; it's already past half past eight, and Jay-Jay starts calling out the numbers.

"He's not coming," says Mira at the double table in the corner by the toilets. She's off sniffing again. Mira, of all people, who's been with Kasper for years, but who doesn't want to give up Nick. "There's just no comparison," she says sadly if anyone asks why she elbowed her way in to reserve Nick every three weeks. She once paid for a hotel room in Kreuzberg, telling Kasper she had a conference to attend. He believed her right away. That's men for you.

"So, let's start! Stop flirting, please!" Jay-Jay's voice rings out in Claudi's taproom. Sunday. Bingo day. The door opens, and who comes in?

Renate. She's late. She rolls up to the family table and looks around. "Where is he?"

"He'll be coming later," says Claudi from behind the bar.

"No, he won't," says Paula, and a tear splashes onto her bingo card.

"Number B67!" shouts Jay-Jay. "Number B67!"

"A good year," says Jürgen. He's also a '67 vintage and he

winks at Claudi, but she wants nothing to do with him.

Hasn't for years, but some people never learn.

How will things be without Nick around? We don't know. We still pass by Schmitz Katze, keep walking through side streets, and hear someone playing "The Thief That Stole My Sad Days" through an open window. We begin to cry uncontrollably.

The nights on Heinrichplatz are simply not what they used to be. There are many fish in the ocean, but let's face it, there's no substitute for some. And we know what we're talking about. We've been to Trinkteufel, to Franken. Almost every night we do the rounds from the Bateau to the Taqueria, from the Elefant to the Goldene Hahn. We're constantly meeting men, having drinks, trying them out. But they're just not the same. We want to be touched the way Nick touched us.

In the Bateau, one of us has written his name on the wall of the ladies' bathroom. And the dot over the *i* is heart-shaped.

KADDISH FOR LAZAR

BY MICHAEL WULIGER

Charlottenburg

"You're Jewish, aren't you?" the editor of *Blitz Magazin* asked me.

"Yes, I am." I felt uncomfortable. "Why do you want to know?" That kind of question coming from Germans irritates me. It runs in the family, I guess.

"Then you must have known Mark Lazar well," he said.

Actually, I hadn't. The closest I had ever come to the man had been last Yom Kippur, the one day of the year even I go to synagogue. Lazar had stood twelve rows in front of me, checking messages on his iPhone, while the cantor intoned Kol Nidre, the holiest of Jewish prayers.

"So what do you think it was?" the editor inquired. "An accident? Suicide? Or murder?"

Mark Lazar's body had been fished out of the Spree River two days ago. His death was the talk of the town. The papers were full of glowing obituaries detailing his storybook career. A penniless twenty-four-year-old, he had come from Kiev to Berlin in 1991, when newly reunited Germany had allowed some 200,000 Jewish immigrants from the disintegrating Soviet Union into the country as a token gesture of historical redemption. Within several years, Lazar had learned German well enough to study law and graduate with honors, after which he joined a prestigious law firm on posh Kurfürstendamm. Simultaneously he got into politics, where he rapidly rose to local prominence. Starting out as board member of the Jewish Community of Berlin, Lazar had progressed first to a borough assembly, then to the city council, and three years ago to the national Parliament, the Bundestag's first observant Jewish member in decades. And it hadn't stopped there. Up until his death, Lazar's name cropped up regularly when possible contenders in next year's mayoral election were discussed.

"We want you to do an in-depth story on his life and death," the editor told me, lighting a cigarette. At *Blitz Magazin* the legal ban on smoking in the workplace apparently didn't extend to the upper echelon. "A cover piece. Around six thousand words. Family, background, career, the whole works. How and why he ended up in the river."

The police had issued the results of Lazar's postmortem that very afternoon. The cause of death was drowning. According to the autopsy report, the deceased's blood-alcohol content at the time of death had been 0.3 percent. In other words, he had been blind drunk. The pathologists had also found substantial traces of tranquilizers in the corpse.

"Something about the affair definitely stinks." The editor gave me a well-trained, encouraging smile. "If anybody can get to the bottom of it, it's you, with your background."

Aha. That explained why *Blitz* had called me that morning. I had never worked for them before, but they seemed to believe that as a Jew I had access to sources their regular reporters couldn't get ahold of. It's a common misconception among gentiles that all members of the tribe are intimately acquainted with each other. I, for one, am certainly not. Of the thirty thousand Jews living in Berlin, I personally know only a few dozen. But I wasn't going to correct the guy on that. An assignment from *Blitz Magazin* was an offer I couldn't refuse. Berlin has several thousand freelance journalists like me, jobs are increasingly scarce, and *Blitz* pays well above the usual rates.

If you want to know what goes on behind the scenes in Berlin's Jewish community, the person to consult is Ruthi Berenstein. Ruthi is the community's resident yenta. She has the dirt on everybody and loves to dish it out. When the medieval talmudic sages condemned *lashon hara*—malicious gossip—they had people like Ruthi in mind.

We met in Café Einstein on Kurfürstenstrasse, Ruthi's favorite hangout. "I won't be sitting shivah for that guy," was the first thing she said, after heaving her ample bottom onto a settee. "No grief here. Lazar was a schmuck. Remember how he fixed last year's Jewish Community of Berlin board election?" Lazar's notoriously incompetent and corrupt henchmen had narrowly defeated a reform slate, thanks to hundreds of dubious absentee ballots from newly registered members no one had ever heard about before. Ruthi had been one of the defeated opposition candidates. "I personally could have killed him just for that," she snarled.

"So you think he was killed?" I asked.

"Don't know, don't care," she shrugged. "Maybe somebody settled a score. Maybe his conscience, if he had one, finally caught up with him. Maybe he just slipped and fell into the river. HaShem works in mysterious ways."

"If not the Lord it might have been the Russian mafia," I suggested. Berlin, like other big cities in Eastern and Central Europe, has a well-established Jewish underworld. Our local kosher mob was even featured in a TV drama series some years ago.

Ruthi shook her head. "No. Lazar wasn't involved in organized crime. He did a bit of legal work for some of the bosses every once in a while. But that was strictly above board. Real-estate deals and the like. Other than that, he had nothing to do with the mob." She took a gulp from her glass of white wine. "Not because of moral scruples, mind you. He just didn't have the balls for that. Behind all that big *macher* posturing of his, our boy Mark was a coward. One more thing they won't be mentioning at the funeral."

Despite the ongoing police investigation, Lazar's body had been released for burial immediately after the autopsy. He was going to be laid to rest in the Jewish cemetery tomorrow. Our strictly Orthodox head rabbi was apparently ruling out that the deceased had died by his own hand. Jewish religious law does not permit the interment of suicides in hallowed ground.

"Of course he would," Ruthi sneered. "Lazar got him his job. Besides, the widow will have seen to that. Probably wants to cash in on the double-indemnity-accident clause of his life insurance. I don't think she gives a flying fuck about the religious aspect. She's not really Jewish, anyway. Aryan to the core. Her grandfather was a general in the Wehrmacht. Before she married Lazar she proselyted on the quick with some rent-a-rabbi in Tel Aviv who charges ten thousand euros per conversion, no questions asked."

Gunhild Merz had been a minor actress on a daily TV soap opera when she had met Mark Lazar eight years ago at a charity event. In their own words, as reported in one of the glossy magazines, they had "fallen madly in love at first sight." Mrs. Lazar, who at 5'8" towered a head over her diminutive husband, was considered one of the assets in his political career.

"Took some of the Jewish edge off him and made him more palatable to the goyish voters." Ruthi gave a nasty snicker.

"Was it a happy marriage?" I wanted to know.

"Not happy, but stable, even if they had no kids," Ruthi responded. "It was a mutually beneficial arrangement. If you're thinking domestic murder, you're way off the mark. He did some occasional screwing around, but she didn't mind too much, as long as he kept her in Prada dresses and Cartier watches. Besides, the prospect of becoming the city's First Lady next year had Gunhild lubricating her panties. She wouldn't have done anything to jeopardize that." Ruthi looked at her watch. "Bye now. Gotta run. See you at the funeral tomorrow. Wouldn't miss that for anything."

Back home I logged on to Facebook for some comic relief. The conspiracy nuts were having a heyday. Lazar had been liquidated by Mossad, one user asserted. Neo-Nazis had done the dirty deed, someone else ventured. Another speculation had the Russian secret service behind the affair: Lazar, who originally hailed from Kiev, had been smuggling weapons to Ukraine. Or possibly the other way around: the weapons he smuggled had been intended for pro-Russian separatists, so the CIA had done him in. The Mossad theory won out by 287 likes and ninety-three increasingly lunatic comments. I closed my computer and went to bed.

Weissensee is Berlin's 130-year-old main Jewish cemetery and, at a hundred acres, the largest of its kind in Europe. Some four hundred people had assembled there to pay their last respects to Mark Lazar, among them nearly all of the city's dignitaries. The men were wearing cheap black polyester kippot that had been handed out at the cemetery's entrance. The skullcaps made them look like movie extras. After eulogies by the rabbi ("loving and devoted husband," "pillar of our community") and the mayor ("trusted friend and colleague," "embodiment

of German-Jewish reconciliation"), Mark Lazar's mortal remains were lowered into the grave. The cantor recited the
kaddish. Like most of the mourners, some of the Jews included,
I didn't know the Hebrew words to the traditional prayer for
the dead, but nevertheless moved my lips as a sign of respect
and to hide my ignorance.

Among the women standing slightly apart from the men,
as Orthodox custom dictates, I noticed an old lady with tears
running down her cheeks. "Who was she?" I asked Ruthi on
our way back to town after the funeral.

"That was Hetty Goldstein," she informed me. "Probably
the only one in the crowd who was genuinely grieving for Lazar. She really loved him."

"Hetty Goldstein?" The name didn't ring any bell.

"The Jewish Community of Berlin's administrative secretary. She knew Mark Lazar from the day he arrived in Berlin.
Treated him like the son she never had, poor old maid. She's
who you should talk to if you want to find out more about his
early years."

"Does Mrs. Goldstein still work for the Community?" I
asked.

"Oh no. She retired years ago. Must be at least eighty by
now. She lives in the Jewish home for the elderly. Phone her.
She'll see you. She's lonely and desperate for company."

The next day I called Mrs. Goldstein. Yes, she would certainly
receive me, she said. Yes, early this afternoon would be fine.
She sounded delighted.

The Jewish Community's retirement home is near Liet-
zensee Park in the uptown district of Charlottenburg. Mrs.
Goldstein's room looked out upon a garden. The couch she
sat on seemed oversized for her frail, tiny body. Her voice,

however, was astoundingly strong and clear, like a young girl's. We had coffee, served in genuine old Meissen porcelain cups. "Family heirlooms," she explained. "It's all I've got left from my father and mother. They and my older brother were deported to Riga and killed there. I'm the only one who survived. Neighbors hid me."

Here we go, I thought. Mrs. Goldstein was going to tell me the sad story of her life. Holocaust survivors have a special place in my heart, but that was not what I had come here for. Luckily, I didn't have to summon what limited empathy I possess to get Mrs. Goldstein on to the subject of Mark Lazar. The old lady came around to it by herself.

"And now I've lost Mark. Such a charming young man. He regularly sent me flowers and chocolates for my birthday, always with a handwritten note, apologizing for not visiting in person. Twenty-six years ago it was that I first met him. He came to the Jewish Community Center right after he arrived in Berlin. And not, like some of those other Russian immigrants, just to sponge off benefits. No, Mark was different. He took religious instruction from the rabbi and got actively involved in the Jewish Community of Berlin's affairs. He told me how grateful he was to be among his own people. You see, Mark had grown up in a Soviet orphanage after both his parents were killed in an automobile accident. He was seven years old then. The only Jew among goyim. No living relatives. They had all been murdered by the Germans. As I told that other gentleman recently, that was why I probably took to Mark. We were both alone in the world."

"What other gentleman?"

"Oh, he was here some weeks ago to talk about Mark, like you. I'm afraid I don't remember his name though. My memory isn't what it used to be." She prattled on about the vagaries of old age. After a few minutes of perfunctory polite conversation, I made my excuses and left.

Fortunately, I didn't need Mrs. Goldstein's failing memory to find out who her mysterious caller had been. Like all Jewish institutions in Berlin, the retirement home has elaborate security measures to protect it from possible neo-Nazi or Islamist attackers. After entering through a bulletproof door, all visitors are required to register with an armed security guard and show their ID cards. On my way out I asked the guard, a burly Israeli with an impressive gun in his holster, to check his log. It didn't take him long. Mrs. Goldstein did not receive many callers, he told me. A social worker from the Community's welfare department had checked on her last Thursday, as she did regularly. The rabbi had visited the old lady the week before. And on the third of the month a certain Erkan Özgentürk had signed in to see her.

God bless Google. I found Erkan Özgentürk with one click on the web. He was special adviser to Harald Liedke. Here was a name I, like every Berliner, knew. Liedke is the city's financial affairs commissioner, an up-and-coming career politician, and, like the late Mark Lazar, a possible candidate for the mayor's office. He has carefully cultivated the image of a tough, no-nonsense guy, stating at every possible opportunity that issues matter more to him than popularity. Whenever he is thus quoted, his approval in the opinion polls soar, of course. It is also common knowledge, though rarely mentioned in the media, that the commissioner likes his beer and chasers—a lot of beer and a lot of chasers.

So why had Liedke sent one of his top staff to see an old Jewish woman?

Klaus Hildebrand and I go back a long way. We both started out in journalism together. While I went freelance, Klaus, who had a family to feed, got a job with public radio, where he worked his way up to head of local affairs. His knowledge of Berlin city politics is encyclopedic, though to his permanent frustration he can't put it to full use. Most of the details he knows are too juicy for publication. Public radio is more or less under the subtle control of the city's political parties and other powers that be.

We had dinner at one of the Michelin-starred restaurants off Unter den Linden Boulevard in the now gentrified center of former East Berlin. Neither Klaus nor I typically frequent places like that. We can't afford them. But today the tab was on *Blitz Magazin*'s expense account.

"Özgentürk is Liedke's hatchet man," Klaus told me over appetizers. "He does the commissioner's dirty work. If he visited that Mrs. Goldstein, something nasty was going on. What exactly, I don't know. I did pick up a rumor a couple of weeks ago that Liedke had boasted to some of his followers that, quote, *The Jewboy is out of the race, he just doesn't know it yet*."

That certainly sounded ominous. The notion of a city commissioner offing his political rival, though, was a bit too ludicrous for my taste.

Klaus agreed. "Liedke is an unscrupulous bastard. Anything it takes to further his career, he'll do. But cold-blooded murder is not the way things are done here in Berlin." He paused while the waiter brought the second course. After a first bite of Kobe beef with pan-seared foie gras, he continued: "Liedke's not a killer. He's a schemer. Character assassination and blackmail are his preferred tools. He's reputed to keep hundreds of detailed dossiers on everybody and his brother. Özgentürk was probably digging up some dirt on Lazar for him."

We changed the subject while eating our way through the

rest of the eight-course menu. When the maître d' brought the check, Klaus whistled through his teeth. "Four hundred and thirty euros. Not bad. I owe you one. I'll check around in case anybody knows what Özgentürk and Liedke were up to with Lazar."

True to his word, he called me the next day. "Someone I know in Liedke's office told me that Özgentürk flew to Kiev just twenty-four hours after he saw your Mrs. Goldstein. That's all I could find out, I'm afraid. Good luck and happy hunting!"

Liedke's right-hand man must have been researching Lazar's Soviet past. Of that, little was publicly known. The late departed had never talked about his pre-Berlin biography. His life seemed to have begun only when he came to Germany. The Bundestag's official membership registry merely mentioned that Deputy Mark Lazar had been born in Kiev in 1967 and relocated to the capital in 1991. Neither his Wikipedia entry nor his personal website were any more detailed.

The Jewish Community's archive in Oranienburger Strasse, though, turned up some additional information. When Lazar had first run for the Jewish Community of Berlin's council in 1996, he had issued a campaign flyer in German and Russian. Beneath the photograph of an earnest-looking young man in an ill-fitting suit, it stated that Mark Naumovich Lazar was the son of Naum Davidovich Lazar and his wife Rosa Moisevna Lazarova, née Roitman, both deceased. After his parents' untimely death the candidate had grown up in the Anton Makarenko orphanage and graduated from Kiev public school number 27.

I needed to check up on that. *Blitz Magazin* could afford to pay for a quick jaunt to Ukraine Kiev is only two hours from Berlin by plane. I called the editor.

"Do you speak Russian?" was the first thing he asked. When I told him that I did not, he immediately nixed the idea. "We have a bureau in Moscow with a very capable stringer in Kiev. Let him do the research. You concentrate on your writing. You've got a deadline to meet. What is it you need to know?"

Cheap bastard! I gave him the details I had dug up in the archive and he promised to e-mail them to Moscow immediately.

Blitz's Kiev stringer was as capable as the editor had claimed. Within thirty-six hours he sent his report. No one by the name of Mark Naumovich Lazar had ever attended school number 27 in Kiev. The Anton Makarenko orphanage had no record of him either. Likewise for the parents. Naum Davidovich Lazar and his wife Rosa, allegedly killed in an automobile accident, couldn't be found in the city's registry of deaths. There was, furthermore, no documentation of their ever having existed. The magazine's Moscow bureau had gone to the additional trouble of consulting the Russian army's central archives. Like all young Soviet men his age, Mark would have been conscripted into the forces after graduating. But no record whatsoever existed of a Mark Naumovich Lazar from Kiev doing his patriotic duty.

Mark Lazar, linchpin of Berlin's Jewish community, promising German politician, subject of dozens of flattering media portrayals, had been a fake.

I shouldn't have been surprised. It is common knowledge that a number of supposedly Jewish immigrants from the former Soviet Union aren't what they profess to be. No one knows the exact figures. In a 1997 report, the former German ambassador to Ukraine speculated that only 40 percent of all Jewish immigrants to Germany actually were Jews in the strict sense of the word. Jewish religious law stipulates that only children born by a Jewish mother are considered members of the tribe. Many of the newcomers came from mixed marriages where only the father was Jewish. They probably made up the bulk of the other 60 percent. The rest, around 10 percent, were Jews by ID card only.

Soviet identification cards not only stated the name of the holder and his or her date and place of birth, but also their ethnicity. The entry "Yevrey," for "Jew," was a black mark. It meant in practice that the holder was barred from prestigious universities and top jobs. But when Germany admitted a large contingent of Soviet Jews in 1991, the infamous "third item" no longer carried the stigma of social discrimination; it was now literally a passport to the West. A flourishing black market for counterfeit Jewish papers soon developed in the crumbling USSR, prices ranging between five hundred and one thousand US dollars. That must have been how whatever-his-real-name-was became Mark Lazar. The story about losing his parents at age seven had been a nice additional touch. It explained his ignorance of Jewish customs and traditions. Lazar had been phony but definitely not stupid.

I wondered whether he'd even gone to the literal pains of getting circumcised to perfect his false identity. His wife would certainly know. I couldn't ask her, however, since Mrs. Lazar had left town immediately after the funeral for an unknown destination, where, in the words of a press release issued by her lawyer, she was "quietly mourning her beloved husband undisturbed by public attention and the media." Not that I really would have quizzed the widow about her late spouse's foreskin. There are limits even to a journalistic death knock.

What I might have found out from Gunhild Lazar, though, was what her husband had been up to in the days before his death and what emotional state he had been in.

The next best source for that kind of information would be Lazar's office. Maybe that actually was the best source. Like most politicians Mark Lazar presumably spent far more time with his colleagues and with his staff than with his family. Perhaps that was also where he had done the screwing around that Ruthi had mentioned. Though probably not with the person who answered the phone when I called Lazar's office in the Bundestag. The voice was definitely that of a male, and Lazar, based on what I knew, had not been gay.

"Martin Kern speaking." Kern was the legislator's chief of staff, he told me. "Or rather, his former chief of staff, now that he's dead. Right now I'm the chief removal man. We're clearing out the premises. The Bundestag administrators ordered us to vacate the rooms by tomorrow. His successor wants to take them over. Come by if you don't mind the mess."

Lazar's former office was on Dorotheenstrasse in a building that had first housed the Nazis' Ministry of the Interior, then Communist East Germany's Ministry of Justice. Now it served parliamentary democracy. I found Martin Kern on the second floor among dozens of moving boxes. "The remnants of my career," he commented. "A week ago I was looking forward to a possible top job in Berlin's city hall. Now I'll be filing for unemployment benefits."

I commiserated with him. He was my age and had, as he told me, the same academic background. Fortysomethings with political science degrees are what the labor exchange calls "difficult to place" on the job market.

"Well, enough about me," Kern said. "What is it you want to know?"

I asked if anything out of the ordinary had happened prior to Lazar's death.

"Yes, actually, there was something. But this is strictly off the record. If I'm caught blabbing I'll never work in politics again."

I promised to keep mum.

"The day Mark died, he had an appointment here with Erkan Özgentürk in the late afternoon. The meeting wasn't long, half an hour maybe. When I went to see him a few minutes after Özgentürk left, the boss was sitting at his desk ashen-faced. I wanted to talk about an important roll call scheduled for the next day. But he just gazed into the void without saying a word, as if he didn't know what I was talking about. Then all of a sudden Mark stood up abruptly, grabbed his briefcase, and stormed out of the office. That was the last I ever saw of him. I tried to call him later, but his cell phone was switched off."

Özgentürk again. It was high time to meet up with the man. I called Liedke's office and asked for his special adviser. A snotty secretary informed me that he was not available and referred me to the commissioner's media spokesperson. I persuaded her to let Özgentürk know I had phoned. "Tell him it's about his visit to Kiev," I said, and gave her my mobile number.

Within twenty minutes Özgentürk returned the call. "What is this Kiev shit you're referring to?" He tried to sound disdainful.

"Let's talk about that face-to-face," I suggested. "You never know who is listening in on phone conversations." In 2013 a whistleblower had revealed that the US National Security Agency was routinely intercepting the phone calls of hundreds of German politicians.

Özgentürk could have called my bluff by simply refusing to see me. Luckily, his curiosity won out over caution. He agreed to a get-together that evening.

We met in a bar on Stuttgarter Platz. "You've bitten off more than you can chew" was the first thing I said to him. "There is more involved here than your local Berlin politics. Lazar worked for us. We're not happy." The plural form was deliberate, as was the large silver Star of David pendant I was wearing around my neck for the occasion. Özgentürk was Muslim. And many Muslims, even some westernized Muslims, are firm believers in the worldwide Jewish conspiracy in general and the omnipotence and ubiquitousness of the Mossad in particular.

He stared at me. "Don't you know he wasn't Jewish at all? Oh, I see, you people got on to him long before. I found out about this in Kiev. Liedke has a contact in the city administration there." He was sweating slightly. "We hadn't planned on Lazar's death, I swear. We only wanted to put the screws on him. I went to Lazar's office and threatened to leak the story of his bogus identity to the media, unless he withdrew from the mayoral race and came out for Liedke. All he would have had to do was cave in. Instead, the fucking fool went and killed himself. I guess he must have panicked. Shit, this really spiraled out of control."

I believed him. For Mark Lazar, or whoever he really was, the shock of being found out must have been devastating. For more than a quarter of a century his big lie had worked successfully; maybe by that time he had nearly come to believe it himself. Now his game was up. Today a celebrity, tomorrow a virtual nobody, with not even his name left. "Acute stress reaction" is what psychiatrists call the emotional state Lazar must have been in. Common symptoms are numbness, emotional detachment, muteness, and derealization. Add booze and downers to that and you have enough to land in the river, be it willfully or accidentally in a stupor.

I peered at Erkan Özgentürk. "I think I should see your boss."

"Is that all you could come up with?" *Blitz Magazin*'s editor was visibly annoyed. "Okay, the false identity bit isn't bad. Lazar was an impostor. But that alone is not cover-story material. If the guy were still alive, yes. But he's dead. That's the big story. We wanted you to find out how and why he died. Who was involved." He ranted on: "No facts, no names, no background. Not even rumors. This could have been your big break. You fucked it up." He let out a resigned sigh. "I can't even give the assignment to someone else now. It's too late for that. The story is already getting stale."

He probably expected me to feel dejected. Actually, I didn't give a shit. This had been my last assignment as a freelance journalist. Beginning next month I had a new job as communications director of the Berlin Finance Department. Harald Liedke had offered me the post immediately when I confronted him with what I had found out. Like Lyndon B. Johnson, he preferred people inside the tent pissing out, rather than the other way around. And I liked the idea of a cushy civil-service position with a steady high salary, paid holidays, first-class health insurance, and a pension. Far better at my age than chasing after badly paid journalistic work and sucking up to asshole editors.

When a Jew dies, the words *May his memory be a blessing* are written as a honorific beside his name. Lazar's death had certainly been a blessing for me. Next Yom Kippur, I promised myself, I would recite the kaddish for him. I'd even learn the Hebrew words to the prayer for the dead. It was the least I could do. After all, I owed the late deceased a lot. Mark Lazar, *alav ha-shalom*—may peace be upon him.

This story was written in English.

FASHION WEEK

BY KATJA BOHNET

Mitte

Thea Stauffer looked at her hands and was surprised at how she had managed to let herself go. Blood was spattered all over the cream-colored bathroom tiles and Ansgar's head was twisted at an odd angle. Thea thought about whether to pull the electric toothbrush out of his throat but couldn't bring herself to do it because she thought the image pleasing. Although she had to leave for work, she found it hard to move. Seconds passed, and Thea felt something strangely soothing in the way blood was pooling under Ansgar. His white bathrobe of ultrafluffy organic cotton was turning pink. Thea relished the silence. It was only now that she realized how much she had missed the peace and quiet. Ansgar's body convulsed one more time, and blood sprayed from his mouth. Thea thought about dialing the emergency number but then decided against it because she was enjoying being alone with Ansgar so much. She sat on the edge of the bathtub and listened to the sounds of the building. A door slammed, the heating gurgled, the boiler slowly cooled down again. Ten minutes later, her heartbeat had completely normalized. Thea got up and pulled the toothbrush from Ansgar's throat. A quick test proved that it still worked perfectly. After that, she began to remove the evidence of Ansgar's unnatural demise.

* * *

The previous day, Thea had walked along Brunnenstrasse toward Gesundbrunnen, appraising the shop windows of the competition one by one: straight cuts, fabrics in single or complementary colors, or patterned with oversize geometric motifs. Each store offered just a few items in its range. It was striking how impossible they were to combine and how much they cost. Anysweet draped individual pieces over driftwood while both Babe Berlin and Paranoia lit up the changing rooms in different neon colors. JuteJule had dressmaking patterns on display and advertised sewing classes. Just before the Bernauer Strasse subway station, Thea realized that each boutique's uniqueness seemed completely uniform. She unlocked her store, which was next to the new coffee shop, Liberace. Coffee was now the golden calf of Berliners: life revolved around caffeine. Thea waved to the barista with a neighborly gesture. Her hand ran over cashmere and an alpaca-mohair mixture in mud shades, bought at Fashion Week two years before from a rep who'd impressed her with his precise language.

That same year, Nebelkind had presented its new collection in a yurt that could only accommodate two hundred people. Thea had managed to get her hands on one of the coveted tickets, and the new editor of German *Vogue*, Sandra Mutterkorn, was sitting two rows in front of her. She was wearing a gray Prada suit that sat snugly on her shoulders. The models had their hair piled up into nests. A fog machine produced dry ice, into which they glided off. The man beside Thea tapped his foot in time to the Mongolian chimes. After the catwalk show, he handed her his card: *Ansgar Möller. Design Director. Fashion Retail Worldwide.* He invited her to a green sencha tea with lactose-free milk. Then he showed her his catalog and samples.

For Thea, it had been love at first sight. She admired the

fabrics imported from Pakistan. No child labor, no chemicals, he emphasized. Nice to work with. Sustainability and fair trade were more important to Thea than anything else. She would have paid almost any price for such exquisite items.

Now, Thea flipped the switch and the light flickered; she turned on the old sewing machine and looked for the price tags. The day before, she had sold a long-sleeved shirt (modal-merino mix) to a tourist who had taken up the changing room for an hour and tried on eight other sweaters. After a thorough consultation (suitable for all occasions, timeless chic, muted colors), the customer let herself be persuaded, not without asking for a discount shortly before paying by credit card. Thea sighed, because yesterday's earnings seemed to reflect the whole month, the one before, and the past half year.

School had been torture for Thea. She preferred handicrafts to academic work. After getting average grades in high school, she had muddled through by selling herbal cosmetics for four years. It was a franchise business with poor margins, and door-to-door selling later on. Then, in the call center of a mail-order company, she advised bad-tempered shoppers who rang to complain about faulty goods. Weekend work, night shifts, no health insurance. Afterward she worked in the perfumery of the KaDeWe department store. Tough shifts, difficult customers, but at least she was paid a Christmas bonus. During her lunch break, she leafed through fashion magazines and catalogs. Pepped herself up with the lives of the rich and famous. Their world was so full of promise. Thea's father had taken a job as a system administrator in Braunschweig early in life. This was the period when her mother was experimenting with soft drugs.

When her father died of a heart attack fifteen years later, Thea inherited his apartment in Brunnenstrasse, where she had already been living. Up until his death, she had paid her father rent. Inheriting that property had been a godsend. She could now save every penny of her salary to fulfill her dream: to do something, anything, in the fashion business. No more selling for others, but her own business, a boutique at last. The competition in Mitte was fierce, but she had already knuckled under for too long and made compromises where there were none to be made. There was no one who advised her against her business idea because she didn't maintain friendships. Others, whether friends or relatives, were always a source of stress. She'd had two brief relationships: Klaus, who smoked too much weed and had completely lost the plot, and Dieter, who sold wooden planks at the hardware store and couldn't get over his ex.

Meanwhile, Thea's mother lived in Hawaii with a Brit who devoted his life to making surfboards, or at least that was the last that Thea had heard. When she took out a loan for the boutique at the Berliner Sparkasse, Thea knew what was at stake: the bigger picture, her life, her personal vision.

But the Curvy Models' calendar was now flipped to the month of November: winter sales wouldn't start for another six weeks. At least Berlin Fashion Week was before that. Thea decided to mark down her prices all the same. She couldn't stay in business if sales didn't pick up soon.

The clock showed eleven a.m. Thea sprayed disinfectant on her hands, although the product was only suitable for surfaces. Afterward, she discarded the sponges, rags, cleaners, and bleach in a dark-blue garbage bag, which she tied with a knot.

She wasn't happy with the result. The blood was gluey and stringy, and stuck to everything. Thea wiped and washed repeatedly, but a red tinge remained. She had the scent of copper wire in her nose. She was sweating because it was proving unusually difficult to wrap Ansgar in the expensive flokati rug. Thea was hoping for the onset of rigor mortis, which didn't happen—Ansgar's body flopped back and forth as if it were made of rubber, and one of his arms always seemed to be in the way. Thea had once seen the procedure in a show with Idris Elba. She wouldn't let these problems put her off what she had set out to do. By the time she finally dragged the body out of the bathroom, it was so stiff in its package that Thea wondered how Ansgar was going to fit in the elevator. Now that rigor mortis had set in, it was a problem. She then wrapped the body in several garbage bags, which she sealed with gaffer tape. In a gap on the outside she wrote in black capital letters: *Careful! Fragile!*—although Ansgar was anything but. He now looked like one of Thea's showroom dummies. She rested briefly and made a call.

When the doorbell rang, Thea jumped because the postman never delivered to her building before two o'clock in the afternoon, and people rarely wandered into the backyard of their tenement by accident.

Omari Sunda had fled the Congo in 2012. For four months he had been the holder of a temporary stay of deportation from Berlin, lived in a run-down apartment share in Wittenau, and picked up above-average German in average-quality language classes. The Boss, whose Italian friend was laid up in a dry-out clinic, had made Omari the barista at the Liberace. The Boss managed whole city blocks in Mitte for a Russian holding company that invested in speculative properties just after the fall of the Wall. He also checked construction sites when buildings were being renovated, complete refurbishments every time. Omari had been working for the cleaning company that serviced the Boss's properties. To Omari's surprise, the Boss waved him over when he was polishing the natural-wood parquet of a luxury apartment on Rosenthaler Platz: he was scrubbing a dark-brown stain that would not budge. A marital argument had escalated and resulted in a knifing. Vacancies in apartments like these only came up due to crimes.

"We'll have to replace it. It's going to be expensive because it's bamboo," said the Boss.

But Omari shook his head. He knew these stains, had already seen them a dozen times. He mixed two cleaners, carefully rubbed them into the wood, waited, scoured, repeated the procedure, and subsequently polished the surface with oil. The Boss was very pleased with the result and Omari's concentration. "Better than any crime scene cleanup job," he said. "And cheaper."

Omari nodded. It was a habit he'd picked up.

"Do you need an apartment?" the Boss asked.

Omari would have liked to own an apartment. But living space in Mitte was unaffordable. And what for, anyway? He didn't even have a family, let alone a wife. "Where does this go?" he asked.

"The garbage bags?" the Boss said. "Straight to the dump."

Omari reminded the Boss of an actor from his favorite TV show: a tall black man with pronounced muscularity and a soft gaze. Omari seemed just as young and energetic. The Boss described his own predicament (a depreciated property, Italian, cocaine, withdrawal) and offered Omari two euros above minimum wage. Omari accepted immediately. The Boss told him about the opening hours and handed him his card, the cash box, a down payment on wages, and the keys to the café. "Good luck!" he shouted to him.

Since then, Omari had not heard much from him.

* * *

"A coffee, please."

Omari poured water into one of the ten filters, which were resting on old-fashioned coffee pots in front of him. Omari liked the foam that this produced. But he was still baffled by the effort it took. "Would you like something to eat with that?" He reeled off his standard pitch.

"Just black coffee." The woman looked at him with a frown. Omari noticed by a gap between her incisors. In fact, her teeth were unusually white. She must brush them very well.

"Cream or sugar?" Omari asked uncertainly. The coffee foam sank down into the filter as he watched.

"Black," she repeated as he added water.

Omari watched as she pushed a strand of her fair hair behind her ear. "Nice sweater," he blurted out, distracted by her pretty face.

"Feel it," she said, holding out a corner.

Two patrons waiting in line complained. A few startled pigeons flew up in front of the window. Their movement confused Omari, but he reached his hand over the counter and touched not only the sweater, but also briefly her hand. "Wool?" he asked.

"Yes," she replied.

"Wonderful," he said, then realized that he was still rubbing the material between his fingertips.

She smiled. Later, they drank coffee together.

Two years ago, a courier had handed Thea a bouquet of flowers. It was already noon that day, but not a single customer had yet ventured into her boutique. The cloudy weather outside the store bathed the city in grayness. The bouquet was colorful and summery—in the middle of February. In sweeping handwriting, the card said: *Fancy a latte?* Underneath there was a phone number. Signed, *Best wishes, Ansgar.*

Design Director, Fashion Retail Worldwide, thought Thea. On the counter of her boutique, the bill for many meters of fabric lay there in the flickering neon light. Premium goods from Pakistan. No child labor, no chemicals. Pleasant to work with. Presumably Ansgar had paid for the bouquet with her money. But Thea was overjoyed because she never gave herself flowers. What's more, she had been living alone in the rear building of the apartment on Brunnenstrasse for too long, so she dialed Ansgar's number on the spot.

They agreed to meet in the store of a popular café chain that could be found in every prominent Berlin location. Ansgar was wearing a loose-fitting business suit. Thea immediately noticed his shoes: finest brogues with leather trims. He seemed confident and elegant. His dark hair was impeccably styled. They talked about the fashion industry and the latest prime-time series. Much like Thea, Ansgar preferred television to cinema. She rarely went out. Ansgar behaved like a gentleman toward her and had a certain worldliness. Two days later, they arranged to have dinner in the restaurant of a C-list celebrity TV chef. Next, Thea invited Ansgar to try some slow cooking in her apartment in Brunnenstrasse.

Ansgar looked around, clucked his tongue approvingly, and praised her choice of furniture. After the perfectly cooked salmon, he wanted to sleep with her and had also brought condoms. Thea agreed, although she found Ansgar's pushiness a little jarring. She chalked it up to first-time nerves. They met with increasing regularity, but never at his place. He lived in a hotel because he traveled frequently. In June, he flew to Pakistan for two months. He brought her back a precious scarf made of the finest cashmere.

Thea had to take out a new loan for her boutique, because a crack in the window caused by frost forced her to replace them all with modern ones. Her bank adviser at Berliner Sparkasse grumbled. He urged her to make quick repayments. Meanwhile, the temperature dropped during the cold months. Thea crunched figure after figure, but the pressure still rose.

One muggy day in July, Ansgar suggested to Thea that he move in. Thea hesitated because she had become accustomed to living on her own. And because the apartment belonged to her and was rising in value. This place was her refuge. The only things Thea owned were the apartment and the boutique. On the other hand, she had not taken any risks in her private life for years. People thought her aloof and not very communicative. Two days later, she agreed.

Three months later, on Ansgar's birthday in October, he proposed to her with a hundred red roses. Thea's present— an ultrafluffy white bathrobe made of organic cotton, which delighted Ansgar—was simply trumped by his flamboyant proposal. She hesitated before replying, because she was very happy with her life in her apartment on Brunnenstrasse and all its freedom. Thea did not like making hasty decisions. On the other hand, Ansgar traveled a lot, which meant that it would be good for them to make a commitment. In the meantime, Thea found Ansgar's sexual appetite too much, almost abnormal. It was overwhelming and made her so sore that even creams and lubricants no longer helped. But wasn't a higher sex drive precisely the difference between men and women? And wasn't a relationship all about risking something? Wasn't Ansgar the perfect partner for a woman like her? They shared professional and private interests, as well as tastes in fashion and pop culture. Working in the boutique meant that Thea didn't meet many men. Not one in years, in fact, except those who accompanied their wives on shopping trips. Thea was thirty-nine years old and Ansgar might be a chance in her life that would never come around again.

Every day at six o'clock Omari closed the café for half an hour. It was a time of day when few Berliners wanted to drink coffee anyway. Today, thick flakes of snow were falling outside and settling on the sidewalk. He shut himself in the storeroom, locked the door, and took a bag from the refrigerator, from which he pulled a pigeon's carcass. Using the carving knife that he used to cut the cooked ham into wafer-thin slices for sandwiches, he repeatedly stabbed the body of the dead animal until its feathers flew up all around him. Bloody snow drifted through the air. It wasn't until there were only a few pieces of bone left on the chopping board that he calmed down. Margarete from the charity had warned him that the thirst for death could come back again and again. Many child soldiers suffered what he was going through. For two months now, Omari had felt the old compulsion. When he awoke at night, the horrified eyes of his victims stared at him. The dead gathered to torment him. His subconscious had gone haywire, not able leave the past alone. Omari missed Margarete and all the others whose lives were far removed from normality. But in the Congo, there was no future for him. The girls all looked past him because they were afraid. It was impossible to find work in Goma. Former child soldiers were considered unpredictable. No one trusted him. Omari was tempted to flee his country; in fact, it became an obsession. An uncertain future did not scare him in the least. He'd already been through every imaginable atrocity. He had become cruel.

From a cabinet, he took cleaning materials, detergent, and bleach. Tomorrow, he would meet the Boss. Once a month,

Omari settled his accounts with him. The Boss appreciated Omari and trusted him fully. With the expertise of a professional cleaner, he eliminated every trace of his fit of rage.

Ansgar waited for Thea to come home, very aroused. As soon as she stepped through the door, he began caressing her. She barely had time to put down her bag before he started undressing her. Thea wanted to tell him that she had found an animal carcass in the trash behind the boutique, but Ansgar's sexual appetite left no room for conversation. After intercourse, he demanded that Thea cook for him. Thea could barely walk without pain. When she asked him for help, he insisted that he liked to watch her as she cooked. There was no beer in the fridge, so Ansgar sent Thea to the supermarket. He said he would clear the table and wash the dishes. When she came back, though, he had fallen asleep in front of the TV so she was left to do it herself.

Later, when she was sewing or sorting her papers, he called out to her. He whispered sweet nothings in her ear as soon as they were lying in bed together. Thea had to get up early, whereas Ansgar always made his appointments in the late morning. "The fashion business," he said sarcastically. He kissed Thea and reminded her what shopping needed to be done by the evening.

Omari barely took notice of the visitors to his coffee shop. He served them politely and efficiently but avoided any close contact. His filter coffee was good, and so was the service. The bills were always spot on, down to the last cent. The Boss said that Omari was his most capable man. Omari stood outside the door on his breaks watching Thea in her boutique. When she sewed or dressed the shop window, he took in every detail. In the summer, she left the door open, and Omari could hear her humming. He saw the tension in her face when business was light; her concentration while she was sewing; her delight when she sold something. He knew she preferred sleeveless tops and didn't wear turtlenecks in winter. He knew her favorite shoes and the exact time she closed up the store. When Thea redressed the window dummies, he offered to help. They seemed heavy and bulky to handle. At first Thea hesitated, but then she accepted his offer. So they sat among piles of arms and legs and unscrewed heads. Pigeons fluttered down in front of the shop window. Omari forced himself not to look at them.

Ansgar raped Thea for the first time on a public holiday. They both had a day off on the Day of German Unity, and Ansgar celebrated it after dinner (slow food, roast pork) by dragging Thea by the hair from the dining table to the floor where he tore open her new blouse (a silk-cotton mix). When Thea screamed, he put his hand over her mouth until she thought she would choke on her own spit. When he heaved himself off her, he slapped her bare thigh and called her a nice piece of ass. With difficulty, Thea pulled up her pants and dragged herself into the bathroom. Ansgar grabbed a bottle of beer from the fridge, then turned on the TV and tuned in to his favorite show. He took another bottle of beer from the fridge. Thea washed the blood from the corner of her mouth and later from her between her legs. Dark bruises appeared on her arms. When she tried to leave the apartment, Ansgar just slowly shook his head. Thea crept back into the bedroom. She sat down on the bed and waited. A little later Ansgar lay down next to her. He stroked her, although Thea flinched at his touch. Soon, he started snoring while Thea tried to stop trembling.

* * *

Four months after their civil wedding ceremony (he wore Lagerfeld, she wore Nebelkind), to which no guests came because neither had close friends, Ansgar had already started raping Thea on a regular basis. Once Thea tried to press charges. But just before she reached the police station, which was not far from her apartment, Ansgar had intercepted her. He escorted her home in the pouring rain, where he beat and kicked her. He took away her apartment keys and threatened to kill her—at any moment, just because he could, just because he felt like it. Afterward he demonstratively ate a banana while Thea tried in vain several times to get up from the floor.

Meanwhile, Thea's debts increased because she had to close her store more frequently and because she still had to accept fabrics from Ansgar, whose prices seemed to rise steadily. Thea was his best customer—he made sure of that. He ripped up letters from the bank as soon as they arrived. Since Thea had started paying his way too, he had given up traveling. She was only allowed to enter her apartment when he let her. He made her cook, shop, and clean, and penetrated her whenever he felt like it.

When Omari waved to Thea from the coffee shop, Thea hardly ever waved back. When he visited her in the boutique, she made excuses for her black eye. Omari listened, nodded, and didn't believe a word. If Thea begged him to leave, he rose to his feet only slowly. One Wednesday, he asked Thea whether she would like to go to an exhibition with him. Outside, the wind was rattling the shop windows, and leaves were blowing about. Thea said she was more of a TV person. Although that was no longer the case, since Ansgar now commandeered her television as well. Omari asked her again one Thursday and the following Friday too. One Monday, when the wind had died down, and a few leaves lay scattered on the ground like victims of a crime, Thea agreed.

In the Martin-Gropius-Bau, there were three exhibitions going on at the same time: a tribute to a pop star who had died all alone in a hotel room, a happening by a Canadian artist who shot holograms with paint capsules, and a presentation about international fashion. Thea was nervous because she wasn't working in the store. She was afraid Ansgar would check up on her. But Omari paid for both of them and carried her padded jacket. He smiled and Thea felt calmed by his presence. She admired a German designer's haute couture, which was currently making a splash in Paris, then the charcoal drawings of the young Coco Chanel. In a separate room, a documentary film was being screened. Thea was drawn in by the absolute darkness. Omari sat down next to her, his presence no more than a shadow. Piles of clothes in Bangladesh and Pakistan passed before their eyes, seamstresses who worked day and night on outdated machines. Workers with scarred faces, victims of a factory explosion. Other young women stirred barrels of the tinted poison that they used to dye fabrics. They gossiped and laughed, as if oblivious to it. Images of women with skin rashes, open wounds, people with respiratory problems, and babies with disabilities. At some point, Omari took Thea's hand. Thea could not tear herself away from the film. Then at one point, she jumped up. A trader was shown buying fabrics from the women for a paltry sum. After that, chain stores flickered across the screen, with laughing customers who paid absurdly small amounts of money for shopping bags stuffed with clothes. At the end, the credits showed the names of international firms who made a living by exploiting others. In the flickering, dim light, Thea tore off her sweater and ran out. Omari followed her. He didn't understand what was going on. She didn't want to wear her jacket anymore, although Berlin was chilly that day. In front of the museum, she stuffed all her clothes into a garbage can. But she accepted Omari's old coat from the charity storeroom, as well as his effort to put it around her shoulders. At the subway they parted ways. Omari offered his help, though he did not know exactly what for. Thea nodded. Omari wrote down his cell phone number. What she didn't tell him was that she had just witnessed a crime.

The next morning, Thea was brushing her teeth in the bathroom. Ansgar was standing in the doorway in his white bathrobe demanding that she leave her apartment. Forever, on the spot. His breath smelled of alcohol, which explained why Thea had found him asleep on the sofa the evening before. Ansgar had discovered the day before that she had not been in the boutique and said he would not tolerate that kind of behavior.

"Do you want to fuck me?" Thea heard herself ask him. White foam quivered on her lips. She was shaking. Slowly, she pulled the head off her electric toothbrush.

Ansgar just watched her. One of her nightgown straps slipped off her shoulder. Ansgar's silence and his heavy breathing signaled that he was about to hit her. Thea had recognized him immediately in the film, although he was hard to make out and only visible from the side. But those were his fine, leather-trimmed brogues, no mistake. Thea would have recognized them anywhere. At that very moment more than ever, she understood the way he corrupted the lives of all the people he met, from top to bottom. When Ansgar lunged for her, Thea lashed out faster. She stabbed him repeatedly with the electric toothbrush until her arm hurt. By then, Ansgar was no longer moving. Her trembling slowly subsided and then she felt quite at peace. Thea was only sorry about the bathrobe.

When Omari entered Thea's apartment, he was surprised by the huge package in the hallway. Thea, a serious expression on her face, invited him to look around her place.

"May I?" he said.

Thea allowed him to shove the package aside.

Omari went from room to room, carefully examining the bathroom in particular for a very long time. He had often seen red smudges like these. Omari thought things over, and Thea watched him in silence. He knew how to clean rooms. An hour later he came back with the right materials.

"It has to be spotless," Thea said, because she loved her apartment.

Together, she and Omari scrubbed the bathroom.

"And that?" Omari asked, pointing to the electric toothbrush.

"I want to keep it," Thea said.

"Better not." Omari shook his head. He leaned against the edge of the tub and made a call. The Boss had a new construction site, and Omari knew the location.

"Perhaps you should know," said Thea, "that I'm pregnant."

"Ah," said Omari.

Afterward they sat down at the dining table and drank black coffee in silence.

For Fashion Week, Thea had renamed her store Showroom. A shooting star from the Czech Republic presented his new collection, which he called "Sale." It consisted of candy-colored plastic pants made of recycled, ecologically certified bike tires. Two window dummies wore designs from Pakistan, rich fabrics in muted colors. Thea's store had never been so full of visitors. The breath of her guests condensed on the glass of the newly installed windows. The Berlin press crowded at the entrance to take photos of German *Vogue's* editor, Sandra Mutterkorn. A city magazine did interviews. Techno pumped out of the speakers.

Thea smiled as she crumpled up the bailiff's letter behind her back. The visitors gathered in groups in front of the store, because there was barely room for any more inside. Thea's financial adviser from the Berliner Sparkasse rapped on the shop window until he got her attention. Thea wiped a hole in the condensation with her sleeve and the consultant pressed a letter to the glass. Thea read the words *foreclosure, sureties, apartment,* and *Brunnenstrasse.* The writing was slightly blurred by the moisture. On the street, pigeons pecked at the crumbs left from the buffet. She nodded pleasantly to her adviser before turning back to the buzz in her boutique. People Thea had never met before patted her on the shoulder and praised her commitment. A man offered her sums that she could have only dreamed of several months ago. Someone issued her a cash check that Thea accepted, although it was too late for that. A fashion legend with peroxide-blond hair, whose name Thea could no longer remember, congratulated her on the event. The legend's lapdog was called Lucky; that much Thea could remember. Sandra Mutterkorn elbowed her way over to Thea and asked if she too had noticed the smell. Thea raised her eyebrows and shook her head. No, everything smelled quite normal to her.

But that evening, Ansgar's body collapsed and slid off the chair that he was draped over in the shop window. The fine goods from Pakistan suited him very well. Ansgar would make an excellent front page.

Omari stood in front of the boutique and shivered. Leaves skipped in eddies across the sidewalk. He watched the commotion, guessing that Thea was right at the center. The screams only dimly reached him. People ran past him.

A pigeon fluttered to his feet and pecked at a piece of paper. Omari scared the bird away and grabbed the paper before a gust of wind could carry it off. He briefly skimmed the content. Carefully, he folded the letter from the Berliner Sparkasse and put it into his pocket. When he heard the police siren in the distance, he turned away. Tomorrow, the Boss would come to collect the monthly take. Quietly, Omari went back into the coffee shop, where the filter coffee was getting cold. But halfway, he turned around again and stood there, thinking. The pigeon was still there.

ONE OF THESE DAYS

BY ROBERT RESCUE

Wedding

"Are you even listening to me, Robert?"

The man in front of me had already had a few. With one hand he was clutching a beer bottle, and with the other he was holding on to the bar. I had to be nice to him because he was the owner of the place.

"Of course, Edgar. I'm all ears."

Edgar was from Wedding, and a little rough around the edges. People in the Bar said that he still lived out of the moving boxes that he hadn't unpacked since 1983. Signing contracts was not his thing; he had more respect for a hearty handshake. He used to own a hauler company, so some said, but others claimed he'd made his money in the red-light district. I once googled him and found out that he had worked as a police reporter for one of the sleaziest tabloid newspapers in Berlin.

"When Wedding was still red, full of Social Democrats and Communists, that was quite something, you know. Every day Nazis drove up in their trucks and tried to intimidate people, but the locals showed them. My father was always getting into brawls and beat up Nazis a bunch of times. After the war, the French soldiers stayed. He started fights with them too when they went on the rampage in his bar. He didn't care that they were our protectors keeping the Russians out of West Berlin. You should handle with things the way he did, believe me, it earned him respect. If anyone's giving you hassle, smash him right in the face. When my father fell down the stairs drunk in 1983 and broke his neck, I moved here from Schöneberg. I was working for the newspaper, and I can tell you, there was a lot going on. Murder and homicide on every corner. I remember a case right here in this building. A son killed his mother and hid the body for four weeks. Then he wanted to bury her in Schiller Park and they caught him. But after the Wall fell, there was peace. For about fifteen years, I guess. Well, now and then a dog got run over, a bank got robbed, or a person got killed. But that was about it. Until a few years ago. Then the place burst into life, in the truest sense. If no one's interested in you, you can lead a quiet life, but when people start turning up for the fancy apartments, you get a lot of lowlifes, believe me. If I was still writing for the newspaper, I think I'd be on the road all day, from dusk till dawn. Stabbings, robberies, and murder, the whole shebang. Just like the old days."

Edgar paused and took a sip of his drink. As he did, he leaned back. I was poised, ready to make a dive for him if he fell off his stool. But he had a grip on himself. For a moment he looked thoughtfully out the window. Then he turned back to me. "And the flashiness of the houses. Don't think much of it. Everything here used to be a different shade of gray. For decades. Didn't bother anyone. And now suddenly everything's blue and red or piss-yellow. And some assholes get rich on high rents, and people who can't afford them have to move away. I earn money on rent, and it's enough for me to live off."

Edgar took another sip. Then he looked at me with a serious expression. "What will happen when I'm gone, Robert? I mean, to the house. It'll go to my daughter in Charlottenburg. And me and her have a different way of thinking."

"You'll be around for a while longer," I said. "And even if it all gets fancy around here, Liebenwalder Strasse 33 and the

Bar will stay just the way they were twenty years ago. We don't have the money for renovations and high rent."

Edgar simply nodded. Then he took his beer and stood up, lurching forward in the direction of the sofa. He sat down, leaned back, and fell asleep shortly afterward. Edgar and I were the last people in the Bar. I sat on my stool, lit a cigarette, and had a think.

It had been quite a few years now since artists had started moving to this poor multicultural district in north Berlin, selling their heating-duct sculptures and paint-splattered canvases on the sidewalk. Speculators—who bought up the art studios, ousted the artists, and threw their extravagant art into containers—thought this was great. Wedding was turning hip. Old stores like the umbrella shop and the music shack, whose inventory probably dated back to 1980, shut down. New stores opened that sold things the locals had never heard of: smoothies, vegan draft beer, and liquor bottled and sealed in jam jars.

Students moved to Wedding but the dream of having their own digs at a reasonable price was long gone. Either they rented a twenty-five-square-meter box for six hundred euros a month or their parents bought some fleapit for a hundred thousand straight off. Those looking for room in an apartment had to be vegan, nonsmokers, outgoing, and female. For all others, or people with vices, speed-roommating in the hottest hipster bar was the only remaining option, and whoever failed the test was forced to return to some outback town and abandon the dream of studying, social climbing, and high life in the capital.

It was thanks to Edgar that the Bar even existed. Anyone who had lived through the past ten years shared his views on gentrification and speculation. There was no speed-roommating or schnapps in jam jars. And no ping-pong table

either. In the back room, which most referred to as the "salon," except one who in ignorance of room sizes called it the
"hall," there was a dartboard; but it was out of use because the
darts had been lost and no one had gotten around to buying
new ones. The house beer bore the dubious name of Pilsator,
cost an unbeatable one euro fifty, and was drunk by all those
who put alcohol content before taste. If you needed to line
your stomach, there were peanuts and pretzel sticks. The joint
had no employees; its supporters were a collective and they all
worked on a voluntary basis.

It was a shabby place, a former butcher's shop, of which
the eye-catching blue-and-white art nouveau tiles remained
on the floor and walls of the front room. The furniture was
old and worn, the toilets uninviting, and the mold creeping
around the walls clung uncomfortably to your clothes after
you'd been in the room for just five minutes. The homemade
stage in the salon groaned under the footsteps of comedians and
bands whose audiences were sometimes big, sometimes small.

The regulars were usually nonconformists who felt that
the atmosphere matched their lifestyles; or people interested
in tiles; or people who loved the name, the simplicity of which
they regarded as an inspired, creative feat until they found
out from the bartender that it was due to lack of inspiration.
Many years ago, the founders of the Bar hadn't been able to
agree on a name, despite the limited range they had come up
with: the dreary Drinking Den, the arcane Basalt, and the
stripped-down Music Café. So they had done well to stick to
a description of what the place really was.

I'd been part of it for five years and was responsible for
the finances. I also took care of the hard liquor. Once a week
I went to the supermarket and spent most of my money on
whiskey, gin, and rum, and a little on pretzel sticks, peanuts,

and cleaning supplies. It was embarrassing because the cashiers probably thought I was a drunk who flushed down the peanuts with the alcohol and wiped up the mess with the cleaning fluid afterward. It was mostly me who used the cleaning products when I was on bar shift, because I was the only one who prized cleanliness.

Cleanliness was in fact my middle name. When there weren't any customers, I cleaned.

Just then, Frederik, Fauser, and Kuba, three of my fellow bartenders, entered the joint. "Edgar didn't make it upstairs again?" asked Fauser, amused.

"I'll wake him up later," I replied. "By then he should be sober enough to manage the stairs."

The three lined up at the bar, and I handed them each a Pilsator. Fauser took out his smartphone and wrote messages, and Frederik and Kuba continued a conversation about their plans to attend a festival in Poland soon. I went to the broom closet and took out the cleaning supplies. My goal was the freezer in the back of the storeroom. It was connected to the power supply, although it wasn't being used at the moment. When the ice machine broke down in the heat of the summer, I fetched ice cubes from the supermarket, reinforcing the cashiers' impression that I was a drunk, and stored them in the freezer. Although the ice machine was still running for the time being, we left the freezer permanently on. Food had once been stored in it for a party but the remains had been left inside and then forgotten. However, someone had managed to turn off the freezer shortly afterward. We had to draw straws at that time to decide who was going to clean up the mess. Since then the freezer had given off a hellish stink that was only halfway tolerable when it was switched on. Now seemed to me like a suitable moment to go at it with the cleaning fluid and, if I was lucky, solve the problem. When I entered the storeroom and went over to the corner where the freezer stood, I saw that the boxes of wine bottles that were normally stored on top of it had been put on the floor. That was strange. I went back out to the front and asked the boys.

"No idea," said Fauser, looking up from his smartphone. "Someone probably had the same idea as you but gave up after moving the boxes."

"Maybe it was you, Robert?" said Frederik. "On your first attempt. Maybe you've just forgotten?"

I didn't rise to his jibe. Our relationship wasn't exactly the best. We'd had a fight recently, because he had kicked up a fuss with Lisa, the neighbor who lived over the bar, which was not conducive to community relations. Frederik was a failed local politician who had turned Wedding and its issues into his cause. He had stood as a candidate at the last House of Representatives election but hadn't earned the required majority. Since then he'd been involved in the Bar, but only until the next election and his victory. After that he'd be too busy.

"It wasn't me," said Kuba. He had Polish roots—his name was actually Jakub, but no one wanted to call him that, hence the nickname. "But I wish you every success." He wasn't being sincere; that was just his way of being polite.

I went back into the storeroom, resenting not for the first time the others' indifference to keeping the place clean.

I opened the lid of the freezer.

Benno was lying inside.

Startled, I dropped the lid. It banged shut. What was going on? Benno, the Bar's hard-core stoner. In the freezer. But could it be that my senses were playing tricks on me? I hadn't slept much the night before.

I propped myself on the lid with both hands, still holding

the cloth in my left hand, and mulled things over. I could go back out to the front and convince myself that I'd imagined it. But that wouldn't work. As if in slow motion, I lifted the lid again. This was really happening. That was Benno.

He was squatting in the freezer, his hands resting in his lap, as if partaking in one of those crouched burials from the Stone Age that I'd recently seen in a documentary. *Maybe he's asleep?* I thought. He could have lain down in there half an hour ago, feeling tired. But I hadn't seen him in the Bar all evening. I leaned over, felt his upper body, then shook him. No, Benno wasn't asleep. I straightened up and carefully closed the lid, like I was scared of waking him up somehow.

As I hurried out to the front, two thoughts crossed my mind. For one thing, I was annoyed that I'd come up with the idea of cleaning the freezer. If for whatever reason someone else had opened the freezer, then *that* person would now have sleepless nights ahead. Secondly, I wondered what the consequences would be.

"Does anyone know what's up with Benno?" I asked when I was back behind the counter. Joe and Tanja had shown up. With Joe's arrival, all the active members of the Bar's staff were present. Tanja, his girlfriend, had pulled out a year ago because the place was too chaotic for her, but she often dropped in, picked up on what was going on, and got annoyed, which is why she kept on saying that she would be avoiding the place in the future. But because she wanted to spend as much time as she could with Joe, she always ended up sitting at the bar anyway.

"Since his girlfriend left him, he's been keeping a low profile," said Frederik. "A break from social life, he texted me. He was here for a while last Saturday. He went into the hall and after that I didn't see him again. Why do you ask?"

"Last Saturday, huh?" Being frozen had prevented Benno from being discovered on olfactory grounds, or else the smell of rotten food from the freezer had masked everything else. "And his girlfriend hasn't shown up since?" I said. "Has she called anyone and asked what's up with Benno?"

"No," answered Fauser. "But that's how it is with breakups—you don't see each other for a while, right?"

This was a typical Fauser question. He knew nothing about breakups. No one had ever seen him with a girl- or boy-friend. No one had ever talked to him about it, not even in a drunken stupor. Everyone assumed that he was asexual.

"Why are you asking about Benno?" Frederik said. I looked around. No guests, and Edgar was asleep.

"Because he's in the back lying in the freezer. Dead. Well, lying in the sense of crouching. Like in the Stone Age."

Joe choked on his beer and spluttered. Fauser put his smartphone down on the bar and looked at me in confusion. It was Kuba who was the first to respond. He set down his beer bottle and went out the back. No one followed him. A short time later he came back. "Robert's right," is all he said. Then Frederik, Fauser, and Joe got up and went out back.

"Benno's not allowed in the storeroom," Tanja complained. "He's not an active member. He's a nice space cookie, but he's not allowed out back." She lit a cigarette and dragged on it violently several times. Then she shook her head repeatedly, mumbling something about a "pigsty."

Tanja had a problem with change. She didn't want to accept that the Bar was changing too. She wanted it like it was five years ago, when things had been run better overall. Sometimes we talked to her about it and tried to make it clear that the Bar would never be the same again, but her persistent refusal to acknowledge this bordered on the pathological.

When Joe worked behind the counter, she helped him and droned on all evening about the good old days.

"Neither Frederik nor anyone else could have known he went into the storeroom," I said, getting annoyed with myself as I spoke. There was no point in having this conversation with Tanja.

"Then the person on shift should have checked," Tanja griped. "The beer store is out back too. People help themselves and don't pay. When I still worked here, that never happened. I always made sure that no unauthorized people went into the storeroom. And now they're even allowed to head out back and kill themselves. This place is really going to the dogs."

Frederik, Fauser, and Joe came back in again. Fauser heaved himself up on the barstool. "Goddammit! Last week, the toilet wasn't flushing, Lisa was moaning about the noise, and now there's a corpse. Can't a week go by without some kind of problem?" He gestured with the beer bottle in his hand and then brought it back down on the counter hard. The beer started to foam and overflowed. "Shit, fucking shit!" he yelled.

Joe tried to roll a cigarette. It took him three attempts before he managed to come up with something that looked vaguely like a ciggy. He fumbled to light it. "Wow," he said, evidently summing up his reaction to the discovery. He was a nerd who spent all day designing websites. His was an orderly world of bits and bytes. He only knew corpses from first-person shooters, and they weren't real. He reached for his beer. His hand was shaking. He raised his other hand and pointed to the door. "Should I lock up the front?" he asked. "Because of Benno, I mean. Well, not exactly because of Benno. I dunno."

"No, that would attract more attention," Frederik replied. "If anyone shows up, they'll ask why we're closed."

"The question is, what are we going to do now?" Kuba piped up.

"We found this in the freezer," Frederik said, unfolding a note. "Written on a computer." He put it on the counter and each of us in turn leaned over and read:

> *Howdy, howdy, friendz of the beloved Bar,*
>   *I no its no good wot I done.*
>   *It meenz Ill go to hell and burn. Peeple hoo cummit sooeyside go to hell. But Cora woz so great to me. She tuk me as I am. But then she didnt wont me anymore. Eazy come eazy go. We wuz both happy here and I thought I was gonna dye here and when she cums she can think of me. Jeses save me!*
>
> *Big sorry!*
> *Benno*

That was Benno, no doubt about it. His dope consumption was remarkable. His first joint of the day was in the morning after getting up, and his last was right before going to bed. By his own admission, he had been permanently stoned for seven years, and the effects of it were visible to everyone. His concentration was shot to pieces and he suffered from mood swings. When he talked, you had to listen carefully to understand what he meant, and occasionally interpret it so it made any sense. He himself didn't seem bothered. He claimed that he felt better than during his pre-hashish period.

"So we're off the hook," said Kuba. "We had nothing to do with it. Pity about Benno, I liked him. But there's still the question: what do we do now?"

"Easy, we call the police," said Fauser. "He's killed himself, no idea, perhaps with pills, and wrote a farewell note. Like Kuba said, we're off the hook."

"But it'll have consequences," I said. "The police will close the Bar, possibly for a few days. We can't afford it. How am I supposed to cover the rent or electricity at the end of the month? A night like tonight blows out the whole budget, and it's not our first bad evening this month. Tomorrow is stand-up comedy night. That brings in good money, as does the weekend. We can't close."

"You don't want to notify the police?" yelled Fauser. "And you're using money as a reason? I mean, that's fishy, right? Did you bump him off or what?"

He can't be serious, I thought. *He's just blown a fuse.*

"Hold on a minute." I leaned over the counter and pointed a finger at Fauser. "Everything was fine between Benno and me, okay? I may not have been his best buddy, but we were cool. You yourself said it was suicide. I just came up with a spontaneous solution to this dilemma from a financial point of view, which I am responsible for."

"I don't understand why Benno had to kill himself here," Tanja interjected. "Why couldn't he have done it at home, in the park, on a bridge, or in the subway? Plenty of people throw themselves in front of trains. No one kills himself in a bar. Now we have all this trouble, just because of him."

Tanja's objection wasn't very helpful, I found, and I wasn't the only one who thought so.

"I agree with Robert," said Frederik. "If the police show up, there'll be problems. The labor inspector might come here too and go over the place with a fine-tooth comb. Then we'll lose customers because people will think it's creepy that someone died in here."

"So?" Fauser argued back. "The dust will settle after a

while, and in the meantime, we'll just do without the fucking money, or one of us can advance the cash for rent and electricity. And the thing about the labor inspector is just speculation."

"Perhaps I haven't made myself clear," said Frederik. "I meant to say that blowing the lid on this business will damage me personally. You know I lost the last election for the Berlin House of Representatives by a narrow margin. If it gets out that someone killed himself in a bar where I volunteer, it'll ruin my reputation. I don't need news like that. Then I'll have already lost the next election. The campaign starts in three months, and the public won't have forgotten it by then."

"And that means?" Kuba now asked. Like everyone else, he knew what that meant, but he wanted to hear it from Frederik.

"We leave things just as they are. We keep looking for a solution. But for now, it'll remain a secret between us. Until one of these days. Well, the day when we know how to proceed."

"If someone finds out, we'll be in big trouble," Fauser cried out. "Because of a cover-up or something. The police will definitely think we had something to do with it."

"If that happens," said Frederik, "then let's just say we didn't know. We'll pretend that anything they find is a shock for us too. Until then, we'll imagine that Robert didn't open the freezer and we'll presume it's empty and smells bad."

Fauser went over to the front door and locked it.

Tanya weighed in again: "What if the ice machine breaks down and we have to store ice cubes somewhere?"

"Then Robert will just put the ice cube bags on top of Benno after his shopping trip," Frederik explained. "Very easy."

I swallowed.

"But if I do a shift with Joe, I'm not getting them out," Tanja said. "I can tell you that right away."

"Why don't we just clean up Benno's body?" Kuba suggested.

"How? And put it where?" Joe asked.

"In movies, they always do it with a carpet," Tanja said. "We used to have a long one lying in the salon. Where is it, actually?"

"We threw it away during the last major cleanup because it was so filthy," I replied.

"I have one at home and I could go get it." Frederik was excited, as if he'd found a solution to the problem. "We can put him in the dumpster after it's been emptied and throw a few garbage bags on top. Then we'll be rid of him."

"That's not going to help," I said. "If we get Benno out of the freezer, he'll start to smell—and a lot differently from garbage. Some neighbor will notice and inform the property manager or the police."

"But then we can just pretend we don't have a clue." Frederik's repeated suggestion to pretend not to know anything was starting to bug me. None of us would be able to keep up such a pretense at a cross-examination, except him, perhaps. "I mean, we're a bar. If someone drops down dead in here, then of course we'd inform the police. They'll think the dead guy's a tenant."

"If the police find out that Benno was a regular here, we'll get busted," said Joe. "And if they find him rolled up in the dumpster, they won't believe he killed himself."

"What about the suicide note?" Kuba said. "It proves that Benno committed suicide, and if they do an autopsy, they'll find out that it was an overdose."

"I don't think it's worth much as evidence," said Frederik. "As I said, it was written on a computer and isn't signed. I don't know whether it can be proven for sure that he killed himself. Someone could have strangled him or given him tablets. Damn it, we don't even know *how* he died!"

For a moment there was silence. Everyone was thinking. For my part, I was ready to agree with Fauser's suggestion. It seemed to be the simplest: we could call the police right now, and in two or three hours the situation would hopefully look a lot better.

"We could carry the carpet up to Schiller Park in the dead of night and drop him there," Tanja said.

"Someone would see us," Kuba countered. "There are always cars on the road, or partygoers. We're not in the country. Two or three people carrying a rug at night looks suspicious even in Wedding."

Edgar and the murder case here in the building went through my mind.

"We could dismember him," Joe said. "Like, piece by piece. Then carry the parts at night out to Schiller Park and bury them. A piece a week."

"Okay," said Frederik, "that's how we'll do it. Will you take care of it?"

"I was only making a suggestion," Joe responded, raising his hands defensively. "I don't know how to do it. We could ask Inga. She's a trained nurse. She'll know for sure."

Frederik's fist landed on the counter. "No way are we going to let someone outside this group in on this. No regulars or their groupies, and certainly not anyone who might, possibly or probably, know how to dismember a corpse!"

Suddenly everyone grabbed their beer and knocked it back. Joe belched loudly, which got him a stern look from Tanja. I brought six new cans from the refrigerator.

"What about a body bag?" said Kuba. "They are definitely

sealed against odors. His parts could be disposed of in a body bag in the dumpster."

"You don't just come across them in supermarkets," I said. "Probably on eBay or Amazon. But what if these things are checked or you have to prove you're a funeral director? And a body bag is certainly more prominent in a dumpster than a carpet."

"None of these ideas help," Fauser said. "We should just call the police. We've got nothing to be afraid of, period! If the place stays shut for a few days, it stays shut. Robert, is it really not possible?"

I sighed. "All right, if that's the way it's got to be. But no longer than a week. Let's just hope business picks up afterward. I'm worried that the reserves won't make up for lost revenue."

Fauser, Joe, Tanja, and Kuba nodded at me.

"We're not going to do that," Frederik said, scanning across each of us. "Or do you really want to destroy my career?"

No one answered him.

Half an hour later I was alone again with Edgar. I went over and woke him up. "Boy oh boy," he said. "I thought I was at home in bed. So comfy here on the couch."

"No problem."

"Anything happen? Did anyone wonder who that bum was lying around snoring?"

"No, no one came. It's been a quiet evening."

At the Bar, decisions took awhile to be made or put into action. The plan to purchase a ventilation system for the mold problem took five years. In that time, a "project group" consisting of Joe and Kuba was set up to examine the issue, but they did nothing for four years, not even managing to meet or discuss anything. It was thanks to Frederik, who looked into funding possibilities, that at least part of the money was collected. I scraped together the rest from the reserves that—disciplined treasurer that I was—I had put aside but hadn't actually intended to spend, at least not to that extent. Yet the mold problem did not disappear with the ventilation system; at most, it was kept from spreading. That was my opinion, but the others had a different one. There were countless other examples of decisions that were discussed but never carried out. With Benno, however, it was different.

The next evening, turnover was very good. The Anglo-American stand-up comedians did their weekly show and brought a bunch of people who were in the mood to drink. But the mood among the team members was tense. While the comedians were having their after-show party in the salon, I collected a new case of beer from the storeroom and hurried back behind the counter.

Fauser continued to insist that we inform the police, saying he wouldn't take any shifts and would stay away from the Bar for the time being. Kuba and Joe declared that until further notice, they would only turn up for their shifts. Tanja no longer wanted to come, which we would have welcomed under different circumstances.

Two days later, on Saturday, the matter escalated in a way which we all should have expected. It was a lousy evening, especially for Joe, who was on shift. No guests until eleven o'clock—but then Benno's girlfriend showed up.

Joe texted for help: *Benno's girlfriend is asking about him. She's worried coz she got a letter from him. He wrote that he's gonna end his life in a place they both know. What should I do? Help!*

No one wanted to have anything to do with it, so we all just gave Joe advice.

Frederik: *Don't tell her the truth on any account. The thing with her and the suicide letter is alarming.*

Tanja: *Sweetie, just say you don't know anything.*

Kuba: *You have to lie to her. You'll do a good job of it, I'm sure. Tell her we haven't seen him in days and that we're sad about it.*

Robert: *Show concern! And make it clear that the Bar is with her and we all hope that they get back together again. Good luck!*

It took Joe an hour to answer: *I managed to shake her off. She's really down. Says she can't stop thinking about him mentioning a place they both know. Convinced he means the Bar. Even showed her around and said it can't be true, Benno must have meant a different place. What should we do now?*

He got no reply. But everyone was secretly wondering what would happen if she came back and became more insistent or even asked the police to investigate Benno's letter.

Four days later, I was in the Bar again in the evening, mainly to pick up the money from the weekend. On Sundays and Mondays, the place is closed. That Tuesday, I had shopped at the supermarket and taken out the empties.

"Has Benno's girlfriend been here again?" I asked Kuba, who was standing behind the counter.

"No. Maybe Joe managed to convince her that Benno didn't mean the Bar. But maybe she's not that sad about him after all and is busy doing something else."

"Maybe she went to her parents' place to get away from it all," said Frederik, who had just come back from the bathroom. "She hasn't been in touch again. I'm friends with her on Facebook, but she hasn't written anything. She's bound to turn up again at some point."

I considered all of this. Kuba's view didn't sound plausible. I had talked to Benno's girlfriend a couple of times and she didn't seem insensitive, so I didn't think she'd brush aside Benno's disappearance like a lost pack of cigarettes or a hair clip. Frederik's view seemed likely if you assumed she wasn't a Berliner. But it appeared that I knew something he didn't. She'd told me that she came from Friedrichshain. It may well be that she had gone to see her parents for some comfort, but that was hardly far enough to be able to forget about Benno. And why, on top of that, would she have given up or taken a break from her search? If she didn't know what to do next, she might have at least contacted the police. I took a deep breath. Had she been here last night? She surely knew that she wasn't likely to bump into anyone during the day. Whose shift had it been yesterday? She must have been here last night. If only to ask whether Benno had shown up or if he'd been in touch with one of us.

"Whose shift was it yesterday?" I asked.

"Mine," said Frederick.

"Was it busy?"

"No, there wasn't much going on. Joe stopped in at around midnight. The cheap beer probably lured him here, despite everything. But today, it's a whole different story. There's a big group in the hall. A birthday, I guess. Here out front, though, it's just a gaping void."

"Okay," I said to Kuba and Frederik, "you're probably both right. We won't have any trouble for the time being, and if Kuba's right too, she might never come back again. Even if it doesn't solve the crux of the problem, we'll manage somehow."

I got up from the counter and turned to Frederik. "Are the takings in the hiding place out back?"

He nodded.

"I'll just collect them then drink up. Feeling a bit under the weather today."

I had to carve a path through the throng of people having a party in the salon. First I went to the hiding place in the far back of the former office, which was now just a storage room mostly for broken things. On one shelf there was a bunch of CDs, including Santana's album *Welcome* from 1973. A strangely inviting title for the hiding place where Frederik deposited the money. Then I went back into the storeroom and stopped in front of the freezer. *She must have been here last night,* I thought again. It had been Frederik's shift.

The thing with her and the suicide letter is alarming, he'd texted.

Alarming, I thought. What a strange word to describe the current situation. As if Benno's girlfriend were a threat. I shook my head and tried to think of something else. I should go out front, say goodbye, and head home. But something wouldn't stop nagging me.

Slowly I put my hand on the lid.

"What are you doing?" I heard from behind me.

I turned around.

Frederik.

My hand moved away from the lid.

"I wanted to see whether our problem had disappeared into thin air."

"I'm afraid not," Frederik said.

"What makes you so sure?" I asked. "I mean, perhaps—"

"I get your wishful thinking, Robert. We all feel the same way. But you yourself know that these kinds of problems don't just disappear. And as I said, this secret stays in the Bar. Everyone is in on it and no one can opt out because we're a community. Or do you want to quit and make trouble?"

"No, no," I said, moving toward him. "She's was here again, right? Yesterday?"

"Monday. Monday afternoon," said Frederik. "I was here to sort the crates in the storeroom."

"And what happened?"

"Nothing happened," he said.

I looked at the freezer again. Frederik had probably told her there was no news. Then she'd left again. Just like that. The idea was comforting, and that was something. Why should I bother myself with another problem?

I went out front with Frederik and drank up my beer. Then I ordered another one. I drank for long enough to believe that everything really was all right.

For four weeks, nothing happened. The team members dropped their concerns and started coming back to the Bar because the beer was cheap and alcohol makes people forget. At the counter no one spoke about Benno and his girlfriend anymore; it was sometimes difficult when one of the regulars asked. Although we were clumsy at first, the lies soon flew off our tongues with ease.

Then Thursday night came around, stand-up night. It was Fauser's shift and also his birthday. As always, it was a lively evening with good revenue. Two of the comedians stayed after the show in the storeroom and got so sozzled that one felt sick and had to vomit. The freezer seemed a suitable place to relieve himself. He simply pushed the wine boxes off. But I suspect that what he saw then really turned his stomach.

A little later, Fauser called the police.

DOG TAG AFTERNOON

BY ROB ALEF

Tempelhof

O n a slight rise next to the pond stands the church, made of natural stone. In the shade of the tall trees there is a little cemetery. A bridge runs across the pond to the other side. A woman in jogging gear sits on a bench holding her face in her hands. Next to her lies a red rose. Behind her the park slopes gently upward.

Red roses float across the water. A bouquet of flowers has spread out across the pond. The woman on the bench has encountered a dead man who is now turning languidly among the dots of red like a compass needle. The corpse is dressed in military uniform. The church clock strikes three times: it's a quarter before six in the morning.

A few hours later, Max Schembart parks his Volvo station wagon in front of Tempelhof Airport. His friend Dirk Ogorski gives a thumbs-up when he sees what is in the back of the car. Schembart gets out and nods in greeting. He is tall, muscle-bound, with dark, mussed-up hair and a rough-hewn face. Ogorski is a head smaller and the beginnings of a belly are showing under his polo shirt. His hair is cut short to hide that it is thinning.

Ogorski smacks his hand on the roof of the car— Schembart doesn't like being slapped on the shoulder. "Nice loot," he says.

Schembart nods.

"Ludwig and Agnes are going to sleep as soundly as angels," says Ogorski.

Schembart normally prefers to take his bike, but in the back of the station wagon are two disassembled cots made of cherrywood. He and his wife Charlotte live with their children, Ludwig and Agnes, in Potsdam. Like her children, Charlotte was born in Potsdam. Schembart comes from Würzburg and the road to Potsdam has been a long one. Schembart and Ogorski met at a baby swim group, just after Ludwig was born. Ogorski's daughter Anna is a month older than Ludwig.

Ogorski works at the German-American Chamber of Commerce. He is their PR man. And he's passionate about his job. The German-American Chamber of Commerce is the main sponsor for the seventieth anniversary of the Berlin airlift. Ogorski is also passionate about the Berlin airlift.

Schembart works for the Fisheries Authority in Potsdam. He is their man for angling. He knows it's called game fishing, but it's not something he cares about. He's not passionate about his job, but about his children. That's something he has in common with Ogorski—the joy of fatherhood.

Ogorski takes Schembart to the airport's old terminal building. An airplane with two turboprop engines and a stubby snout is suspended from the ceiling. It looks like a dog with an underbite, a dog's head with a span of thirty meters. Hundreds of small white parachutes hang from the ceiling as if they are about to land. They carry chocolate bars and other American candy. Schembart recognizes photos of Elvis and Martin Luther King, Eleanor Roosevelt and Meryl Streep, Hemingway and Obama. It's raining heroes.

Workmen labor under the shadow of the plane. Cables, lamps, and tools are scattered around. A black-and-white film flickers on a screen projected onto a pillar; the sound is too low to understand what the man is saying, but his eyes are shining.

Instead Ogorski provides a commentary: "A whole city was supplied from the air for more than a year—a *whole* city. A plane landed every seventy seconds, *bam*, six minutes to unload, *bam*, like the Pony Express. It was incredible."

A wall chart displays a large mounted quote from someone whose name Schembart can't read: *It was an act of the greatest daring*. They clamber over cables and go past panels that have already been mounted. Schembart recognizes Clay, the organizer, Reuter, the mayor, and Halvorsen, the pilot. Ogorski says, "It was an act of the greatest daring."

Schembart grins. Ogorski likes to think big. They step out onto the runway from the terminal building. A catering truck and chairs have been set out under the awning for the exhibition team. Ogorski collects two Styrofoam cups of coffee; they sit down and look out at the expanse of nothingness that stretches for kilometers into the distance.

"Why haven't you got any Raisin Bombers on display?" asks Schembart.

Ogorski sighs. "The Senate didn't want to buy a second one, because there's already one hanging in the Museum of Technology. One of the board members, an American, managed to find a Fairchild Packet. It'll stay here when the exhibition is over."

They slurp their coffee. Schembart knows that the Senate has dragged its feet over the anniversary celebrations.

Ogorski throws his coffee cup into a trash can. "But every aircraft used in the airlift will be on display as a model."

Schembart nods and carves a heart with M + C on his cup. He places his artwork on the table and checks his watch. "Speaking of models, are you coming with me?"

* * *

Across from the airport, on the other side of Tempelhofer Damm, there is a store called Take Off. The interior is hidden from view because the windows are stacked high with model aircraft kits. Inside there are illustrated books, oil-stained manuals in Ziploc bags, photos on the walls, a disassembled altimeter, and other technical equipment on display.

A man sits in a folding chair, leafing through a French book with the title *Aiguilleurs du ciel*—air traffic controllers.

"Do you have a Yakovlev Yak-9 on a scale of 1:72?" asks Schembart. The man looks up. His hair and beard are snow-white, which make him look like a ship's captain. He shakes his head. "Not 72 or any other scale. Only newer models, the whole Sukhoi range. And I have a Tupolev White Swan."

Ogorski nudges Schembart and winks. "How about a Raisin Bomber?" In his hand he holds a model of the Douglas C-47 Skytrain. On the fuselage it says: *Contains 500 grams of finest California raisins.* The raisins behind the windows look like the heads of shrunken passengers on a transatlantic flight.

Schembart shakes his head. He needs a present for his father-in-law, Helmut John, a former GDR diplomat. "Helmut would prefer something that was flown during the Soviet Union."

"Then take a Spitfire by the Tommies," says the store owner. "The Russians had more than a thousand of them during the Second World War."

Schembart nods. "Lend-Lease Act, 1941."

The white-bearded man raises his eyebrows. Behind him on the wall hangs a photo of a barge. Maybe he really is a former captain. Men with military haircuts stand at the railing. They're wearing US uniforms and are laughing and waving with their caps. In the background there is a dark brick building with a square tower and a large clock.

"Churchill supplied airplanes to Stalin?" Ogorski asks.

Schembart nods. "And the Americans paid for it." He leaves the store with a 1:48 scale Supermarine Spitfire kit under his arm.

Ogorski's phone rings and he answers it; Schembart is surprised. Is Ogorski looking desperate? If so, that would be a first.

Ogorski puts his phone away. "Munro is dead," he says.

Schembart shrugs, none the wiser.

"Bill Munro, one of the three veterans we invited for the celebrations. Ninety-six years old. A volunteer, he was one of the first to sign up."

"Heart attack?"

"No." Ogorski grinds his jaws. "He was as fit as a fiddle. He's been murdered."

Schembart puts his hand on Ogorski's shoulder. "I'm sorry. You've busted your ass to get this thing ready."

Ogorski purses his lips. "Well, more to the point, a man has died." He points to the Platz der Luftbrücke subway entrance. "The police want to talk to me."

"I'll drive you there," says Schembart.

The investigator stands on the path next to the pond and taps the ground with the tip of his shoe. "Who's this?" he asks Ogorski.

"A friend of mine, Max Schembart."

"I need to speak to you alone," says the investigator.

"If you want to talk Mr. Ogorski privately, I'll go for a walk," says Schembart.

"Stay away from the pond," says the cop. "It's a crime scene."

There's a diver working in the water. Some long-stemmed

red roses are lying on the bench, as if counted off. Schembart walks up the slope to the top of the park. He watches Ogorski being questioned. The investigator shows Ogorski something in a plastic bag; he shakes his head. There is garbage lying everywhere. He dodges a broken beer bottle, a folded newspaper, and a disposable cup with a lid and straw on the bridge; there are cigarette butts at every turn. *The church is beautiful*, thinks Schembart. *Probably nice and cool in this heat.* The gravestones on the church floor have survived many an inferno. The sparse decoration is no match for the Catholic churches in Würzburg. In the vestibule to the nave there is a plaque hanging on the wall with the inscription:

In honorable memory of the soldiers, pilots, sailors,
and civil servants who worked during the airlift
and lost their lives saving the city.
District Mayor of Tempelhof
Tempelhof, October 21, 1949

Sailors, like the ones in the photograph hanging in the model store. The British landed on the Havel by seaplane. Schembart crosses the cemetery. On one grave, there is a fresh long-stemmed red rose. Two people are buried there.

Hermann Rohde, 17/11/1926–24/08/1948
Hilde Rohde, 04/01/1928–18/10/1973

By the end of August 1948, the airlift had been operating for a month. Munro had been one of the first, said Ogorski. Hilde had died a quarter of a century after Hermann and had clearly never remarried. A grave site is normally discontinued thirty years after the last burial. *So someone obviously tends to this grave*, Schembart thought. *Or the entire cemetery is protected as a national site.* They had married very young; Hermann had died at the age of twenty-one. *Did Munro put the rose here? Or his murderer?*

Schembart looks around. He is completely alone. He takes the rose from the grave and wedges it between the memorial plaque and the wall. Munro might have wanted it that way. Ogorski has vanished from the spot next to the pond. The investigator is consulting the diver. Schembart goes back to his car. Ogorski has sent him a text: *On my way to the office. Have to save the ceremony.*

Schembart lives with his family just outside Potsdam on a small hill called the Golm. He takes the newspaper out of the mailbox and puts it on the shoe rack in the hallway. Sometimes, when he goes jogging very early, he sees the newspaper deliverer with his cart working his way around the cul-de-sacs of the housing estate. Schembart carries the beds up to the children's rooms and puts them together. Then he prepares dinner.

When Charlotte comes home with the children in the bicycle trailer, everyone is thrilled with the new beds. To celebrate, Schembart first reads a bedtime story to Ludwig in his bed and then another to Agnes in hers.

When the children are asleep, Schembart comes into the kitchen and embraces Charlotte from behind. She is sitting at the dining table, preparing Agnes's lunch. He puts his hands on her breasts and whispers something in the ear that wouldn't be suitable for any children's book. He sits down next to her, makes Ludwig's sandwiches, and tells her about his day. Charlotte is horrified by the news. They are close to Ogorski and his wife.

"I feel sorry for Dirk," says Schembart, "but it's also quite exciting."

"My husband the detective," Charlotte says, stroking Schembart's arm. "I'll bet you'll solve the murder. Get right to work. Tonight's your night."

Schembart puts the two lunch boxes in the fridge, kisses Charlotte on the neck, and goes down into the basement. Twice a week, he retires to his office until nine p.m. to do some historical research in peace and quiet. Spread around the room are a few thousand unread archive pages, books both started and untouched, essays, newspaper clippings, and odds and ends picked up at flea markets. There is also a baby monitor, because on one of the two days, Charlotte meets up with friends.

Today Schembart isn't just researching for the sheer fun of it: he has an assignment. Who was Bill Munro, murdered in Berlin Tempelhof?

When he starts up his computer, he comes across an e-mail from Ogorski with Bill Munro's press photo and a short biography. Munro had a wrinkly face, bushy eyebrows, and a distinctive nose that had probably once been broken. Before he can start his research, Ogorski calls.

"Agnes and Ludwig are sleeping as soundly as angels, just like you predicted," says Schembart.

"Nice," says Ogorski. He seems to be in a hurry. "Are you in your cubbyhole? Did you already read my e-mail?"

"Someone broke Munro's nose," Schembart says.

"Yeah, it happened during the airlift, a fight in a bar, he once told the story in an interview."

"How did it go with the police?"

"I'm not a suspect. It was about the timing. Munro arrived yesterday afternoon, as arranged. We were going to meet today because of his jet lag. The inspector wanted to know whether Bill Munro had enemies." Ogorski raises his voice. "Why on earth would an airlift pilot have enemies in this city? These guys have been heroes for seventy years!"

"The roses," says Schembart.

"Not from us."

"I saw a rose in the church," says Schembart. "Someone put it on the memorial plaque for the fallen of the airlift."

"Now you tell me!"

"I didn't want to disturb you," says Schembart. "I thought you had enough on your mind."

"Yes, you're probably right." Ogorski quiets down. "I'll tell Inspector Kugler anyway."

"Maybe the other roses were meant for the big airlift memorial?" Schembart says.

"The *Hungerkralle*," says Ogorski. "Yes, you might be right. The cop thinks the roses have something to do with the murder."

Schembart chuckles softly.

"Kugler showed me something they found in Munro's fist. A soldier's dog tag. The police are investigating it—it's quite old."

"If the police find out who it belongs to, then they'll know who the murderer is."

"That's what Kugler said too," replies Ogorski.

Schembart pushes away the thought of the rose on the grave. Can fingerprints be left on a flower stem? The police would have to have his fingerprints first. He turns to his computer. He types *bill munro pilot* into the search field. He finds a US Navy document. As one of seven pilots, a certain William Delaney Munro was decorated with the Medal of Honor for his achievements in the Battle of Guadalcanal. In soldiers' jargon, these units were known as the Cactus Air Force. Pilot Munro was probably stationed on one of the three aircraft carriers that were involved in the battle. That's why the document came from the Navy. Schembart runs through Munro's biography, sent to him by Ogorski. *Highly decorated in the battles in the Pacific.*

Next he enters: *william delaney munro navy.* The middle name narrows down the search. He finds a scanned directory of matriculation. W.D. Munro studied from 1945 to 1948 at the Naval Academy in Annapolis, Maryland. In mid-June he volunteered to go to Berlin. His mission there ended in September 1948. He gave up a semester of his studies to offer his services to the city.

Next Schembart enters: *hermann rohde 1948 tempelhof.* He finds a newspaper report. "Murder in Tempelhof on the Brink of Being Solved?" reads the headline. On August 24, 1948, Hermann Rohde was beaten to death in broad daylight on his plot of land south of the Teltow Canal. A Pole, Marek S., who was living in a nearby camp on the north bank of the canal, was arrested as a prime suspect. A Pole living in a camp in Berlin in 1948?

He enters: *marek s tempelhof murder.*

"Marek Szczepaniak Executed" reads a headline from November 1948. The twenty-seven-year-old, born near **Poznań**, was sentenced to death by a US military tribunal and executed by guillotine. Szczepaniak and Rohde had known each other. Although Rohde had tilled his half a hectare of land south of the Teltow Canal, he was also a foreman at a large laundry on the north bank. Here, the Pole had worked. In the chocolate factory next door, Szczepaniak had been a forced laborer from 1942 until the end of the war—when Munro was fighting in

Guadalcanal. Where had Hermann Rohde been at the time?

After the war Szczepaniak had stayed in Berlin. Stalin was redrawing the borders: the Polish east-west border was shifted, there were resettlements in Poland, and Germans were expelled. Szczepaniak was allowed to stay in Berlin because his ancestors had been Prussian nationals before 1918. At the time of his execution, Rohde's widow was pregnant.

Schembart takes notes. He prepares a time line and downloads documents, then writes an e-mail to his university friend, Jung-hoon Lee. Jung-hoon's father is German, his mother Korean. He travels the world as a freelance historical adviser. Schembart met him when he was studying history in Würzburg; Jung-hoon was a law student with a focus on constitutional law and history. The Korean Constitution of 1949 was based on the Weimar Constitution of 1919. Why Jung-hoon was studying constitutional law in Bavaria, of all places, remains a mystery to Schembart even today. Jung-hoon also studied some minor subjects, mostly wine, women, and song. He had a punk band called Kim Chi MoFo. Nowadays he spends his time between San Francisco, Busan, and Paris. But he can be found wherever there is an archive. His daily rate is two thousand euros if it's not Schembart making the inquiry. *If Jung-hoon reads my e-mail in San Francisco, I might already get an answer by the time I've finished breakfast tomorrow,* Schembart thinks.

He pulls up the website of the Berlin State Archive, searches the inventory reports, and writes a query to the user service. He writes to the Wehrmacht Information Office. It is shortly before ten p.m. He has a nagging feeling at the back of his mind, as if he has overlooked something important today—but not in this room, and not on this screen. He shuts down the computer, switches off the light. At the top of the house in their converted attic, Charlotte is lying naked in bed, reading. High time to take her in his arms and to whisper in her ear some more.

The next day Schembart takes Agnes and Ludwig to the kindergarten by bike and trailer. He leaves the trailer there for Charlotte to pick up the children later, then cycles to the Central Station and gets on the city train with his bike. In Friedrichstrasse he changes trains and gets out at Eichborndamm. Now he's in Reinickendorf, home to the Berlin State Archive. It is housed in a former munitions factory. On the outside, it's Prussian redbrick; inside are the city's memories. The files are stored in air-conditioned rooms on huge shelves that run on rails. With one hand a ton of paper can be moved through the stack room. But moving a ton of paper is much easier than reading it.

In the reading room, a heap of files awaits Schembart. The file covers are faded and the cardboard is frayed at the edges. *Treasures, baby!* Some files have been given new homes in snow-white folders and the leaves are loose. They have been cleaned, all metals have been removed, and numbers have been added to each sheet, or they have been paginated. *Pagina*, the page: the front and back are numbered consecutively. *Folium*, the sheet: each sheet of a file is given a number in the upper-right corner.

Szczepaniak's death sentence is four pages long. During the police interrogation, he swore on his mother's life that he hadn't committed the murder. Where the mother was at the time is not mentioned in the file. There is no farewell letter. *Brutalized by the horrific experiences in the years of the war*, as it says in the verdict, *he killed Hermann Rohde on his farm*. Apparently he had left his workplace and traveled on a

Neukölln–Mittenwalde freight train over to the south side of the Teltow Canal. The railway ran straight past Rohde's plot, and as the train was traveling at walking pace, the Pole only had to jump down. The death sentence was handed down by a US military court. During those years, German courts were only responsible for acts committed by Germans against Germans. Szczepaniak was a "tolerated Pole" and the crime scene was inside the American sector. But why had Szczepaniak committed the murder? Allegedly he was seized by a great thirst for revenge and Rohde had bullied him. Exactly what Rohde did is not revealed in the verdict.

Schembart works his way through the pile. He smells the acidic paper, deciphers stamps, forms, letterheads, file references, and spidery notes that convey foreign messages from a bygone era, like hieroglyphs or runes. He reads authority reports from the summer of 1948. As during the last years of the war, venereal diseases were on the rampage: syphilis, chlamydia, gonorrhea. Occasional prostitution flourished on every corner. There were temporary marriages between Allied soldiers and German women, sex in return for protection. But for some, these arrangements were more than partnerships of convenience. And the city, of course, did not surrender. The aircrafts landed at steady intervals. The Americans were strapping fellows. The Germans were steadfast. In Charlottenburg, a power plant resumed operations on the Spree River; the parts were delivered by plane, piece by piece. Some of the articles would suit Ogorski's exhibition very well.

Schembart goes to the map room. On a huge table there is a map of the Teltow Canal from 1948. Like a dented equator, it passes through the district of Tempelhof from west to east. In the north is the pond where Munro's body was found, and the airport; in the south, Rohde's plot of land. Schembart compares the former site with an up-to-date city map which he has brought along. The agricultural areas south of the canal are now community gardens or have been developed for housing. Rohde's plot was part of a larger piece of land bordered by the railroad tracks to the east and Rixdorfer Strasse to the west. Today, gardens with arbors have been built on the land and given names like *Clover, Alpine Valley,* and *Carefree.* The laundry where Szczepaniak worked is on there too, on the north shore. The colored marker on the map identifies a partially destroyed chocolate factory. At the time of the airlift, Tempelhof only had three intact bridges over the Teltow Canal. The others had all been blown up by the Nazis. Most of those that exist today were built after 1949. The Red Army first built the city train bridge in the far west, and the railway bridge for the Neukölln–Mittenwalde railway company in the far east. The NME, which branched into a works railway in the industrial areas north of the Teltow Canal, was a lifeline for the districts south of the canal. Those who needed to get somewhere fast traveled on the running board of a freight train. Time and again people were crushed or drowned in the Teltow Canal when a train rumbled over the makeshift bridge.

Schembart goes back to his seat in the reading room and sweeps up the files: a productive morning. He feels as if he has been planting flowers. He has rummaged deep into the humus of the past with both hands. His fingers are black with the dust of the files. If Charlotte, Ludwig, and Agnes are not around, there is no place in the world where Schembart is happier than in the reading room of an archive.

Another reassigned Wilhelmine factory on Eichborndamm is home to the Wehrmacht Information Office, or WASt. There,

Schembart goes looking for clues to shed light on Hermann Rohde's short life. Born in 1926, he was drafted in December 1943, not even eighteen years old. Service in Greece, then in West Prussia, near Poznań. Avoided becoming a prisoner of war; returned to Tempelhof in June 1945. As a soldier he was in the military hospital three times, the last time in February 1945. Despite permanent injury, he was able to till his small field and grow potatoes.

Schembart travels by city train to Tempelhof, and the last stretch by bike. Finally, he stands on the Teltow Canal. Above him is the old railway bridge, and even higher, the double-expressway bridge from the eighties.

To the right of the railway bridge there is a vehicle bridge, which was intact in 1948, as well as a footbridge on the same level as the laundry. But it would have taken Szczepaniak too long to walk. If he had not traveled to Rohde's plot directly by train, he would have needed a motorcycle or a boat.

Schembart cycles along the northern shore of the Teltow Canal. Every few hundred meters, a stone ladder is hewn into the canal wall, which disappears in the water. The laundry and the chocolate factory have been impeccably restored and are protected historic monuments. In the early postwar years there was a displaced-persons camp on the site of the factory. People who had been in the wrong place at the wrong time, driven out and chased away.

In front of Schembart, the masts of yachts moored in Tempelhof Harbor soar into the sky. And on the south bank stands the redbrick building which he saw on the photo with the seamen on the barge. He had not realized that the building was so colossal. At the next bridge, he takes the bike path northward. Shortly afterward, he locks up his bike in front of Take Off.

"Didn't the Spitfire do the trick?" the owner asks.

Without greeting him, Schembart points to the photo: "When was this taken and who are the people in it?"

The man with the captain's beard goes to stand next to Schembart and speaks to him over his shoulder: "Ullstein House. That's where the publisher had its books printed until the Nazis got their hands on the building. And these," he points to a row of trucks on the left side of the photo, which Schembart hadn't noticed, "these are the trucks that brought coal from Tempelhof Airport to the barges." He taps the vessel. "The Americans brought coal to the power plant in Charlottenburg. First along Teltow Canal, then via the Neukölln shipping canal. Then a short way on the Landwehr Canal and, finally, across the Spree."

Schembart opens his city map. He finds the waterway cross point, where all four canals meet. The Neukölln shipping canal bends north from the Teltow Canal. "But the route goes through East Berlin."

The old man nods. "The Russians allowed the Allies to transport coal by waterway through East Berlin, because they didn't make a stop there. The coal was transported from the west to the west."

"Was there no other way?"

"Not by water. Bringing coal to the Charlottenburg power station by car would have consumed more gas than the coal that could be flown in."

Schembart chews his lower lip. He can taste his own sweat.

The owner of Take Off continues: "They mostly flew in coal. Perhaps children imagined it was raisins, but the city had to survive the winter and needed electricity and heating. *Raisin bombers* obviously sounds fancier than *coal bombers*. The most common cause of death was coal dust exploding on the planes. Like in mining accidents."

"How much time and human life was saved by allowing barges to travel through East Berlin?"

The captain shrugs his shoulders. "It was pretty decent of the Russians. It was said that they wanted to bring the city to its knees. But in fact it was all about status. They had won the war. It took them two weeks to advance from the outskirts of Berlin to the Reichstag, during which thousands of soldiers were killed. And then the D-mark was introduced, and half the city was suddenly gone. If they had wanted to starve the western sectors, not a single coal barge would have been allowed to set off from Tempelhof."

Schembart points to the men in uniform. "And the sailors?"

"That's a US Navy supply unit."

Schembart's bike is locked next to a wastebasket. In it lies a folded newspaper. The same that he takes out of his mailbox in Golm almost every day. The same one that was lying in the park on the bridge. People live here at the Platz der Luftbrücke, just as they do in Golm. But no one lives in the park. He sits down in a café and orders his thoughts and his documents. He makes a sketch of the coal transportation route. Were there barges already in operation in the summer of 1948? How often? How many?

He looks up the newspaper publisher's phone number and makes a call: "Hello, I live in Schönburgstrasse in Tempelhof, right next to the old church."

"Hasn't your newspaper been delivered? Please give me your name and customer number."

"On the contrary, I'm very happy with the delivery. Even though I get up very early, the newspaper is always there without fail."

"I'll pass that on."

"That's why I'd like to give the delivery person a small thank you, a gift of ten euros. Who delivers to Schönburgstrasse?"

Silence on the line, then: "That'll be Ms. Rohde."

Schembart's heart thumps all the way up to his throat. He hazards a guess: "Ms. Claudia Rohde?" His voice is squeaky.

"Renate Rohde," says the woman on the line.

"Thank you very much," says Schembart. "I'll send her the money in an envelope."

"Better stick the envelope to your mailbox, it'll just get lost here."

Schembart hangs up, trembling. On the Internet he finds a Renate Rohde. She lives in Blumenthalstrasse 5, right next to the church. Now he has her number. And he can mask his own number when he calls. He has tracked down a murderer. Should he call her right away and ask her questions?

Ogorski interrupts him by phoning. "The police are looking for you!" he shouts.

"The police?" Schembart juts his chin forward.

"Kugler wants to know where you went after he sent you away."

"How come?"

"He found a rose petal on a grave at the church."

"So what?"

"Did you take the rose from the grave and stick it to that memorial plaque? Did you?"

"Me? That's absurd. No way." Schembart had not realized that Ogorski could be so quick-tempered.

"Why were you even in the church?"

"Because it was too hot outside. Because the church is a landmark. Because I was waiting for you. Should I call Kugler?"

This appeases Ogorski, and he gives Schembart the number. "The dog tag was Munro's," he says. "It was his old one from the Second World War. Men normally wear such a thing around their necks."

Schembart nods into his cell phone. Munro's talisman, which protected him in the Pacific and which he took to his watery grave in Tempelhof. "And now?" he asks.

"The police think it was stolen from him when he was in Berlin. But Stagorsky says it's something you guard with your life."

"Who is Stagorsky?"

"Our second airlift veteran. Munro was our only pilot. Stagorsky was with air traffic control. He arrived today and immediately identified Munro's dog tag. That was my idea, I suggested it to Kugler. We picked up Stagorsky together at the airport. "

"Are you sure Munro was a pilot?" Schembart asks.

"Do you think he volunteered as a cook? He was one of the best fighter pilots they had. Why do you ask?"

"Did you know that the Americans were allowed to transport coal by barge through East Berlin?"

Ogorski is silent for a moment. "Well, perhaps the odd lump here and there."

"A fifth of the coal that was incinerated in the power plants."

"Jesus, don't go splitting hairs. Are we supposed to be grateful to the Russians? The city was supplied from the air. For more than a year. Period."

"It's your exhibition, not mine. Was Munro in Berlin again after 1948?"

"No idea. Stagorsky was stationed here for another three years, from '70 to '73. He loved it. Tonight there's a veterans' meeting. A bunch of ancient *Ick bin ein Berliners*. Stagorsky and I are going to the restaurant at the Ullstein House in an hour. Where are you, anyway?"

"If you see Kugler, please tell him I'll contact him." Schembart ends the conversation and calls Charlotte.

Family dinner in Golm is on the schedule for tonight, but before he can speak, Charlotte says, "Hello, darling, our tried-and-true telepathy strikes again—I was just about to call you. We're at my parents', and my mother has made plum compote. There's rice pudding. If you're already on your way home, just drop by."

For Schembart, the home of his in-laws near Krongut has all the charm of an interrogation room. Helmut and especially Dagmar John like seeing him get caught up in the contradictions in his new way of life—not much work, and hours spent leafing through old things. He hesitates. It is surprisingly easy for him to lie through his teeth to Ogorski. But with Charlotte, it's different. In her case he can only bend the truth a bit. "Dirk has invited me out tonight," he says. "To a meeting with airlift veterans."

"Sounds interesting. You really have a good nose for this history stuff." Then she turns matter-of-fact: "The dinner you'll miss will cost you an extra bedtime story, of course."

"Oh yes, of course. Three bedtime stories tomorrow."

"Why tomorrow?" Charlotte asks. "Is the history detective hot on a trail?" Then she whispers lewdly: "You know how exciting it is when you do illicit things. Especially with me."

Schembart clears his throat. This is not the time to be having telephone sex with his wife. First of all, the café is busy, and second of all, he has urgent things to do. "It's all above board." He lowers his voice to a sonorous baritone: "I love you, baby. And I'll think up a whole bunch of illicit things and whisper them in your ear tonight." After their conversation, his head buzzes. Has he just discovered something more important than having sex with his wife? Another woman, to cap it all? Renate Rohde.

When he has a grip on himself, he walks back to Take Off. Then he cycles to the Ullstein House. He mentions Ogorski's name at the restaurant entrance and is ushered into a room with a festively decorated table. Dirk and Stagorsky have arrived ahead of schedule.

"What are you doing here?" Ogorski asks.

"Shaking hands with some 1948 heroes," Schembart says, pouncing toward the veteran. "I'm so happy and proud to meet you," he says, shaking hands with the old man.

Ogorski's eyes narrow to slits, but Stagorsky is happy. He's wearing white sneakers and a yellow cardigan. "Let's talk German, my boy. I spoke German for thirty-nine years with my wife. My name's Stephen." Stagorsky sits between Ogorski and Schembart; the conversation drags.

When the next veteran arrives and joins Stagorsky, Ogorski has a word with Schembart. "Listen, have you lost your mind? You can't just turn up—this is a private event! A former city commander is going to show up at any minute. And you look like you've just been training for a triathlon."

"True," Schembart says. "Searching, reading, and finding. Don't worry, I'll be gone in a minute." He taps Stagorsky's yellow sleeve, pulls out the photo from Take Off, and holds it in front of him.

Stagorsky rubs his chin. "Where did you get that from, sonny?" he asks.

"From a souvenir store."

When Ogorski sees the photo from behind Stagorsky, his eyes pop out of his head, but he has to go greet the latest veterans streaming in.

Stagorsky nods. "It was taken out here on the canal. God, we were really young back then." He looks at Schembart. "The boys did a fantastic job. They were our mules. That's what we called them—water mules. Without them, supplies would have been tight, especially in winter."

He shows the photo to a newcomer. "Hey, Frank, you can sure tell us something about this, can't you?" To Schembart he says: "Frank is our souvenir keeper. He stores everything connected to American soldiers in Berlin since 1945 in his house in Zehlendorf. Much to Rosie's great delight."

Frank and Rosie beam at Stagorsky, then Frank takes the photo. He shakes his head: "Those son of a bitches. Sailing in broad daylight through the Iron Curtain. The winter was no pleasure-boat ride, but before and afterward they had fun. They waved to the Russians at the Landwehr Canal and the Reichstag. And the Russians would wave back."

Stagorsky adds: "When the pilots had time off—they had to have regular breaks so that they didn't go crazy—they would sometimes go along for the ride. They sunbathed and secretly took photographs."

Frank says, "In return they had to help unload in Charlottenburg. And buy beer for the barge crew."

"I heard that sailors died too," says Schembart.

Stagorsky's eyes get a little watery. "Yeah, I remember. One guy suffocated in the hold. Something to do with the vent not working properly. A young kid from Albuquerque, I think. And another drowned. He wanted to swim in the Spree right under the Russians' noses. But he got a cramp."

"No one fell into the water?" asks Schembart.

"Yes, some did," says Stagorsky, "but everyone in the Navy could swim, so we fished them out again."

"Even the pilots?" asks Schembart.

"Sonny, you have to know how to swim when the Pacific is below you."

The veterans stand up and stretch their old backs. The

former city commander enters. Schembart sneaks over to the door. "The police phone number was always busy," he whispers to Ogorski.

At half past eight in the evening, a grubby father reads three stories to his two children, who have just been bathed. Schembart keeps stumbling over the words.

"You're not concentrating, Papa," says Agnes, and tweaks his nose with her small fingers. Schembart pulls himself together, but his thoughts fly back and forth between the Teltow Canal and Blumenthalstrasse.

After he has showered and is lying in bed next to Charlotte, she asks whether he's taken something. "You're practically palpitating," she says.

"Too many files in one day," says Schembart. "I'm not used to such a high dose anymore."

"Do you actually work now and then?" Charlotte asks, stroking his neck with her fingernails.

"Of course I work," says Schembart. "Nonstop. But to be at the fisheries at nine a.m. tomorrow, I have to leave at four in the morning. You'll have to bring the kids to kindergarten."

"At four?" Charlotte says. "What are you up to?"

"All kinds of illicit things," says Schembart, and nibbles her earlobe.

At just before five, Schembart is at the pond in Tempelhof. He finds a spot for his folding stool so that he can see Blumenthalstrasse and Schönburgstrasse while keeping hidden. The church clock strikes once at a quarter after five. Shortly afterward, an e-mail arrives from Jung-hoon. He's not in San Francisco, but in Washington, DC, and says he had to use more than just charm to get the information Schembart requested.

Schembart nestles into his thermal jacket and reads. William Delaney Munro was a great swimmer. Jung-hoon found him on one of the lists of college championship winners. Munro won third place in 1948 in a long-distance swimming contest for the Naval Academy, over a stretch of 1,650 yards. He was beaten by a certain Bill Heusner who was the local hero of Michigan State. The photos of the winners were published in a Michigan State University student magazine. One of the three men posing in swimwear has a distinctive but straight nose. The caption identifies him as William D. Munro, *a strong contender for the US Olympic swim team.* The college competitions had taken place in March 1948, the first post–Second World War Olympic Games in London in July. But Munro had been in Berlin, not entirely voluntarily. At the end of May 1948 there was an incident: Munro sexually harassed a woman in a bar in Annapolis. That was when he got his nose broken. It was likely that he was going to be indicted. But before it came to that, he signed up for the airlift. Jung-hoon also included the report from the Disciplinary Commission in the appendix, but the reference to the archive and the signature is missing. What a Kim Chi cool MoFo.

There was a rattling on the cobblestones. *She gets around well for her sixty-nine years,* Schembart thinks. She is wearing an anorak, sturdy shoes, and is pulling a cart with newspapers. After she has almost walked past him, he asks, "Did Munro give his dog tag to your mother?"

She turns and looks in Schembart's direction. He gets up and shows himself.

"Who are you?"

"And your mother left you the dog tag?" he asks.

She nods. "Are you from the police?"

"Not at all. I am just a curious person who is interested

in history. Your history too. Did Munro put the rose on your mother's grave?"

She shakes her head. "That was me. We met, on the bridge. I knew he would be in town, it was in all the newspapers. He was a hero. But when I bumped into him here so early in the morning, I got a terrible shock. We both got a shock."

"Why did you have the dog tag with you?"

"I don't know. The anniversary stirred up many things. I was conceived during the airlift and my father was murdered. My mother lost her husband. She kept the dog tag in her jewelry box until the very end, along with her wedding ring. He wanted to put a bouquet of flowers on my parents' grave. When he recognized me, he pulled a rose from it and handed it to me. But I didn't want anything from him. I never wanted to see him again. So I gave him his dog tag back. I didn't want it either. I'd only kept it because of my mother. But he tried to stuff it into my décolleté. He wanted me. At ninety-six years of age! He forced himself on me. Then he fell. When he was floating around on the water, I realized how relieved I was."

"Munro murdered Hermann Rohde."

"My father? No, that's . . . Why are you telling me this?" She props herself on the handle of her cart and stares at the pond.

"Because I figured it out," says Schembart. "Bill Munro was an Olympic-level swimmer. On August 24, he sailed a short way along the Teltow Canal from Tempelhof Harbor on a Navy barge transporting coal. He jumped into the water, swam to the nearest ladder, and walked two blocks to Hermann Rohde's plot of land. Then he smashed a hoe into his skull."

"That was the Polack."

Schembart shakes his head. "He wanted your mother for

himself. And because she was already married, he had to eliminate Rohde. After the murder, he climbed back into the canal and the next barge taking coal to Charlottenburg picked him up. "

"My mother sensed it," says Renate Rohde. "She didn't want to see him anymore. On August 24, he visited her and gave her his dog tag. *So that you know I'll always protect you*, he said. But she sensed it. She refused to see him after that. And in September, he went back."

"Did she tell you that?"

She nods.

"But Munro kept coming back to Berlin."

"He came because of me: in 1968 and 1973. When my mother became an alcoholic, he wanted me." She drops her head against her chest.

"And Rohde?"

"My mother was fond of Hermann. And he of her. And there was me to remember him by." She sniffs.

Schembart gives her a handkerchief; he has brought along an extra one.

"Will you go to the police now?" she asks.

"No, I won't. I'm not a judge. Besides, you've probably suffered enough."

"What do you mean?"

"You just turned sixty-nine, right?"

"Yes, on May 24. Why do you ask?"

"Why are you delivering newspapers?"

"Because I don't have enough to live off otherwise. After my father's murder, my mother had to sell the land. And she was completely swindled. We were poor. I still am."

She turns and walks off toward Schönburgstrasse. From the cart she removes the newspapers, and a big bunch of keys from her anorak pocket. She disappears into a corner house.

Schembart takes his folding stool and walks along the pond. Hermann Rohde was in a military hospital three times: once for gonorrhea, twice for syphilis. The third time, the Wehrmacht doctor noted that he was infertile. A good thing at least that Renate Rohde does not know this.

ABOUT THE CONTRIBUTORS

ROB ALEF, born in 1965 in Nuremberg, is a freelance legal historian. He is the author of several highly acclaimed crime novels inspired by Berlin's mad everyday life, featuring elements of horror and fantasy and a hint of the grotesque. His most recent publication was *Immer schön gierig bleiben* (2013). Alef lives in Pankow, Berlin.

Andrew Mogridge

MAX ANNAS was born in 1963 in Cologne. He was a journalist, film critic, and nonfiction author. With his three award-winning novels—*Die Farm, Die Mauer,* and *Illegal*—he has developed a distinctive voice and is widely regarded as one of the best German-language crime fiction writers. His latest thriller is called *Finsterwalde* (2018). After many years in South Africa, he now lives and works in Berlin. *The Wall* will be published by Catalyst Press in 2019.

V Tomaschko

ZOË BECK, born in 1975, writes, translates, and manages the CulturBooks publishing house together with Jan Karsten. She was formerly a creative producer for international TV films. Since 2004 she has been an editor, dialogue writer, and director for dubbed productions. Many of her novels have won awards and have been translated into several languages. She is one of most celebrated German-language crime fiction writers. Her most recent novel is *Die Lieferantin* (Suhrkamp, 2017).

Benedikt Ernst

KATJA BOHNET, born in 1971, studied film theory and philosophy. She has traveled widely and has had many jobs, living for a long time in Berlin, Paris, and the United States before moving to the countryside. She is a former TV presenter and author. Since 2012, she has been a full-time writer. *Messertanz* was her first, highly acclaimed crime novel. Her most recent is *Kerkerkind* (2018).

LCviia Cohen

UTE COHEN, born in 1966, studied linguistics and history in Erlangen and Florence. She is a former management consultant for a company in Düsseldorf and Frankfurt, and has worked for an international organization in Paris. Since 2003, she has worked in concept development, customer communication, and journalism for various media. Her debut novel was the psychological thriller *Satans Spielfeld* (2017). Cohen lives in Berlin.

Nils T. Ninkler

JOHANNES GROSCHUPF, born 1963 in Braunschweig, works as a freelance journalist for *Die Zeit*, *F.A.Z.*, *Tagesspiegel*, and *Berliner Zeitung*, and has traveled widely throughout the world. After a helicopter crash in the Sahara, he wrote the NDR radio feature *Der Absturz* in 1999 based on this experience, for which he received the Robert Geisendörfer Prize. He is an award-winning young adult novelist and thriller writer. His thriller *Berlin Prepper* will be published in 2019. He lives and works in Berlin.

Julio Rodríguez

KAI HENSEL, born in 1965, is a copywriter and comedy writer for television. He has written screenplays for numerous television films and three feature films. With *Klamms Krieg* and *Welche Droge passt zu mir?* he became one of the most performed playwrights, and his plays have been translated into thirteen languages. He has been awarded the German Short Crime Award, the German Youth Theatre Prize, and the Schiller Memorial Prize.

Nikolas Toeliigaard

LUCY JONES was born in England and has lived in Berlin since 1998. She studied German, film, and applied linguistics in the UK. Her translations include works by Annemarie Schwarzenbach, Silke Scheuermann, and Brigitte Reimann; she also writes book reviews of German literary fiction, coruns the translators' collective Transfiction, and hosts a reading series called the Fiction Canteen. Her own writing has been published by *Pigeon Pages NYC* and *SAND Journal* in Berlin.

Brauseboys

ROBERT RESCUE, born in 1969, is a writer, reader, and (founding) member of various public reading platforms, including the fabulous Brauseboys. He has given countless live performances and has published numerous short stories and other work since 1995. He is also a novelist. His latest publication is *Das ist alles eins zu eins erfunden* (2017). Rescue is a chronicler of the district of Wedding, where he lives and works.

Stefan Kobel

SUSANNE SAYGIN, born in 1967, has a doctorate in medieval history. She has spent long periods in the UK, Italy, and the United States, working various jobs in university administration and at PR agencies. Her debut thriller, *Feinde* (2018), is a novel about modern-day slavery in Germany. She lives and works in Berlin.

MATTHIAS WITTEKINDT, born in 1958 in Bonn, studied architecture and has worked in that field in Berlin and London. He also studied philosophy of religion. He is a theater director and has written numerous scripts for television films, radio plays, theater plays, and TV documentaries. He has published four excellent novels to date. His most recent work is *Die Tankstelle von Courcelles* (2018).

Thorsten Wittekindt

ULRICH WOELK, born in 1960, grew up in Cologne. He studied physics and philosophy and earned a doctorate in physics. He is an award-winning novelist (including crime novels) and a playwright. He also writes short stories and nonfiction, and is at the forefront of German contemporary literature. His most recent book is *Nacht ohne Engel* (2017). He lives and works in Berlin.

Bettina Keller

THOMAS WÖRTCHE, born in 1954, is a literary scholar, critic, and was director of several crime fiction publishing imprints. He is currently responsible for a crime line with Suhrkamp Verlag. He lives in Berlin.

Christine Fenzl

MICHAEL WULIGER was born in London in 1951. Until 2015, he was the features editor of the *Jüdische Allgemeine* newspaper. He is the author of the nonfiction book *Der koschere Knigge: Trittsicher durch die deutsch-jüdischen Fettnäpfchen* (2009), essays, and columns. Wuliger lives in Charlottenburg, Berlin.

MIRON ZOWNIR was born in 1953 in Karlsruhe to German-Ukrainian parents. Since the midseventies he has lived and worked as a photographer, director, and writer in Berlin, New York, Los Angeles, London, and Moscow. His photographs have been published and shown in numerous photo books and exhibitions. He is the author of crime novels, short stories, and poetry. His latest publication, cowritten with Nico Anfuso, is *Pommerenke: Ein True-Crime-Roman* (2017).

Nico Anfuso